Editorial Reviews for *Th*

"The Bottom Line: A perfectly crafted conspiracy thriller with a truly noble hero at its core, *The Deadly Deal* is the twisty tale we've been waiting for. Highly Recommended." — ***Best Thrillers Book Review***

"*The Deadly Deal* is a fast-moving, page-turning thriller propelled by rapid scene changes, frequent plot twists, and an enemy that grows more powerful and menacing as the full extent of the conspiracy. Fans of plot-driven thrillers will find plenty to like…" — ***Windy City Book Review***

"*The Deadly Deal* evolves superb characterization, satisfying twists of plot, and a focus that will keep even seasoned thriller readers guessing about its outcome." — ***Midwest Books Book Review***

"J. Lee does it again with *The Deadly Deal*. Fans of mysteries and thrillers will love this new cliffhanger. I was immediately hooked as the story began to unfold and this fast-paced and intriguing mystery kept me guessing until the very last page. Impossible to put down, I finished the book in days and loved every minute of this captivating read!" — ***Nicky Steinberg, Publisher of Downers Grove Living Magazine***

"J. Lee is a must-read new talent." — ***Mike Lawson, Edgar Award Nominated author of the Joe DeMarco series.***

"Action packed and sharply written. Grabbed me from the start and wouldn't let go. I've already made room on my nightstand for the next J. Lee thriller." — ***Davin Goodwin, author of PARADISE COVE and the Roscoe Conklin Mystery Series***.

"*The Deadly Deal* is my kind of thriller. Clever premise, complex characters, a pulsating plot and a satisfying, but in no way predictable, ending. Easily J. Lee's best work, and that alone is saying something." — ***Drew Yanno, author of In the Matter of Michael Vogel and The Smart One***.

i

"A terrific follow-up to *The Hubley Case* and *The Silent Cardinal*. J. Lee lays out an explosive tale of political intrigue, government conspiracy, and murder. If you haven't yet read Lee's thrillers, it's time to jump aboard the bandwagon." — *Alfred C. Martino, author of Pinned, Over The End Line, and Perfected By Girls*

"Regardless of how you feel about the pharmaceutical industry, this book is a must read. J. Lee pulls you into a fast-paced thriller of good vs. evil that never ever lets up. Extremely tight writing, intricate plot, believable characters, and a sharp, fast-moving dialogue that gels it all together. Put this one on your reading list!" — *Jesus Leal, author of True Diversity*

"Set yourself some time to read *The Deadly Deal*, because once you start, you will NOT want to stop turning the pages. J. Lee's third book is not only as good as his first two suspense novels, it's the best one yet! The twists and turns are unexpected to the very end." — *Pamela S. Wight, author of Twin Desires, The Right Wrong Man, Flashes of Life, Birds of Paradise, Molly Finds Her Purr*

Editorial Reviews for *The Silent Cardinal*

"A twisty, fast-paced novel-intrigue of the highest order. Highly recommended!" — *Ward Larsen, USA Today bestselling author of Assassin's Strike*

"THE SILENT CARDINAL is a taut, complex thriller that grabs the reader on the opening page and refuses to let go until the last." — *James L. Thane, Author of A Shot to the Hear, Fatal Blow, South of the Deuce, Crossroads, Tyndall, and Picture Me Gone*

"J. Lee picks up right where he left off in *The Hubley Case* with this latest thriller. *The Silent Cardinal* packs a powerful punch with a looming terrorist threat, multiple kidnappings, unexpected killings and some high level political infighting. Lee keeps the reader guessing right along with the hero, struggling to determine who to trust, the payoff coming at the very end with a twist I never saw coming. You won't be disappointed." — *Drew Yanno, bestselling author of In the Matter of Michael Vogel and The Smart One.*

"Millions of lives hang in the balance in this fast-paced nail-biter. J. Lee delivers a thriller with constant twists and turns, taking readers on a thrill ride that is hard to put down." — *Steve Brigman, bestselling author of The Orphan Train*

"Ben is back! Those who read J. Lee's first spy suspense, *The Hubley Case*, will be thrilled that the main character, Ben Siebert, is back in action. *The Silent Cardinal* is a standalone novel, though, and it's a standout. A crew of people need Ben to solve this race-against-time case: the FBI, CIA, military, and terrorists all stake a claim on the skills of Siebert. But his family, friends, and ultimately, his country are at risk as Seibert fights a lethal enemy to unravel a deadly mystery." — *Pamela Wight, author of The Right Wrong Man and Twin Desires*

"Fans will not be disappointed with his follow up thriller, *The Silent Cardinal*. Readers will cheer the return of former marine Ben Seibert, while enjoying the wild ride of espionage and murder in this taunt page-tuner. — *Alfred C. Martino, author of Pinned, Over The End Line, and Perfected By Girls*

**Editorial Reviews for *The Hubley Case*
Winner of the New York City Big Book Award
And "Best Book" Award for thrillers**

"A terrific debut. I look forward watching Lee continue to develop as a writer." — *Kyle Mills, #1 New York Times Bestselling Author*

"*The Hubley Case* is intricately plotted and the action never lets up! A great read that fans of Kyle Mills and Michael Connelly won't want to miss. — *Ward Larsen, USA Today bestselling author of Assassin's Run*

"*The Hubley Case* will blow you away and J. Lee is a must-read new talent." — **Mike Lawson, author of the Award Winning DeMarco Series**

"With *The Hubley Case*, author J. Lee has spun a yarn of intrigue that captures readers from the opening pages – with audacious murder of a seemingly innocuous US businessman in Sao Paolo – and brings them on a wild ride involving the FBI, Interpol, a shadowy millionaire, and the PCC, a ruthless Brazilian drug cartel. A very smart, fast-paced thriller." — **Alfred C. Martino, author of Pinned, Over The End Line, and Perfected By Girls**

"Move on over Lee Child and Jack Reacher … J. Lee and his main character, Ben Siebert, take the reader on a page-turning ride through cyberattacks, spyware, malware, and twists and turns that keep you guessing to the end. As a reader and writer of romantic suspense, I give this well-written book a whole-hearted five thumbs up." — **Pamela S. Wight, author of Twin Desires and The Right Wrong Man**

"*The Hubley Case* is everything you want in a thriller. Killer opening, breakneck pace, smartly-drawn characters, startling reversals and, best of all, a truly satisfying ending. You'll be left hoping J. Lee is busy working on the follow-up. I know I am." — **Drew Yanno, bestselling author of** In the Matter of Michael Vogel **and** The Smart One

"Has the pace and the stakes of a Brad Thor or David Baldacci novel. Dynamic characters, vivid settings and intrigue that keeps you guessing until the end make this one a must read. J. Lee has burst onto the scene with brand of storytelling that is hard to put down. I look forward to more like *The Hubley Case.*" — **Steve Brigman, bestselling author of The Orphan Train and The Old Wire Road**

THE DEADLY DEAL

J. Lee

Moonshine Cove Publishing, LLC

Abbeville, South Carolina U.S.A.

First Moonshine Cove Edition September 2023

ISBN: 9781952439582

Library of Congress LCCN: 2023907333

© Copyright 2023 by J. Lee

Cover provided by the author; interior design by Moonshine Cove staff.

For Steve, my greatest literary supporter and wonderful father-in-law, who welcomed me into his terrific family and has treated me like a son from Day One.

Acknowledgments

This one was different. The first draft was inked sixteen years ago, then sat in the proverbial drawer as life flew by and two other books got published. So though it's #3, in a lot of ways it feels like my first. Even after several significant rewrites, a serious editorial overhaul and a new title – all pointing out just how much a person's writing and perspective can change – seeing it in print evokes a lot of reflection.

There are a few people I really want to thank: my wife Kristen, who doubled down on editing this one; Kyle Mills, who gave me excellent advice about it over a pizza in Jackson Hole; Alfred Martino, who twenty years ago administered a hard dose of reality I still use today; and Dr. Andrew Lane, who read a very early draft and provided some much-needed medical expertise. Thank you all so much.

Pam Just, Mike Lawson, Drew Yanno, Dave Goodwin, Jesus Leal, and Nikki Steinberg — thanks for taking time out of your very busy schedules to help me out. I owe you one. Thanks also to Gene Robinson and the Moonshine team for its partnership.

To my family and friends – you know who you are – you have been so encouraging. Thanks for the kind words, launch parties, wide smiles, sincere handshakes, heartfelt hugs, and for caring enough to ask. It means so much. I hope you like this one.

The
Deadly
Deal

1

David Centrelli, Director of Business Development, stepped into the CEO's office at Medzic Pharmaceuticals like a rookie into the batter's box determined not to let the veteran pitcher intimidate him. He stayed focused on keeping his 6'2" frame posture perfect. Slightly adjusting his new navy Peter Millar suit jacket with a tug on the lapels, he tried to project confidence and belonging.

On the inside, he felt weak, out of place and a nervous wreck.

"Good morning, Mr. Patera. How are you, sir?" It was all he could muster.

Seated in an exquisite fine leather chair at the head of a beautifully polished granite boardroom table, the 58-year-old CEO of the 44,000-employee, global powerhouse pharmaceutical company that did over $60B in revenue last year smiled with a mouthful of half-chewed apple.

"Just fine for a Monday."

Alvin Patera accomplished more in one day than most people did in a week. While David made an honest effort to get to ProFitness Gym once a week, Alvin ran five miles before getting to the office by six-thirty and usually worked until his eight o'clock evening racquetball match.

Overachiever.

Not afraid to flaunt his wealth, Alvin employed a private barber who groomed his graying hair each morning as he read *The Wall Street Journal* and shaved his face every night while he listened to the latest broadcast from The Met Opera. His strict adherence to an egregiously expensive diet seemed certain to ensure that Alvin would never need the drugs that made him so rich.

The door opened and the final two members of the meeting, Medzic's COO and CFO, entered the room. Martin Richardson, the CMO, was already seated. Checking his watch, Alvin said, "It's seven-twenty-nine gentlemen. Let's get started."

Just like that, David thought. *Right down to business.*

This meeting, his first of every week, always made him feel like the little kid who had somehow wandered over to the grown-ups' table at the Christmas Eve party. It was comprised of the company's top-level executives ... and him. Every one of these gentlemen had thousands of people reporting up to them, more money than David would know what to do with, and twelve-hour daily calendars filled with sixteen hours of meetings.

"David, how's Previséo coming?" asked Larry Bonnelson, the Chief Operating Officer. He said it with a slight shiver, perhaps because Alvin kept the corner office's thermostat set to sixty-five degrees.

Previséo was slated to become the next wonder drug for Medzic Pharmaceuticals. And the men in this room stood to gain or lose the most, depending on whether or not it actually did. Administered in three equal doses over six months, its promise was to fully cure Type 1 diabetes. If successful, the drug would likely end up being responsible for sixty percent of Medzic's sales. With a wave of generics ready to flood the market and cut into other revenue streams, pressure was mounting for Previséo to realize its potential.

Larry, forty-six years old, was short and stout. Already on his fifth ultra-caffeinated espresso to wash down the daily apple fritter, he glared at David through thick, black glasses so big that they rested dangerously close to his bushy mustache below. One inch lower and they'd be in the mealtime splash zone. Larry was tough but fair as well as notorious for ensuring targets were hit and deadlines met.

"It's still on track," David replied.

"We're going to need more than that, David," Larry said. "We've got forty percent of our revenue coming off patent protection this year and Previséo's the only real winner in the pipeline."

"I have the charts ready to review."

"Gentlemen ..." Larry interrupted David's passing out of the bound report, before turning to the CEO, "I don't need to remind you that the projected cost to bring Préviséo to market is over three *billion* dollars. That's fifty percent higher than the average drug and we still don't know if it'll make it. Remember those two turkeys from last quarter that our scientists said would work? That could still happen with Préviséo. We don't get our ten billion in annual sales until this young man tells us it's done."

Alvin didn't say a word, but nodded his head slightly to cue David to continue distributing the weekly report.

"There's still high confidence in these projections and timelines?" Alvin sought clarification.

"Yes, sir." He felt a trickle of perspiration slide to the small of his back.

"Maybe we should pull Dr. Mallick into this meeting?" Larry asked.

Taking a seat, David rested his right ankle on his left kneecap. He knew it wasn't personal. In fact, having the lead scientist most directly responsible for Préviséo's development in the briefing made a lot of sense, but he also couldn't help but feel a bit as though leadership was questioning his work.

"I think David's got it," Alvin replied. David focused intently on not smiling. Despite not fully understanding the CEO's decision, he was grateful for the support.

"You're talking with Mallick every day?" Larry asked.

"Yes sir. Every day."

"And do you have any reason whatsoever to believe Préviséo will fail or be delayed?"

There it was. The inevitable question of every weekly meeting, and also the reason for David's unsettledness. Despite his tendency to think that their need for constant reassurance was redundant, the concern was completely understandable and well placed. There were a multitude of ways a drug could fail and often did — development glitches, FDA politics, unclear documentation, unexpected late-stage performance, the list went on — but there was only one way it could succeed. Préviséo was no exception. But David didn't have a crystal ball. Larry of all people knew that he couldn't say with absolute certainty that nothing would get between the leadership team and its billions of profits, but that didn't stop the COO from asking him each and every week.

He cleared his throat and looked straight into Larry's bulbous face. "No, sir, I do not. Dr. Mallick and several members of his team have confirmed multiple times that our budget and timelines are on track. Based on their status reports and projections, I don't see any issues right now."

"Then you're a damned fool," came the swift response. But it didn't come from Larry, who merely nodded.

Instead, it was uttered by the last person David wanted to hear from.

2

Medzic's top two executives, Alvin and Larry, CEO and COO, were very different people. Alvin was an extrovert and extreme health nut; Larry was a recluse with a diet that would soon require him to take Previséo. Their jobs were just as discrepant. Alvin was responsible for three-year plans, selling the sizzle to investors and bringing in the cash, while Larry flexed his muscle to meet those three-year plans. Which was why Larry's skepticism was predictable.

But Jonathan ... his skepticism was cause for concern.

"What makes you say that, Jonathan?" Alvin asked. "How are the forecasts looking?"

Straight-faced CFO Jonathan Debil didn't speak much, but when he did people listened. David knew from eight years on Wall Street that all paths eventually led to the CFO. Organizational charts notwithstanding, companies' financial gurus were the end of the line for a lot of ideas. And Medzic practiced that notion to the extreme.

"They're very favorable, which is what scares me."

David pretended to understand what that meant with a slight nod, secretly trying to decipher it. Over the past six months, he'd watched the CFO suggest, with alarming regularity, ideas such as elimination of free employee coffee and soda, lunch-hour break reductions, and the reorganization of company holidays in order to further cut costs. Less was more; efficiency was his religion.

And he was quite devout. Two years earlier, Jonathan created an enigmatic vendor-managed inventory system out of Mexico to eliminate three hundred warehouse employees. He then transferred the goods to a Medzic facility on paper and saved the company eight million dollars in taxes. The CFO thrived on finding ways to improve financials at any cost and, or so it seemed to David, the more ruthless the idea, the more he liked it. Recognizing the value it could bring, two months ago Alvin directed Jonathon to apply that pessimistic focus on Previséo and look for any reason to be the voice of doom.

"What do you mean by that?" Alvin asked.

Even the CEO doesn't understand you, David thought.

"Yes, the market is very encouraging," Jonathan answered deadpan. "Some thirty-four million Americans have diabetes now, just over ten percent of the population. Scientists project that by 2050 one in three could develop Type 2 alone based on current dietary trends. Listening, Larry?"

The COO offered no reply. Being a smartass to Jonathan didn't pencil in.

"In the USA, there are just under one-and-a-half million new cases diagnosed every year, and some 250,000 deaths. Worldwide, there are over 420 million cases. And while the projected growth curve isn't as steep globally as in the USA, it's still directionally favorable."

David peripherally observed that Jonathon said all this with a gleam in his eye, while Alvin smiled.

"Even with conservative sales price assumptions, Previséo will be the most profitable product in the company's history halfway through its sixth year. More than three quarters of a trillion dollars over its lifespan, assuming it remains the only viable solution on the market."

"And there's still no reason to think it won't be," responded Martin Richardson, the Chief Marketing Officer and David's direct superior. "Even if competitors reverse-engineer Previséo, we'll still have patent protection from the copycats." David couldn't help but feel Martin was trying to force a word in just to feel like a contributor, a feeling he knew all too well. He could just imagine the sweat working its way around Martin's neck beneath that silly looking yellow bow tie.

"Regardless," Jonathan continued, "there's already a multibillion-dollar market out there just to create more convenient ways to take insulin. Competitors are getting rich making diabetes more manageable. If Previséo really cures it, actually removes it from the body altogether, we'll make a killing."

Now the dollar signs danced in David's head too.

"Sounds pretty good, Jon. What's the problem?" Alvin asked.

Jonathan looked straight at David, not Alvin, when he gave his answer.

"The problem is that the forecasts are contingent upon successful development and launch of the drug. Ever since Previséo got in the pipeline, our shareholder value has escalated with each step towards its release-to-market. That's all fine and dandy, but it's only temporary. If the drug doesn't launch on time, shareholder confidence will plummet and so will the stock price. So you'll forgive me if I don't simply take your word for it that everything is on schedule and will go according to plan."

"What else would you like to see, Jonathon?" David said with as much confidence as he could muster.

"You're the Director of Business Development. Convince me it's on track. Show me it's on track with FAQs and mapped out projections versus forecasts. Give me specific dates for each step; include as much information as you can. No detail is too small. Throw data at the problem to make it go away."

Jonathon rose from the table and walked over to the wet bar adjacent to the floor-to-ceiling window. The sun reflecting brightly off his shiny bald head, he poured himself a glass of water and removed his rimless glasses as he turned to the four of them. "Very difficult investor questions are coming, gentlemen. And all of our asses will be on the line. Convince me now, David, and I'll convince them later."

3

Two hours later, David re-entered Alvin's office not thinking about Previséo, Jonathan, projections, forecasts or anything else related to Medzic. He was no longer concerned about his imminent at-bat against the veteran pitcher or whether leadership thought highly of him. An hour before, he'd taken the single worst call of his life. His outside must have matched his inside, at least in part, because all four executives immediately ceased conversation as he stepped into the room.

"Martin, I need to take a couple days if that's okay," he forced out through the slim opening between his teeth, barely moving his lips.

"What's going on, David?" Alvin asked softly, cocking his head and furrowing his brows. He seemed almost preemptively irritated at the suggestion of schedule disruption, no matter the cause.

"One of my old coworkers at Clearwater Funding died on Saturday night. He ... he was my best friend."

"Dear Lord," Martin breathed out, his face visibly softened. "How?"

"There was a fire in his apartment. Sometime in the middle of the night. Police don't know how it started. Both he and his wife are dead."

Saying it out loud somehow made it feel more real. His speech felt slow, but his mind was racing. He'd just seen Jake and Mary LeMoure a few months ago. They'd met up after his conference in New York City for drinks and reminisced until almost one o'clock in the morning. It was the last time he could remember actually having fun. Jake's smile flashed in his mind.

"I'm very sorry, David," Alvin said.

Larry and Martin nodded in sympathetic agreement, and they both frowned as well. Jonathan nodded but otherwise remained stoic and silent. He felt the tears forming and knew he needed to get out of there.

"Take whatever time you need," Martin said.

"Yes, David. Go," Alvin replied. "We have your figures, and Martin will send out the reports to the broader team. Let us know if you need anything."

Their compassion was appreciated, but walking out of the palatial office all David could think about was the simple fact that Jake was dead. His only real friend in life, the one person who really knew him, and really understood him, was gone. He'd felt abandonment before and those memories had surfaced in his grief as well, but this was different. This wasn't by anyone's choice and there was no one to be mad at. His best friend was gone, and he didn't even get to say goodbye. He beelined it towards the bathroom to privately unleash the tears that were already on their way.

4

The four men sat on the two fine leather couches in Alvin Patera's 800-square-foot office at a quarter past twelve, surrounded by authentic impressionist paintings and handcrafted Egyptian sculptures. Three of them — he, Larry and Jonathan — had been in the room since early that morning as CEO, CFO and COO of the company. The fourth was the one that concerned him.

He went by Marcus, though Alvin doubted that was his real name. He stood about 6'6" and was far too thin for his towering height. His cheeks were sunken, and his unusually long eyelashes swept across a deep black eyeline. His long, pointed chin would have benefitted from the covering of facial hair, but it matched the rest of his clean-shaven face.

The unwelcome truth was that Alvin wasn't privy to any of Marcus's background.

He guessed Marcus was former military based on his no-nonsense attitude and buzz cut, but that was just speculation. The fact he knew so little about the man only augmented how unsettled he felt. But one thing was certain: Marcus was no businessman.

They stared uneasily at one another, waiting for the conversation to continue. The only one of the bunch drinking, Alvin then rested the crystalline glass on his stomach and rolled his shoulders forward, as if to somehow protect the drink. Then he pushed his lower back deep into the fine supple leather.

This was not going to be pleasant.

"It's a problem we're going to have to deal with sooner or later," began Marcus, rising from the couch to accentuate his towering stature as he ran his bony hand through his thin black hair. Then he further compressed his already naturally squinty eyes, to the point that Alvin thought he was trying to bring something distant into focus.

"Not necessarily," Alvin replied. "David knew Jake LeMoure well; they were good friends at Clearwater, and he was pretty broken up about losing his buddy, but there's no reason to suspect that he knows Jake's death wasn't an accident."

"It's my job to suspect when there's no reason to suspect," Marcus said matter-of-factly.

"Let's take a step back here," Alvin said holding up his right hand. "David's thirty-two years old, has been here six months and makes two hundred grand a year for a job he knows he's lucky to have." He turned his palms upward to match his incredulous look and punctuate the fact that surely both he and Marcus could feel confident in the matter of David knowing nothing and feeling indebted to this company.

"His career is of no concern to me."

"He works hard, he plays hard. Performs well and gets paid for it. Owns a four-bedroom house and drives a fast car. Chicks in Richmond can't get enough of the guy. He's successful and he's hungry. Why do you assume he's a problem?" Alvin now felt on the defensive. It was unfamiliar territory.

As usual, Jonathon had remained completely silent until he uttered few, soft-spoken words that commanded respect. "Perhaps it's best to let Marcus do his job, Alvin. The biggest problems rarely advertise themselves early on; let's hear him out."

"For all his success, he doesn't speak to his family?" Marcus phrased it as a question, but it was clear he was making a bigger statement.

"That's not exactly strange, considering what happened eleven years ago."

"Is it strange to you that he sees a shrink?" Marcus asked, retrieving a manila folder from the briefcase by his feet. Flipping through its contents, he kept his eyes down and continued speaking. "Five sessions a week at twenty-two seems steep enough, but eleven years later he still has a weekly appointment?"

"Is that his medical file?" a bemused Larry Bonnelson interjected. "What about Doctor-Patient Privilege?"

Marcus paused to briefly smirk before continuing. The message was very clear: he was above such confidentialities. "Centrelli's background demonstrates grit. Lost his mom at only eight years old and didn't have a father worth his salt, yet somehow managed to graduate valedictorian from high school with a 4.0. Founded a peer mediation group at his community center that's grown and is still being used statewide today."

"What do Centrelli's high school transcripts and credentials have to do with Previséo?" Alvin asked.

This time Marcus kept going as if he didn't hear the question. "He busts out of Lincoln County, Minnesota and a town of two thousand people on a full academic scholarship to Cornell University. Graduates with honors and serves as President of the Big Brother/Little Brother chapter, and in November of his senior year he saved two kids who fell into a frozen pond. Spent three days unconscious in the ICU but made it out relatively unscathed ... only to have his world completely fall apart two months later."

"Getting back to your question ... so the guy is in therapy," Alvin said, noticeably louder. "And yes, he has for the past decade, just like a lot of other people in this country. What's your point?"

"Don't raise your voice at me, Patera. You may run the show for the cameras, but you will respect my situational authority." Marcus said it in a quiet, monotone voice, which only added to the dread Alvin felt. Such a lack of emotion outwardly made him wonder what was on deck inwardly.

Alvin took a slow sip of Russell's Reserve, letting the liquid linger long enough in his mouth to elicit a burning sensation on the rear of his tongue. He wished he could swallow this whole meeting right down with it. He didn't like being on the defensive, being reprimanded, having to respect someone else's authority, particularly *this* someone else, or a host of other hierarchical subtleties playing out here either.

"It matters," Marcus continued, his hands now on the back of the couch. "Everything matters. From his opposition to the death penalty now, to the fact he hooked up with a random chick on Friday night, to the reality that he's become what he claims to despise. Nothing's irrelevant."

"How do you know that?" Alvin scratched the back of his neck and blinked too many times in succession.

"I know because it's my job to know."

"Perhaps he could join us," Larry Bonnelson nearly whispered into the silence. "He's very intelligent and obviously motivated by money. He might be of use to us."

"No," Jonathon replied plainly.

"Maybe we should consider the possibility," Alvin said softly, lacking conviction.

"It concerns me that a man can go from where he was then to where he is now. From being the model high school and college student and volunteering with the Salvation Army and doing charity work for the elderly to not giving a damn about anyone or anything, all because of what happened eleven years ago when he was still in college. If he can do a 180 like that, he can turn on us, too."

"Isn't that a bit of a stretch? His personal life fell apart because of people he loved when he was transitioning to adulthood. Who can blame him for becoming cynical? What he went through would mess a lot of people up way worse."

"You're breaking my heart, Patera."

Alvin audibly began grinding his teeth as Marcus reengaged. "What's relevant here, gentlemen, is that a guy like Centrelli can turn on a company, go digging where he doesn't belong, take risks he otherwise wouldn't in the name of loyalty, and become a major liability to us given the situation we are in."

"I'll ask again ... is it really so hard to imagine his path from A to B? Yes, he was the all-American boy with the noblest of intentions, but life threw him one too many curve balls, and he got cynical. It's got nothing to do with us or with Previséo," Alvin answered, this time with more confidence. Guys like David weren't a threat, even if their best friends were dead. He'd seen it before. They got power hungry, money hungry, jaded, caught up in the rat race. And in David's case, add in bereft. But they didn't become major liabilities. And they certainly didn't warrant this kind of scrutiny.

"If he can shift that quickly, he can turn on us in a heartbeat. It's an unnecessary risk."

"It was eleven years ago, Marcus."

"I don't understand why you care, Patera. You'd sell ecstasy to recovering drug addicts to make a quick buck, so don't give me your compassion for poor David. What is it? Will you just miss his brown nose being up your ass all day? If you want an admirer, get a dog."

Alvin felt the anger begin to bubble up within. He could feel the ire working its way up from his stomach into his throat, leaving an acrid trail and the taste of heat in his mouth.

"It's true that he's not worth the risk," said Jonathan Debil. "But perhaps you should consider something in the middle. Dealing with him now, in any manner, could raise some questions. The police have already connected him to LeMoure. And two ... accidents ... in such a close timeframe might arouse suspicion."

"Finally, one of you cream puff executive jackoffs has demonstrated a shred of intelligence," Marcus answered. "You're absolutely right, and that's precisely why we need to be very careful in how we figure out what to do with Jake's best friend. How has David's demeanor been, Jonathan?"

"Alvin's dead on about that. Centrelli loves it here. He's got a good job, enjoys the light traffic, and sure doesn't miss freezing his ass off in January like he did in New York. He has regular access to the CEO and other top executives, and to your point earlier, he certainly plays the schmoozing game well." Jonathan mentally replayed his answer and thought he'd said it all too fast.

Marcus turned back to Alvin.

"What do his coworkers think of him?"

"Most think he's going places at Medzic and with good reason, and very few would object if he did. Despite being as cutthroat as he is, he's won a lot of them over rather quickly. Trick of the trade he probably learned on Wall Street."

"He does have rapport with employees," Larry agreed. "And there's a soft spot most folks don't see."

"Is that so?" Marcus said.

"Three months ago one of our interns shared with her coworkers over lunch that she had a twelve-year-old niece with cystic fibrosis. Things were headed downhill fast, and the family didn't know what to do. David heard about it and reached out to his buddy from Cornell, a top pulmonologist at Hackensack University Medical Center in New Jersey. The doc confirmed she needed a double lung transplant and pushed her to the top of the donor list and performed the transplant, saving her life. On top of that, Lacey, our intern, told me in confidence that David gave the girl's family thirty grand to help pay for it but insisted he remain anonymous. No one knows. The only reason I do is because I happened to walk by Lacey's desk as she sat there crying, literally weeping with joy, just after her sister had called to tell her what David had done. The raw emotion got the better of her and she spilled the beans."

"Yeah ... this guy seems like one real cutthroat son a bitch, Patera," Marcus replied with a sideways glance towards the CEO, then put his hand up as if he knew what Patera would retort.

"My point is that we don't really know who Centrelli is. He comes across as hardened and definitely has reason to be, but there are plenty of examples of behind the scenes of altruistic behavior that tell me he's much more compassionate. That is a viable threat to our primary objective."

"How so?" Alvin questioned. "What am I missing here? His e-mails, office and telephone lines are clean, right? He's been super predictable and hasn't given any indication he's a threat to the plan. When he found out his best friend died, he almost broke down right here in this office. You think he could've hidden it from the three of us if he knew LeMoure's death wasn't an accident? He'll never connect the dots."

"Of course you don't get it, Patera." Marcus shook his head rapidly as if to shake off their collective stupidity. "There's no reason to add Centrelli to the mix. I believe in running a tight operation, and I'm not going to change the way I do things just because you don't understand it."

After a brief pause, Marcus continued.

"We plan for the worst and hope for the best, Alvin. You just run your company like a good little boy and leave these matters to me. I don't want any more resistance. My superior, whom we all ultimately report to, is not willing to take any more chances. You know precisely what I mean."

Alvin took a deep breath and stared back in defeat. He did know what it meant.

David was as good as dead.

5

Anne Halavity watched surreptitiously from across the street through the tiny, black binoculars she'd taken from her closet.

Her bony elbows rested against the Kia Stinger's black leather steering wheel, and when she saw him, she felt herself gasp. This was the moment she was simultaneously waiting for and dreading.

David Centrelli hurriedly exited Medzic Pharmaceuticals corporate headquarters wearing a heavily starched white dress shirt and a navy-blue tie that matched the suit jacket he'd thrown over his shoulder. He walked quickly and focused on the pavement, resembling a New Yorker stuck in the slower Richmond, scurrying through the private garage and emerging a few moments later in a slick 4 Series BMW convertible.

Surely a company car.

But something was off. His handsome face was now drawn, his body language slumped. He must have already gotten word somehow. The 4 Series peeled out of the circle drive like a drag racer from the start line, as if David was running away from something. Escaping.

She knew that look and she knew that feeling. She'd felt the need to escape as well. The real question was: why did David Centrelli feel that need to escape? Was he in the same boat she was, or ...?

She wouldn't be taking any chances.

The loaded gun concealed under a light coat on the passenger seat didn't make her feel confident, nor did it remove the fear that she felt. She turned on the ignition and followed him two cars behind, exactly as instructed. And as she drove, she restated her objective out loud over and over, reminding herself not only why she was doing this, but more importantly whom she was doing it for.

It's almost time. You can do this.

* * *

David stared at the menu, but he couldn't really read the words. They blurred together in sort of a fuzzy haze, and he lacked the ambition to make them clear. Twenty-five miles from the office in a Cheesecake Factory sure to be free of other Medzic employees, he motioned to the waitress to bring his third double Jack and Coke in just over an hour.

The restaurant was relatively empty during lunchtime most days and definitely not a popular haunt for coworkers, which was exactly why he chose it. He could actually hear the soft piano music playing from the speakers above while he drank his meal. The sun's reflection on the table next to him was blinding, but he didn't care to move. Rotating his neck and running his fingers through his light brown, wavy hair, he sat still and soaked in the quietness engulfing him.

Or was it loneliness?

The restaurant was connected to the Hawthorne Suites via a hallway corridor, meaning folks staying at the hotel were led to pay forty bucks for a meal without even considering other options. It was a clever business idea that worked, but it annoyed him. Perhaps because it felt like deception. Or perhaps, because he was no different.

Money had become all that mattered, and he hated himself just as much as he hated The Cheesecake Factory and Hawthorne Suites. One minute he was a money-hungry executive, the next he was pissed off because others were too.

How hypocritical.

And he hated hypocrites.

Not Jake, though. Jake was above hypocrisy. Jake was above him. He'd somehow maintained his dignity over the years; he'd possessed a moral fiber seemingly not subject to the pressures of money and power. His best friend didn't turn cynical when the going got tough. Instead, Jake filled his life with love, trust and compassion, and David had both cherished and envied him because of it. He was a rare gem of warmth in a cold, relentless world. A special person, the type who never left your side. The only friend he'd had left.

And now he was dead.

MAN, WIFE KILLED IN APARTMENT FIRE

The New York Times headline had him grinding his knuckles into each other in between increasingly large gulps of Jack and Coke.

"That's nice," he spoke aloud, ignoring the waitress's glare as she delivered drink number four. "Capitalize it. Bold it. Put it in big, black letters, you greedy son of a bitch. Highlight the fact that two of the best people in the world just burned to death just to sell more newspapers."

The avarice bandwagon was big enough for anyone to hop aboard. And with money as fuel, it could run forever.

6

Lost in all his pessimistic philosophizing, David Centrelli didn't see her.

But she saw him.

Sitting quietly at the bar fifty feet across the room, wearing a Chico's straw hat with a small red flower on top, Anne studied him closely while nursing a club soda and pretending to flip through a tabloid magazine. He looked very similar to the picture she'd been given: straight nose, strong white teeth, broad shoulders, thick quadriceps, well dressed in a navy business suit, sleeves now rolled up past the elbow and tie loosened. Attractive for sure. She could see why she was told he did well with the ladies.

She watched him for over an hour, but when he started on his fourth drink and began cursing aloud and then suddenly threw his newspaper on the floor, she knew it was time. She'd already been warned not to let Centrelli draw attention to himself before she made her move, and he was certainly doing that now. Precious seconds were slipping away as the fool got tipsier and louder. This needed to happen. She gripped her leather bag, feeling the bulge within, and inhaled deeply.

For me. Do it for me.

The words unapologetically rang in her ears as she fought through her trepidation and walked straight towards him, exhaling slowly in an unsuccessful attempt to simmer down. The gun's presence continued to offer zero comfort.

When she reached David Centrelli, it was apparent that he was not expecting her.

Staring at the ground, he appeared sad, angry, confused and helpless all at the same time. Beneath his notoriously hardened outer shell, she could immediately sense the tenderness she'd been told about. Even the way he slouched in the booth conveyed a sense of vulnerability. But his fourth drink also confirmed he wasn't embracing that vulnerability, but rather ignoring it. The term used to describe him was "emotionally immature." This was a man who would likely continue to bury his emotions deep inside until one day, in a predictable yet unpreventable and uncontrollable fashion, they would be ferociously unleashed on someone completely undeserving.

Like her.

She had not been misinformed. He looked to her like a ticking time bomb; one that would go off at precisely the wrong moment.

Like right now.

For me. Do it for me.

"David Centrelli?" she almost whispered.

"Who's asking?" he replied nonchalantly, still looking down and attempting to scratch something off his right trouser leg that didn't exist.

"You need to come with me right now."

His head rose slowly, as if it took monumental effort to fight gravity.

"And who the hell are you?" David hissed, rotating his neck while wincing in pain. His eyes were crimson red and very swollen.

"Now, David."

"Look lady, I—"

The gun, now in her right jacket pocket, formed a sizable bulge as she hovered over the table and leaned in towards his face. His open mouth and the mixture of confusion and alarm on his face made it clear she now had his undivided attention. He knew what that bulge was, or at least what it could be. She forced herself to be strong and confident to seize that moment.

"You're coming with me now, David. I don't want to hurt you. But believe me, I will if I have to. Get up and start walking towards the lobby. Slowly."

7

As David made his way through the hotel lobby and into an empty conference room, he thought about pulling a James Bond, shoving the innocent bystander waiting in line at the main desk into his assailant and stylishly dashing out of the building unscathed, escaping into a maze of people much to the viewers' delight. But then it occurred to him:

There were no viewers.

There was no maze of people.

And he wasn't James Bond.

Once in the room, the woman shut and locked the door before turning to face him. She then vigorously whipped her straw hat towards the wall with surprising and impressive force, then motioned with the gun for him to take a seat. He chose the one at the far end of the dated grey laminate conference table just to be as far from her as possible. Its hard mid back and unpadded steel armrests made him feel even more uncomfortable.

Thankful that he probably met the requirements to be a functioning alcoholic, he fought through his buzz to focus on the woman without too much struggle. He guessed she was about fifty. Her hair looked like autumn on a windy day, light brown with streaks of gray and side swept bangs that fell across her left eyebrow. She was attractive, but the hat head wasn't doing her any favors. Maybe 5'7" and slim, with a chiseled face and soft lips. She was in tight-fitting jeans and a light brown jacket that concealed a white shirt and presumably a gun, and she also had a camel-colored leather satchel slung over her bony right shoulder. Her shaking hands indicated she was just as scared as he was, but that didn't much matter. She had the gun, and it was pointed at him.

"I've been following you for the past two days," she said as if this kind of thing was common.

"That's comforting," he said, unable to look away from the general direction of the gun.

"Sorry about that," she said, withdrawing the weapon and dropping it on the table, shaking her head in disbelief. It was a Glock of some sort, though his novice marksmanship knowledge couldn't decipher which.

"I had to make sure it was really you," she said very softly, so softly he could hardly hear her. "I ... I don't do this kind of thing. I was really scared."

"Try it from my end, lady."

"I know, and like I said, I'm sorry. But you need to listen to me."

"I've got to tell you, for someone claiming to be so afraid, you sure didn't hesitate to point that gun at me. Who the hell are you?"

"We'll get to that."

"We'll get to it right now."

"It's about Jake."

David stared into the woman's eyes, curiosity replacing his fear. "Jake...?"

"Now's not the time to play dumb, David. Jake LeMoure. Your best friend. He sent me here to find you."

"Who the hell are you?" he raised his voice and widened his eyes.

"My name is Anne Halavity. I'm ... I used to be Jake's secretary at Clearwater Funding Company."

"Bullshit. Nancy was his secretary's name."

"She quit a month after you did."

"How many people work there?"

"Fifty-five full-time employees, twenty part-time. Ten college interns join us every summer."

"Name a few."

"Matthew James, Nina Olverson, Edwin Abraham, Issa Gordon."

"Where's the office's happy hour hangout?"

"Rafferty's Pub, on the far other side of the office complex. Ground floor. Good ambiance. Great Guinness."

He remembered the cracked wooden sign that hung above Rafferty's entrance displaying those exact words, but he continued to shake his head in disbelief.

"I used to work at Clearwater, lady. It isn't that huge of a company, and I think someone would've told me if Nancy quit."

"Can't help you there, bud. But I can tell you that Jake told me all about you. About how you were best friends and saw each other every day until you got the job six months ago at Medzic Pharmaceuticals, one of our biggest clients. Director of Business Development. That's very impressive. He told me about how the two of you used to grab lunch at Fisher's Deli every Thursday."

She now spoke with a subtle confidence that started to chip away at his disbelief.

"So you memorized some things you probably pulled off of social media sites. That doesn't prove anything."

"He said you were best friends for ten years, ever since you joined the firm on the same day. And if that's true, you need to listen to me."

"How do I know any of this is true?"

She reached down into her bag and withdrew a white binder, three notebooks and stationary pad, each adorned with Clearwater's logo.

"These are from the stock room, next to the IT department on the 33rd floor. Padlock combination 11-16-12."

Over the next few minutes Anne rattled off the names of several other Clearwater employees, talked about their families and provided enough details to convince him she either really knew those people or had sources much more impressive than the Internet.

But of particular interest to him was how she spoke of Jake. She did so in a way that seemed only someone close to him could. Not just his likes, dislikes, pet peeves and tendencies, all of which a secretary would probably learn on the job, but his long-term plans for retirement, his family plans with Mary, and his involvement with the Cerebral Palsy foundation. She sounded like a big sister, or even a young mother, proud and protective.

"Fine," he finally replied. "But if Jake sent you, and you know all this about me, why did you come here and stick a gun in my face?"

"Because he told me you'd react like this," she said, blowing out a sigh of frustration.

"Excuse me?"

"Excuse you! I didn't come here for you, so don't flatter yourself. And I don't even like guns ... yet somehow I'm finding that I like them more than you." He leaned back in obvious surprise by her sudden outburst.

"I brought the gun because Jake said that was the only way you'd listen. He gave me your address and picture, told me how and where to find you, and what to say when I did. But he also said you wouldn't listen. That you'd be standoffish, even after I mentioned his name. He said that I had to do it this way because of how important it was that you listened. I resisted and he insisted. It was the last thing he said to me."

"It can't be," he said burying his head in his hands, then springing up from his chair to pace between the table and the wall. His mind was like a pinball machine.

Rotating both hands around each other in small opposing circles as if he were a football referee calling a false start, he pointed his head towards the ceiling and closed his eyes. He thought about Jake and their long history together, everything he knew about his best friend. Would Jake really instruct his secretary to point a gun at him? The very thought was alarming, but he couldn't deny the possibility existed. Remote, and definitely out of place, the kind of thing Jake would only do if he absolutely had to. But deep down, he knew it was possible. If Jake felt the ends would justify the means, it was even borderline likely.

But what on earth would justify that?

He turned towards Anne with a grim expression on his face to express his doubt and frustration.

"I still think you're full of it, lady. And when I find out for sure, I'm going to have your ass arrested."

She didn't say anything, just looked back at him with wistful sadness that replaced her earlier passion. Her eyebrows angled down, and her mouth quivered slightly. If she wasn't genuinely shaken over all of this, she deserved an Oscar.

"But for now," he continued, "what is it that's so important?"

She took a deep breath with her eyes still closed before responding. "I know this is sudden, David. But Jake and Mary didn't die in a fire. And it sure wasn't an accident."

8

David could only stare at Anne Halavity, her mystique growing by the second. Her face, devoid of makeup, looked tired. Purple rings hung beneath her eyes like hammocks beckoning sleep to come rest. The whites of her eyes were haphazardly streaked with red, as if a toddler had gotten into the paint cabinet. And yet, there was a draw there for him. Was it her quiet confidence? Her fierce loyalty to Jake? Maybe it was a strength of character that seemed to slip out through all of the cracks, a beautiful light on the inside, warming the exhausted exterior.

"What do you mean Jake's death wasn't an accident?" he asked

"A few days before the fire, I was leaving the office when he met me at my car and asked to go for a walk. It struck me as odd right off the bat because Jake had never suggested that before. He also looked tense. *Real* tense. He was looking all around, jumping at car horns and acting kind of skittish. I asked him what was wrong, but he said he just felt like going for a walk and wanted me to come."

"So you went."

"That's right. Jake liked cold weather even less than I do. So the idea that he actually he wanted to go for a stroll in New York City in the middle of January didn't add up, but I wanted to see what was on his mind and he clearly wanted to wait until we were walking to reveal it."

"And?"

"And for the first ten minutes, I thought I'd read him wrong. We chitchatted about random, everyday stuff. Things like how much I liked working at Clearwater, how Manhattan was treating me, my commute time, different subway routes I could take, a vacation he was planning ... stuff like that. He still seemed really jittery, but he didn't say anything substantial. So I waited for whatever it was he really wanted to talk about for a few more minutes, but thinking this really was just a walk to catch up, I asked to head back. The wind was bitter cold, my nose and ears were freezing, and I hadn't remembered to slip my gloves on before we'd left the office."

"And? ..."

"And when I asked to head back, he didn't respond to that part. Instead, he took me by the shoulders and spun me to face him, paused for a second to check our surroundings and said almost imperceptibly, "I need your help.""

Anne looked around the room, on edge about whatever she was about to say. She checked every corner of the meeting room twice, as if they wouldn't have noticed any new entrants to the tiny space. Her skyrocketed nervousness had more than jumpstarted his own. David wondered if Anne had just given him a glimpse into the moments just before Jake confided in Anne.

"He told me I was the only person he could trust," she said in a softer voice. "He said he couldn't give me any details, but that he was worried something might happen to him."

"Like what?"

"That's what I asked. Again he said he couldn't give any details."

"Why not?"

"For my safety."

"Oh," was all that came out of his mouth. Stunned, he took a seat on the table and decided to just shut up and let Anne finish telling the story.

"I was terrified. I didn't know what to do or even think. But I was even more confused, and frustrated that Jake wasn't giving me any real information. It wasn't like him at all. He was usually very thorough in our professional exchanges, and the whole tell-me-this-but-not-that thing was confusing and concerning."

Having been his best friend for nearly a decade, David knew Jake didn't mince words.

"I asked him again if he could just tell me what was going on, but he wouldn't. Then I suggested he call the police if he was worried about his safety."

"That's what I would've done," David said.

"But when I did, he said that if he was in the trouble he thought he was in, telling the police wouldn't help."

Now it was his turn to scan the room. He didn't necessarily believe Anne yet, but she certainly had his attention.

"He told me that if anything happened to him, I needed to find you. That no matter what, I *had* to do it. And give you this."

As she spoke, she reached into her satchel and withdrew a large manila envelope. It looked like a standard 10" X 13" and the top seal hadn't been broken. That meant that despite what had to be raging curiosity, Anne hadn't looked inside. She handed it to him slowly, almost as if reluctant to give it up despite having come all this way to do so. Her dark brown eyes were wide, and her lower lip trembled as they made the exchange.

"He gave me your name, picture, a description, and told me where I could find you. He told me about your history at Clearwater and how you moved down to Richmond six months ago."

"Then he said there was no way I'd believe you," David whispered.

Anne nodded. "That's why he told me about your lunches and walks and anything else that might help convince you. Then, just when I was about to tell him I wouldn't do it unless I knew why, he handed me this gun."

She looked at the Glock as if the pistol were some sort of radioactive poison that was dangerous to the touch. She closed her eyes and shook her head side to side with a slowness that unnerved him. He imagined being in her shoes and immediately rejected the notion.

"What'd you say?" he asked.

She opened her eyes and then stared over his head at the projection screen in front of the room, as if forgetting he was there. "I flipped out at first. I told him there was no way I would take a gun. Jake tried to calm me down, but I just got louder. I don't do guns."

"But you obviously wound up taking it."

Anne sighed. "I got to know Jake while working with him at my old company. I'd known that man since he entered the workforce a still-wet-behind-the-ears twenty-year-old intern who couldn't send a fax or brew a pot of coffee without my help. That was over twenty years ago. Even after he left Morecroft Investors for Clearwater Funding, Jake and I kept in close touch. I met him for lunch a few times a year and we exchanged e-mails almost every week. I got to know Mary so well that the two of us would get together without him. I met his parents for goodness' sake, kind of became the big sister he never had."

"And that's why he called you when Nancy left."

"Nancy?"

"His old secretary."

"Oh, yeah. And it was great working for him again. I left the law firm in Pennsylvania the day he called and didn't regret it one bit. Until now."

"But ..."

"But in all those years, he never had anything to do with guns. He was pro-gun control for heaven's sake, and he wanted nothing to do with them. It scared the living daylights out of me when he handed me a loaded gun, but he insisted that I take it and stressed how important it was that I get this envelope to you. He said, 'For me. Please, if you trust me, do it for me.' What was I supposed to do?"

"Did he ever say why?"

"Only that a whole bunch of people would die if I didn't."

They both absorbed the enormity of that statement in their own way. David felt unbridled curiosity and fear. The combination of alcohol and this farfetched-yet-believable tale created far too much spinning for his head to handle. Anne just stared back at him, probably assuming he would have information from Jake to help piece things together and likely disappointed that he didn't.

"So, I took the gun," she continued, "and the stack of cash that he handed me. And I listened to him when he told me that if something happened to him, I needed to get to Richmond right away. He said that I shouldn't use my credit card, and that no one could see us meeting. So I did it. All without knowing why ... because of how much I loved and respected Jake."

David stared at the envelope she had passed to him and slowly picked it up. There were no labels or writing on either side. About five pounds heavy, it felt like it contained a large, hardcover book of some sort.

Dabbing at her eyes with a tissue she'd fished out of her bag, Anne fought through the last part of her story, sniffing after each period.

"When I asked him what he meant by something happening to him, all Jake said was that if it happened, I'd know. And that I should assume it wasn't an accident, no matter what I heard or read to the contrary. I didn't ask any more questions..." she paused before closing her eyes taking a shaky breath, her hand on her chest.

David just quietly stared, waiting for her to finish.

"And I've regretted it ever since."

9

Four full minutes of silence stretched between and over them, like a weighty netting of sorts. Its invisible ropes were filled with a kind of liquid tension that ebbed and flowed like a terrible tide.

For most of that time, while Anne wiped her eyes and chewed on her lower lip, David sat fingering the envelope as he contemplated her story. And despite his best intentions, he couldn't find any holes in it.

It felt very much like a point-of-no return moment, as if the option to walk away from whatever the envelope contained would disappear the moment he broke the seal. But until he did, he was free and clear to wash his hands of Anne Halavity and this entire bizarre day. He couldn't help but wonder if he should do just that.

"I wasn't supposed to show it to anyone else and neither are you," Anne finally said. "Jake told me to physically hand it to you, not leave it at your house or office. No snail mail either. Had to be in person. Had to be private."

The more he considered Anne's story, the more he believed her. One more question just to make sure.

"I don't understand why you didn't just call the cops. Friend or no friend, Jake put you in a pretty tough spot here. Why take it all on yourself?"

"I already told you."

"So you would've jumped off the Brooklyn Bridge if he'd asked you to?"

David froze. He always regretted saying the very words his mom used to say to him the second they left his mouth. Doing so brought emotions back into his head he wasn't prepared for and couldn't deal with right now. He could tell Anne noticed by the way she raised her eyebrow, but she left it alone.

"What would you have done?"

"What we're going to do now. Call the cops and give them this envelope."

"The hell we are, David!"

This was the second time in the past hour one of her sudden outbursts caught him off guard. He checked the door and sternly put his finger to his mouth.

Anne carried on in the same volume, undeterred. "Listen, I don't know you, I don't particularly like you, and I certainly don't understand you. I know this is a shock, but it was for me too. Whatever's in this envelope meant more to Jake than his own life, and maybe even more than Mary's."

Anne paused briefly, as if contemplating something. Then she narrowed her eyes and honed in on him like a laser beam. "Jake told me all about you, David. He told me you'd come off like an ass at first, and that I needed to know why. He told me all about your past, and it is awful. But frankly, even with what happened with your fiancé, I'm surprised you and he were such good friends"

"What makes you say that?" He tried to conceal his disappointment. Jake had been the one bright spot in the past ten years of his social life, and it stung to hear it challenged.

"You're night and day. Jake was a happily married man; you dump any woman who wants to get close to you. Jake was a proud volunteer and philanthropist who sat on the local food pantry board of directors; you contribute just as much time and money but go out of your way to hide it. Jake was super tight with his parents; you haven't seen your dad in over ten years, though I understand why."

Anne stopped talking, as if to let his own life story soak in. "The thing is, it's not that you're a bad guy. You've done some amazing, generous things. Jake told me about that little boy's surgery ... the one who needed the tumor removed and couldn't afford it ... paying for that is one of the nicest things I've ever heard. But then you made the family swear not to tell anyone it was you? And when you took the entire Big Brother/Little Brother group to the Yankees game. Why did you categorically deny it when your coworker saw you there and asked about it the next day? It's like you *want* everyone to think you're a jerk, even though you're really a good man. Why would you do that? Are you that afraid of getting hurt again?"

"Maybe because it isn't anyone's business."

"But just because I don't understand you, I'm not going to dishonor Jake by sitting here quietly while you go against his wishes."

Until that rant, David had considered simply telling Anne about the "I had to make sure" plan, but then decided against it. She wouldn't appreciate being tested and might even re-launch into assaulting his character. It wouldn't matter to her that he'd learned to have a trust but verify mentality. Plus, he didn't necessarily want her to know what he was thinking. He had to know if he could trust her. Because the frightening thing was, once he opened that envelope, he and Anne were in this together.

"One last question. Did Jake say why he wanted you in particular to give this to me?"

Anne exhaled deeply before answering. "I'd like to think it was because he trusted me, but he didn't say. I don't really think my part in this is all that relevant. At least it doesn't feel that way. I was actually hoping you could fill me in on what this is about."

"I know less than you do."

"He was adamant that it had to be you. He begged me not to look inside the envelope. And after I give it to you, I'm supposed to go back to New York. That's not happening, by the way."

"I really think you should."

"You honestly don't have any idea what's going on?" She asked, then gritted her teeth.

"No, I honestly don't." He sighed, running his left hand through the hair at his temple, and then using it to support his head. "I went to Clearwater straight out of college. Jake was my assigned mentor. We became good friends that first year and have been ever since. I got to know Mary and before long the three of us were spending almost every weekend together, always on some adventure. Like that time we went spelunking on a whim. The tide came in unexpectedly so we rushed to the highest ledge we could find only to sit there for three hours, waiting for it to flow back out. We sang every Beatles song we could think of that night. But in all those years he never mentioned anything like this. I don't even know what *this* is."

He thought of his last visit to New York City just a few months earlier for what turned out to be his final night with Jake and Mary. Their infectious smiles and happiness felt so contagious. He recalled the laughter at Barcelona Bar as *Banned from the Zoo* jammed out punk rock covers in the background, and the smirk on Jake's face when he ordered David a specialty "Full Metal Jacket," which had him doing thirty pushups between shots while being yelled at by a "Drill Sergeant." He remembered falling asleep at their apartment and waking up the next morning for breakfast burritos. There had been no hint of danger whatsoever the entire visit. The word "last" stuck in his mind, its significance finally registering.

He'd never see Jake again.

"Why did you leave Clearwater?" Anne asked.

"Because I got a great job and was ready for a change. Look ... not to change the subject ... but are we about done here?"

"Nothing left to do but open the envelope."

"I'll open it at my place in private. Thanks ... I guess ... for bringing it to me. You should head home."

"Have you heard a word I said?"

"Anne ..."

"Not a chance, David. I'm staying right here. I know it's dangerous, but it's probably just as dangerous for me to go home now, and there's no way I'm not seeing this through."

He let a loud sigh escape and rolled his eyes. He knew he probably wasn't going to shake this woman.

"Besides, you're coming back to my hotel room to open it."

"And why would I do that?"

"Because Jake said it wasn't safe to open it at your house."

10

The ensuing half hour was one of the most awkward David had ever experienced. He and Anne agreed not to discuss the envelope until they got to the hotel, but that didn't stop his mind from producing an unending string of questions as they drove. The silence between them only heightened the suspense.

"Why wouldn't it be safe to open this at my house?"

"I already told you. Jake said I shouldn't give it to you at your house or office. He said you should open it somewhere away from your everyday life. I have no idea why."

"This is getting better by the minute."

"Don't shoot the messenger. I didn't volunteer for this."

He changed lanes while trying to figure out the woman who'd turned his world upside down in a mere forty-five minutes.

He briefly considered the possibility that she and Jake had once had a fling, but then quickly discarded the notion. Jake would never do that, and Anne's compassion for him seemed to go well beyond that kind of relationship.

Not everyone is as heartless as they are, he reminded himself. That awful January night rushed to his mind, when he lost the two people he cared most about without actually losing them. The sad realization that his therapist had helped him say out loud years later was that their deaths would've been easier to accept.

"I'm sorry," she whispered. "I certainly can understand what you're feeling right now. Believe me." Her large brown eyes were sincere and empathetic, and she extended her arm to place a surprisingly gentle hand on his forearm.

He didn't respond but internally acknowledged that he appreciated the gesture.

They finally arrived and he parked the car. He looked around in all directions as if he'd know what to do if he saw something unusual or even knew what to look for in the first place. Futile as his surveillance was, he still felt an obligation to scan the near-empty lot.

The Red Roof Inn on Commerce Drive was a small two-star hotel surrounded by four other motels, a Shell gas station and a boarded-up auto repair shop. Located a mere 200 feet from I-95, it was mundane and cheap, sporting a pungent odor of re-grown mold throughout the building. Its trademark tan-colored exterior had faded considerably in areas exposed to the afternoon sun, and two of the red letters in the hotel's namesake weren't lit at all while a third flickered. The wooden railings looked rotten and he wouldn't be caught dead barefoot on the hallway carpet.

One thing was certain: Anne had listened to Jake's request to live frugally on cash alone. He obeyed the urge to hold his breath as they walked through the lobby towards the elevator.

Before they entered the third-floor room, each turned around a final time to make sure they were alone. Once inside the ordinary room, with a queen bed, desk and uncomfortable looking chair all arranged on a blue carpet that had seen better days, Anne dropped her bag on the bed and removed her jacket.

He couldn't help but notice her figure. Curves in all the right places but not in any of the wrong ones, accentuated by her cotton tee and dark wash skinny jeans. *Kind of hot,* he thought, but his mind flicked back to the matter at hand as she withdrew the envelope from her bag. He regrouped, silently chiding himself.

"One last time," he stared right at her, "did Jake say anything else?"

"Only that you shouldn't trust anyone."

"Yet here I am trusting you." He carefully ripped open the envelope's seal.

* * *

Only one item was inside.

And as David had guessed, it was a book.

But the type of book was very unexpected. His fear of the unknown was immediately augmented by bewilderment. He blinked in disbelief, certain there was more in the envelope. There wasn't.

He stared at the high school yearbook, dated 24 years ago.

And it stared right back, looking like any other he'd seen. With Anne equally perplexed, he quickly flipped back through the pages but didn't notice anything all that unusual. The only aspect of any interest whatsoever was a short note scribbled in pen on the upper right corner of the inside back cover, in what looked to David like Jake's handwriting:

Remember the good times with Julie from the swim team? X marks the spot, eh? I'll say! Well, you gotta admit: you can't judge a book by its cover.

That was it.

He and Anne stared at each other with confused looks as David flipped to Jake's senior portrait. They both saw that Jake's appearance hadn't drastically changed since his last year of high school. He was younger, of course, but even back then he had short hair combed to the side with a cunning smile and looked sharp in a dark jacket and tie.

Underwhelmed if not outright disappointed, David flipped through the yearbook again. This time he did so slowly, page-by-page to make sure they hadn't missed something glaring. But each turn of the page offered nothing new until they reached the back cover, and he slammed it shut. There were no other notes or signatures or personalization or references. No additional messages or phrases on either cover.

It looked like a completely typical yearbook, and David had no idea who Julie was or what the handwritten message meant.

"This is it?" he said shooting a puzzled look at Anne.

"I'm guessing it doesn't mean much to you...?"

"Not a thing. I didn't go to this school. I didn't even graduate this year. I was in elementary school halfway across the country when this was printed."

"Watkins High," Anne read on the cover. "Is that in New York?"

He flipped to page 3 where they saw a picture of the front of the building with a brief caption underneath.

WATKINS GLEN PUBLIC HIGH SCHOOL

"Watkins Glen ...Yeah, that's the town where Jake grew up. Downstate New York. Small village. His parents are still there."

Anne took the yearbook and flipped again to Jake's senior portrait. He could tell that the picture momentarily reminded her of what'd happened to their mutual friend, but she didn't linger on the sentiment.

"How do you know that?" she asked warily, as if for a second time she sensed treachery.

"Relax, Anne. We were best friends. He took me to Watkins Glen a few years ago to meet his folks. We took their boat out and spent a Saturday afternoon on the lake."

"When was that?"

"Maybe five years ago."

She didn't respond, but a slight nod and bent lower lip indicated she'd cooled her conspiratorial jets.

"I don't see what any of this has to do with me," he said dejectedly. "The note isn't addressed to me. Or anyone else for that matter."

"Jake wrote it, and he wrote it for you."

"How can you be so sure?"

"He wouldn't have given me the envelope and insisted I give it to you for no reason, David. And besides, I know his handwriting."

Shaking his head he said, "Well, I don't know Watkins Glen. I don't know the high school. I didn't know Jake when this yearbook came out, and I don't know anyone named Julie from any swim team. I went to high school in rural Minnesota. We didn't have a swimming pool let alone a team, and I sure didn't have good times with someone named Julie. So, you tell me what I'm supposed to do with this."

"Well ... it says, 'you can't judge a book by its cover.' Maybe we should take that advice."

11

After carefully flipping through every page twice, Anne still didn't have any clue what to make of the twenty-year-old yearbook from a school neither of them had gone to in a town she'd never been to or heard of before. In that time, David had grown noticeably agitated and twice had abruptly jumped from the desk chair to splash cold water on his face. She couldn't blame him though, because even she was starting to doubt that the yearbook held any answers they could figure out.

In fact, only one thing seemed to support her theory that there was something to find at all, and she played that card to break the silence that had ensued.

"You know what's weird about this?" she asked slowly.

"What's that?" David replied with his eyes closed.

"It's too new."

"Huh?"

"It's brand-spanking new. Look at it. The pages are crisp; the outside is still glossy and shiny. Not even the binding is bent. It looks like it hasn't been opened more than a few times."

David moseyed over from the bathroom sink and she handed the yearbook to him.

"Yeah, I guess it does seem pretty new."

"But? ..."

"But that doesn't mean anything. How many people really look at their high school yearbook? I haven't opened mine since the day I got it."

"Sure, but I'll bet yours has at least a few creases in the spine."

"Mine wasn't this thick. There wasn't much to say about a worn-down hillbilly lumberjack high school in a Minnesota cornfield. They should've just called it the shack school."

"Look at this," she said, grabbing the yearbook back from him. "The spine is pristine. There's no way this was Jake's original copy from twenty-four years ago."

"This is going nowhere fast. So it looks new, and maybe that's a bit odd. Great. Fantastic. It still doesn't mean anything. Maybe Jake never looked through it. Maybe he got it, put on a shelf, went to college, and it's been in a box ever since. Who knows why? But more importantly, who cares?"

"And what don't you see anywhere?" She flipped through the pages again.

"I'm sure you're going to tell me."

"Notes, signatures, friends' best wishes, all that crap. There's nothing in this. My yearbook, and everyone's that I've ever seen, has all sorts of farewells and good luck messages. Even the jocks weren't too cool to get their yearbooks signed."

David turned to the two blank pages following the cover. "It doesn't matter how well-liked a person was," she continued, "everyone had at least a few signatures. I've got pages of farewells, and I'll bet you do too. And imagine Jake in high school!" She was gaining steam fast. "Given how popular he was in adulthood, for his senior high school yearbook to not have at least a few goodbye notes from his friends, well that just doesn't make sense. There's nothing in this entire book except one little note scribbled on the inside back cover!" Her exclamation brought a color and life into her face that had been missing up until now.

David's expression changed from completely disengaged to ever so slightly interested. He moved his lips slightly but no words came out, as if he was whispering thoughts to himself and the lip movement was a byproduct. His eyes scanned up and down like he was searching his memory, clearly deep in thought.

"Okay, you've got a point there. It's probably not the same book he got twenty-four years ago. That still doesn't tell us what we're supposed to do with it."

"No, but it confirms there's something to find."

Her excited proclamation was loud enough to prompt David to check the window and look through the door's peephole. He shrugged his shoulders and shot her a WTF kind of glance before taking a seat on the footrest he'd moved next to the desk chair a half-hour ago.

"Sorry," she said.

"Let's check the swimming team."

They flipped to ATHLETICS and found a four-page spread that covered girls' swimming. Team photos of the junior varsity and varsity squads came first, followed by a few action shots, mainly of swimmers gasping for air, the Win-Loss record, and opponent schedule. Finally, the head coach proudly showing off a gigantic Interscholastic Athletic Conference championship trophy. The group photo's caption revealed there were three girls on the team named Julie.

"Well, we know the swim team was pretty good," she said, sounding disappointed.

The smartass comment she expected from David didn't come.

Instead, he was looking closely at one of the pictures, his left hand holding the book open and his right tugging rhythmically on his earlobe as he squinted his thoughts into cohesion.

He didn't say anything, but Anne could tell that David was on to something.

12

"What is it?" she finally said, unable to hold back.

"Maybe we'll get lucky," he muttered to himself as he flipped to the back of the yearbook.

"David? ..." she opened both of her arms, perhaps to catch the new information she solicited.

"The back index in my yearbook listed all the students and faculty alphabetically and gave the different page numbers where you could see their pictures."

Her excitement dwindled.

"I already thought of that, but there were three Julies on the swim team alone. How many do you think there were in the entire school?"

"I'm not looking for Julie." He pointed to a page:

LeMoure, Jake; Sr.: 13, 17, 21, 27, 29, 39, 43, 44, 49, 55, 59, 64

That meant there were twelve pictures of Jake in the yearbook, and David flipped to page 13 obviously hoping to find something. And although she didn't know what it was or think it would go anywhere, at least he was trying something. She held her breath when he landed on the Homeroom Study Group page and sighed when nothing came of it.

Each page led to more disappointment. Together, they saw their good friend's highly photogenic face in different settings. In all of them, Jake looked young, bright-eyed, and always appeared to be having fun, full of promise and potential. But in none of them did they find anything helpful.

Not until page 64.

"SENIOR LIFE" was a ten-page, full-color section at the end of the yearbook dedicated to the eighteen-year-olds ready to embark on a new life's journey. There were several action shots of graduation along with a series of candid photos showing students sitting together, laughing and posing for the camera. Some were large group pictures, like the one of the senior class trip; others were more intimate, like the close-up of a boyfriend and girlfriend pointing at class rings on each other's fingers.

The photo that mattered was easy to miss because it was dwarfed by a half-page memento of Senior Cut Day above it. One-eighth of a page in size and at the bottom left-hand corner, it offered no description and could've easily been overlooked.

Three high school students posed for a picture on what appeared to be a beautiful sunny day, with tall oak trees and two clouds in the background. They each had wide smiles, locked their arms, and leaned into one another, verifying the appropriateness of the picture's title:

SENIOR FRIENDS SUPPORT EACH OTHER

Under the photograph, the small caption listed their names.

Jake LeMoure, Julie Lerner, Patrick Tomilson

To Anne, there were two things noteworthy in the picture. The most obvious was Ms. Julie Lerner. David was evidently thinking the same thing because he flipped back to ATHLETICS, and they read together that Julie Lerner was captain of the varsity swim team. That had to be the Julie referenced in the handwritten note on the back cover.

But the more intriguing aspect of the picture had nothing to do with Julie Lerner or the swim team or Jake LeMoure. She looked closely at the photo to make sure she wasn't seeing things, and felt like an idiot for not catching it sooner.

According to the caption, the boy standing on the right was Patrick Tomilson. On the surface he looked like any other eighteen-year-old senior from twenty-four years ago. Short black hair similar to Jake's, glasses, a thin, lanky frame, and a wide smile that augmented a skinny face.

It was his outfit that jumped out.

David's open mouth told her that he had the same thought.

Patrick Tomilson wore dark blue jeans and a black T-shirt featuring a large white skull with crossbones behind its mouth. It looked like the standard hazardous chemicals symbol she'd seen many times before:

"You think? ..." her thoughts drifted.

"The bones," David replied.

"Yeah ..."

"Yes, I do think."

She gasped.

"X marks the spot."

13

"The note on the back cover," Anne whispered. "X marks the spot. Who is that guy?"

"Evidently his name is Patrick Tomilson," David said.

Anne shot him a sideways glance and tilted her head, confirming his attempt to use humor to lighten the mood hadn't worked.

"I don't know who he is."

Part of him thought it was just a strange coincidence. Plenty of kids wore clothes with that symbol and it didn't necessarily mean anything relative to Jake, but it also certainly didn't feel like happenstance. In contrast, the sequence of clues in the old yearbook felt deliberate and intentional: the lack of other notes, signatures and distractions on the otherwise clean copy of the yearbook started them on the back cover note. The note led to Julie Lerner of the swim team. Julie Lerner in turn directed them to "X," who turned out to presumably be Patrick Tomilson.

The question was: where would Patrick Tomilson lead them?

"We still don't know what it means to not judge a book by its cover," Anne interrupted his thought.

He looked at Anne, who was resting one elbow on the hotel desk, while gesturing excitedly with the opposite hand.

"I've been thinking about that," David replied. "It's possible it just means don't dismiss the yearbook, the way I did at first."

"Possibly ..." Anne said, but sounding skeptical.

"Or maybe it doesn't mean anything at all."

"What do you mean by that?"

"Well, Julie Lerner's not very attractive. Would you agree?" he asked hesitantly, almost nervously. He'd seen Anne's erratic emotions unleash already and didn't need another outburst right now.

"What?" she said with raised eyebrows and a look of disgust on her face.

"Julie Lerner. She's not ..." he let silence fill in the blank.

"You think Jake wrote that as some kind of joke about how she looked?"

"No, I'm saying it's possible that—"

"Possible that what?"

"That Jake would make a quip about some high school girl from twenty-four years ago right before being murdered? What's wrong with you?"

"Just hold on a second," he put his hand up.

Anne slumped back into the chair and nodded. Her immediate submission surprised him, and he figured he must look more terrifying than he felt when upset.

"What I was *trying* to get in edgewise was that there's a lot we don't know. We're making some assumptions that right now seem to be leading somewhere, but we don't even know where that somewhere is. And I'm just trying to talk through every angle of this. But one thing we do know for certain is that Jake would want you to be safe. And that means he would've taken whatever precautions he could've to protect you. Protect you from people who probably couldn't make heads or tails of this yearbook."

"I don't understand," Anne replied.

"I'm speculating here, okay ... but let's play this out. Let's say Jake was trying to tell us something. And for the moment, let's assume that whatever it is, someone out there doesn't want us to know. If they found you before you got here, what would they do with the yearbook? Probably shrug it off. Because on the outside it looks like a typical high school yearbook."

"But if I had the whole message ..." she continued.

"Exactly. Having the whole message would've put you in danger."

"Because it would prove that I know whatever the something is."

Just then an eighteen-wheeler travelling south on I-95 blared its horn for about five continuous seconds, making both of them jump. David instinctively turned towards the window facing the interstate, took a deep breath and regrouped.

"Maybe that's why Jake went through the trouble to leave cryptic clues in this yearbook. Think about it. He could've just given you the message directly. Even if he didn't want you to know what it was, he still could've written a letter in plain English to me."

"Unless he didn't trust me not to read it," Anne said aloud what he'd already considered.

"True, but I think we have to assume he trusted you. Otherwise, he wouldn't have asked you to deliver this in the first place. On that basis, the easiest thing to do would've been to just mail me a letter. But he didn't do that. Instead, he took the time to encrypt the message in this yearbook so we'd have to sift through swim team pictures and Skull and Crossbones t-shirts to figure out what he really wanted to say. Then he asked you to personally hand deliver it. It all adds up to Jake taking extra precaution to protect you."

Anne twirled the ends of her hair around her index finger while nibbling on her lower lip again. He knew the slight nods of her head indicated she thought his theory made sense. He remained silent so she could process the possibilities of what it meant.

And so he could as well.

"So you think he wrote that bit about not judging a book by its cover to make people think he was referring to Julie Lerner's looks? To throw them off, so they wouldn't look any further?"

"I'm saying it's possible."

"And I'm saying I think there's more to it than that."

"There may very well be. But for now, let's follow the X like the note tells us to."

Anne agreed and then flipped back to the index, her jittery fingers struggling to separate the pages from each other. He reached for the book to help and she snapped it away.

"I've got it," she said.

Yikes, he thought. He leaned back on the footrest and watched her work to regain her composure before landing on the index page they were both wondering about:

Tomilson, Patrick; Sr.: 16, 23, 30, 35, 40, 51, 64, 68

It meant there were only eight photos of Patrick Tomilson in the yearbook, and he hoped at least one of them would help decipher Jake's riddle. Together, they approached Patrick Tomilson's pictures the same way they had with Jake's: one at a time and very slowly.

Yet, each page brought new hope followed by disappointment.

None of the photographs suggested anything about what they should do next. The first picture was Patrick Tomilson's senior portrait on page sixteen. Following that were photos of him in the Latin Club, Scholar Bowl, and on the Math Team. There was a candid shot of him running track, mouth wide open, with his senior-voted tagline below:

MOST LIKELY TO SUCCEED: Patrick Tomilson

It was an impressive award, especially considering Jake was in the class.

Out of curiosity, David checked his best friend's:

MOST ATTRACTIVE: Jake LeMoure

No wonder. There was probably a limit of one award per student, and Jake's stellar looks had won out over his stellar brain.

Following the tagline photo was the picture with Jake and Julie that they saw earlier. As Anne turned the page to Patrick Tomilson's eighth and final picture, he wondered if the answers would all come at the end, like the gold treasure chest found where X marks the spot.

No such luck. Instead, they saw a snapshot of Patrick Tomilson waving to the camera as he climbed into his car. The title read:

SENIORS: A FINAL GOODBYE

It was the final page of the yearbook. They'd gone through all the
Patrick Tomilson photos and come up completely empty-handed.

14

Around four o'clock they put the yearbook aside to do a fast food run. Filling their stomachs wasn't going to fix their metaphorically empty hands, but at least it was something they had control over. A problem they *could* solve. David felt simultaneously exhausted and wired. Not only had he left the office and a pile of work unexpectedly, but the more he thought about it and considered Jake's possible perspective, the more convinced he became there was something for them to find. And it annoyed him that he was missing it.

But that was a Catch-22 in and of itself. He was pretty sure that if there really was something more, and Jake had gone through all this trouble to conceal it, it was frightening stuff. Maybe it would be best if they never figured it out.

The McDonald's across Commerce Road suited him just fine and he ordered two double cheeseburgers with extra fries. Anne, making a remark about how greasy carbs weren't her thing, settled for a packaged salad and bottled water from The Pit Stop, a convenience store and gas station connected to McDonald's. When they reached the hotel and opened their spoils, David eyed her salad's wilted lettuce and bruised mini tomatoes and offered an exaggerated shiver paired with a "yuck."

"Don't yuck my yum," she replied, revealing a smile for the first time that exposed a small dimple on her right cheek. He momentarily took in how attractive she was despite the roughly twenty-year age difference between them.

"You've got order envy and you know it," he said.

One satisfying bite followed another as David wolfed down the first cheeseburger without so much as a sip of Coke. Anne pushed her wilted leaves around with a flimsy plastic fork, reluctant to actually eat the prepackaged disaster. David hoped that physically refueling would help them mentally refuel as well to catch what seemed both elusive and dire. When he finished his second burger, fries and thirty-two ounces of high-fructose corn syrup, he looked over at Anne again. She immediately nodded; they both knew it was time to get back at it. He got up from the bed and took his seat on the footrest next to Anne, the desk lamp's bright bulb illuminating the open yearbook in front of them.

First, they reviewed all eight Patrick Tomilson photos again and didn't see anything that caught their attention. Searching for a common thread, all they found instead was variety. No two pictures included the same person aside from Patrick. A few featured him alone, others had up to ten different people. In a couple of shots he was smiling, and in two he bore the serious game face that all high school boys across the country were determined to put on for team sports photos. Though Tomilson's overall appearance — hair, baby face, etc. — remained the same, his clothes changed with each photo. And the settings were all different too, and neither Anne nor David noticed anything unusual about any of them.

Once they were convinced that approach was a dead end, they turned back to page 64 with the picture of Tomilson, Jake, and Julie Lerner to see if it had more significance than the "X" on Patrick's shirt. As the sun began to set at just past five and the room grew darker as a result, he couldn't help but feel the symbolism. He looked at Jake's infectious smile and a wave of heavy sorrow swept over him. When the photo was taken twenty-four years ago, there was such youthful vigor and promise in Jake's face and life. There was potential beyond one's imagination. And now, he was gone forever. David blinked hard and forced his mind back to Patrick Tomilson.

There were no more "X's" on the page, or clues to be followed as far as he could see. Exasperated, he rose and began pacing the room, mumbling to himself and intermittently squeezing his eyes shut. When he re-opened his eyes, he saw that Anne had pulled the yearbook to within inches of her face and was squinting intensely, her mouth hanging open a bit.

"What's this?" she asked with a slight upturn of her mouth, pointing to a small, handwritten mark at the bottom right corner of the page. It was in print almost unreadably tiny, but it was there. And it appeared to be a mark of some sort. Now it was his turn to squint, and as he did, the mark came into focus. He duplicated it on the hotel notepad:

é

Anne agreed with his rendering, basically an "e" with an accent above it, and they both stared at the napkin with a mixture of hope and befuddlement.

"Mean anything to you?" he asked.

"Is that supposed to be an aigu accent mark?" Anne asked.

"What are you talking about?"

"That thing above the 'e.' I think it's a French accent mark."

Then it hit him. Like a Mack truck.

The accent mark above the "e." He snatched the yearbook back.

Could that be...? No ... no way.

Very excitedly, David quickly flipped to another page with a Patrick Tomilson photo, now full of vigor. Sure enough, there was a different mark in the same lower right corner on that page. Then he checked another page from the list of Tomilson photos and saw it again.

"I'll be ..." his voice drifted.

"What is it?"

"Impossible."

" *What?*"

"The whole time ... we were staring right at it didn't even see it."

Anne forcefully bit her tongue as he flipped to each of the eight pages with a picture of Patrick Tomilson and wrote the markings from the lower right corners next to each other on the notepad.

He knew halfway through that they weren't markings at all.

Put in order, the symbols, or letters, as it turned out, spelled:

Previséo.

15

"David ... what does that word mean?" Anne asked.

Almost as if waking up after nodding off, he abruptly stirred from his inner thoughts and returned to reality.

"I've asked you three times now. Préviséo ..." she said it slowly, sounding out its pronunciation incorrectly. "What does it mean?"

"I ... I don't understand. How could ..."

"David!"

"Sorry," he replied, shaking his head. "Préviséo is a new drug that's in development at Medzic. It's supposed to cure diabetes and the plan is to launch it in the next two years."

Neither of them spoke for the next few seconds as Anne absorbed the information. While he felt more in shock than anything else at the moment, Anne's wrinkled nose, wide-open mouth and squinty eyes spelled bewilderment.

"What the..."

His thoughts exactly. What possible connection could Jake have to Préviséo that would prompt this? Sure, Clearwater Funding was one of several investment firms that traded Medzic stock shares, but it certainly didn't have any information beyond the typical forecast reports and development updates readily available to the general public. Alvin and Jonathan provided those documents along with an overview at quarterly shareholder meetings in accordance with the Securities and Exchange Commission, and there was nothing in them that was cause for alarm.

Not once had he and Jake discussed Préviséo in the six months he'd worked at Medzic. In contrast, Jake had actually gone out of his way to avoid asking David any specific questions about his work because as an investment bank representative, it was entirely possible Jake could have inadvertently learned something that would lead to an allegation of insider trading. Though the chances of that happening were very remote, it simply wasn't worth the risk.

What's going on, Jake?

He had absolutely no idea, but he knew he wasn't going to figure it out in this tiny hotel room. All of a sudden, he felt claustrophobia breathe its hot breath in his face, while pushing on his chest with one hand and covering his mouth with another.

"I ... I've got to get out of here," he stammered, taking ragged pulls of air.

"You're leaving now? Do you think that's—"

He held up his hand and cut her off. "It's not a matter of think. I need to get away from this room and this yearbook. Right now."

She paused for a second and then nodded.

"When do you want to meet again?" she asked in a near whisper.

"I'll come back tomorrow. Eight o'clock."

"You're not going to work? Won't that draw attention?"

"My boss told me to take some time. For Jake."

"Oh."

He walked towards the door with no destination in mind. It felt unimportant. What mattered was escaping this jail cell disguised as a hotel room.

"What should I do, David?"

It was a plea for help and he knew it, but he wasn't in a position to offer her any assistance.

"Just stay here. I'll call you tomorrow."

"All right. I'll be here."

Just then he thought of something.

"How did you get to Richmond, Anne?"

"I drove."

"Your car?"

She shook her head. "No, I borrowed a friend's car. Jake told me to leave mine at home and not rent a vehicle. I would've taken the train if nothing else."

"Where is it?"

"In the parking garage next to the Hawthorne Suites."

"Can you hold on to it for a while?"

"Yeah, she's out of town for the week."

"Okay, we'll leave it there for now."

As he turned the door handle, she said, "Remember what Jake said. Don't do or say anything you wouldn't want anyone to know about."

She was right. As he hightailed it down the stairs, he remembered wondering to himself if he might regret figuring out Jake's true message, if such a message existed. That perhaps it would be better to not know. Now, the answer was painfully clear. Everything had changed. He didn't even feel safe in his own house.

And where he needed to go was far more dangerous.

16

"Is it time for Plan B?"

"Well," Jonathan Debil spoke into the receiver, "if I'm hearing you correctly, the situation is under control. LeMoure's death was officially declared an accident, all things at Medzic remain in order, and every individual we've identified as a risk is responding accordingly. I don't think Plan B is necessary, or prudent, at this time."

"I thought you said Patera was slipping."

"He'll come around. He's a tool; tools always come around."

"Keep an eye on him," Marcus replied. "He's the CEO. Not exactly a low-profile job. It could spell trouble if he falls out of line."

"Of course. And if that were to happen?"

"Then he would be my problem. And I'd deal with him my way."

"That could have fiduciary consequences," replied the CFO.

"That's precisely why it's best that he remains your problem."

"Understood."

"What about Dr. Mallick?" Marcus asked.

"He's been docile ever since he met you. Very predictable, even more scared."

"I'm sure he is ... but watch him as well."

"Will do ..." Jonathan paused. "When are you going to move on Centrelli?"

"After we have the insurance in hand."

"I agree. Better to be safe than sorry; it's pretty good insurance. Let me know if you need anything."

"Just watch those assholes you work with. I'll call you when I obtain the insurance. Soon after that, this will all be over."

With that, Jonathan Debil smiled for the first time that day.

17

David had taken enough Nyquil to knock out a small elephant the night before, but it hadn't provided the solid night of sleep he so desperately needed. Jake and Mary's deaths, and the fact that he didn't feel safe in his own home, kept him up well past three in the morning each of the past two nights. Reading, watching television, and doing push-ups until his arms felt like jelly hadn't helped. When he finally did nod off, the nightmares that ensued made him wish he didn't.

He answered the phone while yawning, a steaming McDonald's coffee in hand because the nearest Dunkin was fifteen minutes away. The call he knew would come at some point was finally here.

"Hi, David. I just spoke with Kimbra ... you're not going to your friend's funeral?" a concerned-sounding Martin Richardson said softly, skipping the formalities. "Her notes say you'll be back tomorrow."

He wanted to believe that Martin's overall compassion was sincere. His boss had always seemed like a decent guy in the six months he'd known him, and he had no direct evidence to the contrary now. He pictured Martin frowning on the other end of the line, softly stroking one of his bright bow ties with a wrinkle in his fair-skinned chin.

But he didn't know what to believe now. The words "don't trust anyone" danced in his mind like the hippos in *Fantasia*. Flustered, he turned to the sheet of paper on the kitchen table next to him:

1.No Previséo (or Medzic). Nothing about where you've been/are.
2.Keep Anne out of it. And the yearbook. No details, keep it vague.
3.Be nice, say thank you. <u>Keep it short</u>.

While writing it last night, the note felt so unnecessary. It all seemed so obvious, and heaven help them if it fell into the wrong hands, so why take the risk of writing it at all? But now that the phone call was actually happening, and he felt his mind go momentarily blank and panicky, he was immensely grateful for having jotted down some reminders.

"Hi, Martin. That's right. I'm really not a funeral guy, I might visit his parents in a few weeks, but they know how I felt. Not going to the funeral won't change that."

"I understand, David. You doing okay?"

"I'm hanging in there. Thanks for asking. And for understanding."

"Take all the time you need, David. If there's anything I can do, let me know."

"Thanks, Martin. I'll be in touch later this week."

After hanging up, he tore up the paper and threw it away. Then reality set in: he really wasn't going to go to his best friend's funeral. He shook his head and stared down at the large crack in the tile floor, internally chiding himself for how asinine his decisions seemed.

So ... you're going to miss Jake's funeral because it doesn't feel "safe," but then you're going to shine a bright "here I am" light on yourself the next day at Medzic? It doesn't make sense. Those two decisions don't go together, dude. Wake up!

* * *

On the way over to the hotel, David thought of Jake's parents, Mike and Jess. That lovely elderly couple would never know that Jake's death, mourned as a tragedy, was actually a murder. For the rest of their lives, both Jake's and Mary's families would go on believing their children were the victim of bad luck. Unfortunate bystanders of the infamous shit cloud that floats around in the sky above, adjacent to everyone but directly over only a few. It might make them mad at the world, or God, wondering *why*? But they'd never know there was such a specific answer. Yet the painful irony was that as depressing as that was, their ignorance was more humane than the truth.

After a quick look in all directions, he gently tapped his knuckles on the door, wondering what scary revelations might come today.

"Who is it?" Anne answered on the other end of the surely double-locked door.

"It's me."

"Who?"

"David," he replied.

"What's Julie's last name?"

"Huh?"

"You heard me. What's Julie's last name?"

"Lerner."

The Glock was in her hand when Anne opened the door.

"Whoa," he said when he saw it.

"Sorry. Had another rough night."

"Me too." He entered, locking the door behind him. "Every time I walked in a room, I wondered if there was some camera watching me. Every time I heard a creak in the floor ... every time the wind rustled, I jumped. I took a sponge bath with shorts and a T-shirt on instead of a shower just in case I had to jam quickly. I've got a packed bag by the door with a week's worth of supplies ready to roll."

She nodded sympathetically. "I left every light on all night long," she said, which he confirmed with a quick scan of the room. Her eyes were wide and red. She'd changed into white pants and a black, long-sleeved top, but everything except her clothes looked worn and ragged.

"We have something in common after all."

"What are we going to do?" she asked. "You still don't know anything about this Previséo, right?"

"I know plenty about it."

"I mean as far as Jake's note."

"We both know what I have to do."

"You really think that's a good idea?"

"We've got to try something, Anne. Sitting in this room thinking about it hasn't gotten us anywhere. We spent all day yesterday doing that and aren't any closer to knowing what this is. The yearbook served its purpose, which was to point us towards Previséo. There's only one way we can find out why."

"But what if Medzic is the lion's den?"

"Then I wish my name was Daniel."

Anne sighed, not appreciating the quip. He no longer questioned her sincerity, as he had at first. He reminded himself that Anne had been alone for four days, away from her home and everyone she knew, and that those days had probably been the most difficult of her life. He wasn't much to her, but at least he was someone who knew her plight and someone she could talk to about this nightmare. And if he made the wrong move at Medzic, he'd end up like Jake and she'd be alone with the weight of it all.

"Anne, we've only got two choices and you know it. We either duck and cover and run away as fast as possible, or we to take the next step. And we both know I have to take it."

She closed her eyes and nodded ever so slightly.

"When?"

"Tomorrow."

"Tomorrow!" she shouted before hesitating. "Why so soon?"

"Because waiting any longer won't make it less terrifying, and the anticipation will make it worse."

"You'll ... be careful, won't you?"

He nodded. "Remember, I don't expect to find anything."

"Just like you didn't expect to find anything in the yearbook."

"Come with me. There's something we need to check out."

"Where are we going?"

"Just follow me." He took a few steps towards to the hotel room door, then paused and looked over his shoulder, reaching backwards to offer her his hand. Anne both understood and appreciated David's sincere gesture of solidarity. And so she took his hand with a mixture of reluctance and gratitude and followed him out the door.

18

"It's a long shot, but this whole damned thing is a long shot," David mused once they'd made their way through the lobby and entered the hotel's business center.

"What's a long shot?" Anne said.

"The note in the yearbook led us to Patrick Tomilson. We've been assuming that was strictly to guide us towards Previséo, but what if Tomilson knows something? It could be nothing, but let's see if we get lucky. We can look him up and if nothing else, we can reach out to him. For all we know, he's waiting for us to make contact."

Anne smiled, suddenly encouraged. "Yeah, of course. That's not a bad idea! And like you said, we've already spent a day getting nowhere. Why not give it a shot?"

He didn't necessarily share Anne's optimism because if Jake had really prepped Tomilson in advance, there wouldn't be much reason to involve her in the first place. Tomilson could have simply contacted David directly. But her logic matched his in that there wasn't much to lose at this point. The thought came to him last night and he was tempted to check then, but decided to wait until he could use a public computer. He didn't want to use his cell phone to search for any name connected to Jake's yearbook clues if he could help it. On the one hand that felt incredibly over-the-top cautious and, he hoped, very unnecessary.

But the other hand was the one he was worried about.

There was no one else in the hotel's business center, which boasted a tiny cluster of three outdated computers atop a semi-circular wooden table. He took a seat behind the middle one and tried not to look directly at the keys. A slurry of dust particles and something sticky eclipsed the "E" and "R" in QWERTY, as well as the "N-J-M" triangle at the bottom of the keyboard. The Dell monitor had to be ten years old at least and the screen boasted more fingerprints than a crime scene. Anne rolled the chair from behind the third computer over and sat down to his right.

First, sort of as a warm-up, he typed "Previséo" into the Google search bar.

Numerous hits came up. The first hits were links to dialogue and debate on whether total eradication of diabetes from the human body was possible. Plenty of supposed medical experts as well as laymen were happy to weigh in, some with data and most without. There was also no shortage of human-interest stories sharing the challenges of having the disease, ranging from challenging insulin administration regimens to the effects of the blood-sugar illness on other parts of life. The stories were compelling and, in some cases, seemingly exaggerated. One even labeled Previséo as the saving grace for millions of people across the globe. Financial sites discussed the drastic effect of shareholder value and what that meant for both savvy and novice investors.

Then he tried "Tomilson Previséo."

That search was besieged with hits, but none that offered anything worthwhile. Numerous references to people named Tomilson and others to the drug, but nothing that connected the two. The results page had indicated as much by the way Google had crossed off one of the two search words he'd typed in all cases.

Despite having grown up in the Information Age and always having perpetual access to the Internet, David was still amazed by its volume of information and an innate irony that now existed. One click, and endless data on almost any subject were at a person's fingertips. Thirty years ago the Internet didn't even exist; people had to go to the library or brick and mortar bookstores to buy encyclopedias. Now, the average American ten-year-old had a search browser at his or her fingertips through a cell phone. Google alone had hundreds of billions of web pages from which to choose, and the 5G networks made it lightning quick, especially compared to old-school modems and their annoying dial up noise that anyone who lived through the late nineties knew all too well. And yet, because of all that interconnected information and its extreme ease of access, the problem over time had morphed. Now, sifting through all the hits to find truly useful and reliable information was often nearly impossible. The facts went from being the prize in a scavenger hunt to hiding in plain sight.

Anne continued looking over his shoulder. She remained quiet as he tried several other searches attempting to connect Patrick Tomilson to Previséo or Jake or both. Previséo Tomilson, Tomilson diabetes drug, Tomilson Medzic, Tomilson Richmond, drug Tomilson, and about a dozen others were all checked on the one hundred million gigabyte Google Search Index.

They all turned up nothing. Agitation stood him up and he pushed his hair back with a heavy sigh.

Anne saw his frustration and wordlessly tapped him on the arm, while gently scooting her chair towards his.

"It actually makes sense, David," she said centering herself in front of the screen.

"What makes sense?" he asked.

"That there's not some readily findable connection between Tomilson and Previséo. If there was, there wouldn't be much use to all the yearbook secrecy."

Anne was right, and he knew it. Walking into the room thirty minutes earlier, he'd half-hoped they'd find the smoking gun on the hotel business center's dirty old computer via a simple Google search, but he knew that was pretty unlikely.

"Fair enough," he said. "Let's just look Tomilson up. We can decide later if we should contact him or not."

Anne nodded and laid her long, skinny fingers gracefully across the keyboard, at the ready. It was a stark contrast to his trademark hunt-and-peck-with-two-clumsy-index-fingers method. After a few empty search attempts, she tried "Patrick Tomilson Watkins High."

Initially, an old intermediate high hurdles record and a dated photo offered little relief. But when she scrolled down to the page's fifth hit, they both stared at the screen in shock of the Google SERP snippet:

WATKINS GRADUATE KILLED IN CRASH

Anne eagerly clicked on the link, and though the hotel's Internet was surprisingly fast, it felt like it took hours on end to load. David violently scratched the back of his neck, as suddenly he felt itchy all over. It was like bugs were crawling down his shirt and into his hair. His hands on the back of Anne's chair, the endless possibilities of what this meant crashed into each other like lottery balls in a drum.

The article was a short blip from *Watkins Glen Review & Express*, which appeared to be a local newspaper, and it was less than a month old.

> Patrick Joseph Tomilson, a Watkins Glen High School graduate and senior associate attorney at MacArthur, Barry and Tain Insurance Agency, based in Houston, TX, was pronounced dead late Tuesday night after a one-car accident on northbound I-45 near Oak Ridge North. Tomilson was driving alone, and no other people were injured or killed. Initial reports claim alcohol was not involved, but the cause of the crash has not yet been determined and an investigation is underway.

They sat in silence for a few moments, and David read the short article for a third time with his fingers gently covering his lips. Terrified, he focused on the two alarming coincidences the article contained.

And he contemplated whether or not to tell Anne.

19

The article was only a month old.

She stared at the screen for a few minutes and then at David, who'd remained silent since reading it. Soaking in news that felt very unlikely to be a coincidence, she tried to get a read on her new "partner's" reaction. David had a good poker face in general, but she played poker too and she'd spotted his tell: he'd start repeatedly scratching his wrist. There was no doubt he was turning something over in his head, and she suspected it was more than just Tomilson's death. Could he be hiding something from her? If so, what was it? And why would he ... unless he was a conspirator in all of this. The thought made her shiver.

Because Jake hadn't dated the message in the yearbook for obvious reasons, she didn't know for sure when he'd written it. However, he gave it to her in the sealed envelope just a few days before his own death, so it felt extremely likely that Tomilson's death preceded Jake preparing the yearbook. It even offered a possible explanation for the note in the first place. After Tomilson got killed, perhaps Jake realized his own life was in danger and he needed a plan in case something happened to him. So, he got his hands on a fresh yearbook, laid out the hidden message in plain sight for his best friend (as well as someone who worked at Medzic), and arranged for it to be delivered a few weeks after Tomilson's car accident just in case. He probably felt he couldn't contact David directly in case he was being watched, but he knew that whatever this secret was couldn't die with him.

What on this earth could be so important?

"Poor Jake," she whispered to herself, tears forming in her eyes.

She thought back to the previous month before the fire, recalling Jake's overall behavior and mannerisms around the office. He certainly seemed very busy and preoccupied, but that was par for the course at Clearwater Funding. A bit less chatty than usual in hindsight, but she'd chalked that up to Jake's demanding job, and the fact he didn't want to spend any more time away from his beautiful wife than he had to.

And yet, his smiles every morning when he came in must've been forced. His supposed interest in her previous weekend and her plans for the upcoming one must've been manufactured. It felt sincere at the time, but it was probably Jake just protecting everyone in the office, including her.

He needed to appear normal, despite knowing whatever it was that he knew. Not once did she imagine he was even having troubles, let alone the kind that would make him fear for his life. Yet that entire time, Jake must've felt death's presence lurking in the shadows. Perhaps he didn't know how close it was, but to harbor that feeling and pretend like everything was hunky-dory ... it must have been awful.

And if they didn't figure out what was going on, it would all be for naught.

"Penny for your thoughts, David." The emotional turmoil in her mind and David's silence had proved to be too much. She needed to find out why Jake did what he did.

"What?" David replied.

"A car accident? Can we at least both agree there's no way Patrick Tomilson's death is a coincidence?"

He said nothing.

"What aren't you telling me?"

"We don't know anything for sure, Anne."

"We know Tomilson and Jake went to the same high school. They were obviously friends twenty-four years ago and probably were until they both got killed. And before Jake dies in a *random* fire in his apartment, he writes a note leading us to Tomilson and it turns out Tomilson himself died in a *random* car accident a month earlier. Are you honestly trying to tell me that we don't know anything?"

Now, it was clear to her that David was thinking about something that had nothing to do with the obviously connected deaths. He visibly shook his head, as if in some sort of disbelief. It was almost like he was looking for some explanation for something not to be true, yet knew in the pit of his stomach that it was. He wiped the beads that had formed at his brow with the back of his hand, staring at the screen.

"David!" she continued, "this proves Jake knew he was in danger but still went through with his plan. That means—"

"Do you honestly think I don't know what it means?" David said in a snarl while jerking both hand hands up in the air.

She realized his anger wasn't meant for her, but still she felt heat in her cheeks. She waited quietly for his next move, not wanting to invite more wrath. David took a deep breath and blew it out a "sorry" on the exhale that could've easily been mistaken for "hurry." Without waiting for her acknowledgment, he carried on as if it had never happened.

"There's something else. MacArthur, Barry and Tain ... that's the insurance company that'll cover Previséo when it gets released to the market."

"What do you mean 'cover?'" she raised an eyebrow.

"They'll insure it. In case something goes wrong, like if another Vioxx were to happen. Drug companies have to protect their assets in the event of a major issue, like a recall. They might pay out a huge settlement, but that's what the insurance is for. No blockbuster drug ever gets released without insurance."

"Because the more people who buy it, the more potential lawsuits?"

"Bingo. Tort lawyers would have a field day. Medzic bought a ton of coverage from MacArthur, Barry and Tain for Previséo's release."

"Help me understand the relationship between Medzic and this insurance firm. The firm represents other drugs that Medzic makes though, right?"

"Actually, they don't."

Her interest was piqued by the revelation and she leaned in closer, motioning for him to go on.

"Because of the amount of dollars involved, drug companies have so much risk in their portfolios that one insurance provider won't cover everything. And if they already cover a blockbuster, they often don't do anything else. It's a numbers game. Hedging their bets by taking on too much usually doesn't pan out."

"Because in the worst-case scenario, they'd go out of business if they put too many eggs in any one basket?"

"Exactly. It can cost insurance companies billions depending on how widespread the failure or how extreme the issue is."

"So how does the insurance work?"

"At a high level, it works a lot like any other kind of insurance. Like health insurance or car insurance. Nobody wants to have to use it, but they know they need it just in case. And because of the risk they're taking in doing so, they usually handle one pharmaceutical company's blockbuster at a time or take on a few lesser-risk opportunities that add up to the same potential risk and reward."

"That's pretty ironic considering drug companies and insurance companies are fighting all the time."

"That's when the insurance companies are covering the consumer. Totally different when they're on the same side."

"I bet," she replied, nodding her head. "So Previséo would be the only drug a firm would insure at a time?"

"Definitely. If the drug is successful, it will be very lucrative."

"And MacArthur, Barry and Tain is that firm?"

"Yeah."

"How did Medzic choose the lucky winner?"

"I don't really know. I wasn't with the company when they made the selection. But I do know there's a ton of cost-benefit analyses, actuarial tables, forecasts, projections, and never-ending calculations back and forth between the firms."

"I would've guessed it was a fixed agreement at the very beginning," she said.

"No, it's like Vegas. As the game plays on, the odds change. It's constantly moving based on the status of the drug's development, which is one of many reasons it's watched so closely. Picture a sliding scale of risk versus reward that gets updated in real time. I don't get into the insurance details of the sliding scale, not my job, but I know it's a huge undertaking that involves big bucks. And for Previséo, Alvin and

Jonathan would definitely have been directly involved in the selection process."

"Who are they?"

"The CEO and CFO."

* * *

Sticky keys notwithstanding, David shifted one computer down and they hit the web hard from their separate stations to find out as much as they could about MacArthur, Barry and Tain.

Nothing seemed out of place to him on the surface. Headquartered in Houston in lavish corporate offices with a few regional locations throughout the USA, it was a reputable firm with strong leadership and high credentials. Compared to the well-known insurance companies he crosschecked it against, it employed fewer people and offered less information on its website, but that didn't mean it was less effective or less reputable. It actually just meant its profit per employee was higher, something the market greatly values in publicly traded companies.

The firm had paid out very few claims that he could find, which indicated it chose what it represented wisely. The selection process outlined on the website was pretty general overall and appeared similar to other firms, but the management team was impressive. Experience and intelligence radiated from each profile page, and he couldn't find any glaring red flags.

Numerous other searches seeking controversial issues, settlements, or any other form of conflict involving the insurance company didn't offer any new results. After two hours of research, all David could find were satisfied customer testimonials from throughout the country and exuberant praise for the small, privately owned firm. It certainly seemed qualified to insure Previséo, he concluded. And he found nothing to indicate that its employment of Patrick Tomilson, and hence two-pronged connection to Jake, was anything more than happenstance.

While David focused on the insurance firm strictly from a business perspective, Anne had spent most of that time researching Patrick

Tomilson as a person. The results of her search were very similar to those David had uncovered. The first article's brief description of his death had disappointingly turned out to be the most descriptive she'd found on the subject. An online obituary stated that no wife, children, or immediate family survived him, and that his closest relative was a distant cousin who lived in Los Angeles. A Lutheran church website posted the details of the funeral but provided no next of kin.

There was a small blurb highlighting Tomilson's graduation from Stanford Law that mentioned his experience at Watkins High and undergraduate degree from NYU, but nothing that jumped out as unusual. A few years at a private law firm apparently drove him away from private practice, and he landed the job at MacArthur, Barry and Tain as lead corporate counsel. He'd been working there for a little over five years when the accident occurred, and the company put out a heartwarming statement asking members of the community to pray.

Despite the dead ends, he knew that there was something to find. Too many things didn't add up, and the lack of answers on the Internet didn't change that.

Previséo, Medzic, the insurance firm, Patrick Tomilson, Jake LeMoure, Clearwater Funding — there was a dangerous connection somewhere. And though unearthing it seemed overwhelming, he knew he needed to find it.

As he leaned back in the metal desk chair and crossed his arms in contemplation, rhythmically grinding his teeth, three things felt certain and equally difficult to face.

One, something was there. And to honor Jake, he had to look for it, even if the chances of him finding it were razor-thin.

Two, he had to take the next step alone. Anne couldn't help him no matter how much he relished her company.

And three, if he did find something, he would wish he hadn't.

20

Jonathon Debil looked at Marcus from across the booth but tried not to stare. He didn't want to lock eyes with Marcus, and he sure as hell didn't want Marcus to lock eyes with him.

He didn't know Marcus's real name, and he didn't want to know. The less he knew about the tall, overly thin man who sat centered in the tiny booth across from him, the better. From the moment he met Marcus through Alvin, he'd done his best to avoid him whenever possible.

Marcus had insisted that they meet alone before the workday began, but didn't give a reason. To be sure, the anticipation of a one-on-one, face-to-face meeting with the man was scary, but physically being here was really terrifying. To get a lay of the land and try to calm his nerves, Jonathan had made a point of arriving thirty minutes early ... only to find Marcus already there and waiting.

They sat in a quiet, empty Denny's restaurant in a so-so part of Richmond. The pre-dawn darkness and no other customers meant there would be no help if he needed it. People disappeared from this part of town from time to time, and he was quite certain Marcus could make that happen now. Except for two aloof middle-aged waitresses, a teenage hostess who was glued to her cell phone, and one cook in the back working with his head down, it was just the two of them.

The waitress poured them each another cup of coffee, the brown liquid sloshing up and over the rims in her haste. Usually this kind of thing annoyed Jonathan and he'd let her know about his dissatisfaction, but today, it seemed insignificant. The only thing on his mind was why Marcus had asked for a meeting.

"Jonathan, we have a problem," Marcus said.

"What is it?"

"Jake LeMoure's secretary is missing."

"Missing?"

"Her name is Anne Halavity. She didn't come to work on Monday or Tuesday, and she wasn't at LeMoure's funeral yesterday. No note or messages or phone calls to anyone at the office. No one at Clearwater Funding knows where she is."

"It's only been a few days since her boss died. They knew each other pretty well. How do you know she's not just grieving somewhere near family for a bit?"

"Don't you *ever* underestimate my thoroughness again," Marcus replied.

He tightened his calves to give his tension an invisible outlet.

"You're right. My apologies."

"Now let me begin with what I know. She hasn't been back to her apartment since Sunday despite the fact that the lights are still on and the music is still playing. It's as if she wants to give the impression she is home."

"Maybe she just forgot to turn the radio off."

"I won't tell you again to not interrupt me."

"I thought you were finished, sorry."

"Her car hasn't moved in over a week, and she didn't fly anywhere. She hasn't been to any of her favorite restaurants, and she skipped her Tuesday evening Yoga class for the very first time since moving to New York City six months ago."

"What about her family?"

"No calls, e-mails, texts, or social networking messages. We already started surveillance on her closest extended relatives, but she doesn't have any immediate family and I don't anticipate we'll learn anything."

"Marcus," he nearly whispered, "I mean this with all respect. You're the expert and I'm not." He paused, and Marcus remained stoic. "But not everyone talks to people or goes to funerals after a loved one dies. Not even Centrelli went to LeMoure's funeral."

"Funny you should mention that."

Now he didn't try to conceal his curiosity. Or fear. He had no idea what Marcus's notion of "funny" was.

"What do you mean?"

"Is Centrelli still coming into the office today?"

"As far as I know, he is. He hasn't contacted us since he spoke with Martin on the phone the other day."

"Keep a very close eye on him. Let me know of anything unusual."

"Unusual?"

"Any suspicious behavior, changes in body language, an inordinate number of private phone calls, that kind of thing. Anything you find even remotely out of place or uncharacteristic for him, you are to tell me about it immediately. Here is a new number for you."

Marcus slid a small piece of yellow paper across the table, and he stuffed it into his pocket. Marcus's contact information changed on a regular basis. He couldn't remember ever calling the same phone number twice.

"What's going on? I thought you were going to ... proactively address the problem."

"Now that LeMoure's secretary is missing, I'm going to wait to move on Centrelli until she's out of the picture."

He gulped. This was unexpected, even for Marcus.

"You have the insurance policy that you mentioned yesterday?"

"Oh yes."

He looked up briefly to make sure both waitresses were still well out of earshot. "And ... LeMoure's secretary?"

"She's a red light that needs to be eliminated."

"Don't you worry that'll raise flags? Some potentially big flags? A boss and his secretary ... in the same week?"

"That's my concern. Your concern is watching Centrelli. I'm not dealing with Alvin any longer."

He nodded, not quite sure what that meant.

"Jonathon, do not let me down," Marcus said, monotone.

He could tell something was wrong. Near certain he wasn't being told the whole story, he thought through the possible explanations and could only come up with one that made sense.

"You think the girl contacted Centrelli, don't you?"

"I think it's a distinct possibility. And I don't want to eliminate him until I know for sure that she didn't. Because if she did, we need to find out what he knows and if he told anyone else."

"How will you do that?"

"There are plenty of ways to deal with him. His background file has provided me with a number of options to learn what we need to know before eliminating him."

He recalled Centrelli's past and knew Marcus's mind had gone to places he didn't even want to imagine. Beyond getting metaphorical chills, he physically shivered.

"And you'll ... deal with the girl ... regardless?"

"The girl doesn't work at Medzic."

"It'll call attention to things."

"Accidents happen, Jonathan. Innocent people die every single day in this unjust world we live in."

For the first time since he'd met him, he saw Marcus smile.

21

David's main goal from the moment he pulled his 4 Series BMW into Medzic's coveted, heated indoor parking garage was to make it look like any other day. He didn't know if anyone was watching him, but he had to assume they were and act accordingly.

Follow your routine, he silently implored himself as he checked his hair in the rearview mirror. *Time for the everyday game face.*

The reason for his absence had unsurprisingly made its way through the headquarter grapevine, at least within his department. After four compassionate smiles, three sympathetic head tilts, two condolences expressing remorse for the loss of his best friend, and a partridge in a pear tree, he walked into his private office and quickly shut the door. Initially, he felt relieved to be alone, but he then reminded himself that his office was their turf now, whoever they were. Settling into a leather desk chair that reminded him of just how uncomfortable the hotel business center seating had been for the past few days, he turned his attention to the computer atop his desk.

At just past eight o'clock in the morning, his INBOX had over a hundred unread e-mails that he mostly ignored, nine Outlook meeting requests that he promptly rejected or marked as tentative, and four missed calls through the VOIP system that he wouldn't be returning any time soon. David rested his head against the top portion of his chair and briefly closed his eyes. He was already emotionally spent and the day had just begun.

Suddenly, he opened his eyes and sat up with a start. He had the unsettling sense that he was being watched. *Time for the everyday game face*, he mentally chided.

After a quick touch-base call to his boss, Martin Richardson, David grabbed his notebook and headed out the door towards R&D. That was when he spotted Jonathon Debil slowly walking toward him in his standard $3,000 black Tom Ford power suit. Neither smile nor frown upon Jonathon's face, the CFO walked right up to him.

"Good morning, David," Jonathon said, extending his right hand. "Welcome back."

"Thanks, Jonathon," he answered, shaking Jonathon's hand while trying not to appear as uncomfortable as he felt.

"I'm sorry again about your friend," Jonathon said, slightly shrugging his shoulders with a sort of contrived sympathy.

Funny, he thought, *you never said sorry in the first place.*

"Thanks."

"Had you seen him lately," Jonathon asked, removing his black-rimmed reading glasses and tucking them into his breast pocket.

"Not for a while. A few months ago was the last time."

Jonathon nodded his head and then turned to business. "Bummer. Hang in there, kid. Oh, by the way, can you get me a Previséo update sometime this afternoon? I've got to review some things with Alvin for an investor conference call next week."

That was more like Jonathon. "You bet. I'm headed to R&D now."

"Sounds good. Take care, David."

As he walked further away from his office and Jonathon, he already regretted coming back to Medzic. Anne's voice echoed in his mind.

Lion's den.

* * *

The concept for Previséo initially came from Medzic's Research & Development department, more specifically from Chief Development Scientist Dr. Peter Mallick. Whenever David read Mallick's executive biography online, he was reminded of how amazing the doctor really was.

Mallick had earned impeccable credentials from the most respected institutions his entire life: runner-up national spelling bee champ in third grade, National Merit Scholar out of high school, summa cum laude at Harvard, with a double major in biology and chemistry and a music theory concentration.

Mallick was an MD–PhD graduate and second in his medical school class at John Hopkins University. He'd headed up a private research lab at Dana Farber Cancer Institute for about ten years, where he became nationally recognized within the medical community as one of the foremost experts on the body's biochemical reactions to new drug treatments. On the side, he was talented enough to play the violin for the Richmond Symphony Orchestra. The orchestra's director had publicly stated "Dr. Mallick could have been a career musician."

In what was left of his spare time from his private medical practice, he got his second PhD, this one in Immunology, from Yale University. He'd earned the degree in two years, faster than anyone else in his class. After that he took a job at Medzic and had been there ever since ... for twelve years now. And if ever there was such a thing as job security, Dr. Peter Mallick had it.

His accomplishments at Medzic over the past decade outnumbered most scientists' full career achievements. Numerous patents, repeated publications, ever striving to push the very boundaries of medicinal development, and a generous list of philanthropic donations to area colleges and local libraries to boot made him one of the most prolific representatives of the Medzic community and a textbook example of outstanding corporate governance.

Dr. Peter Mallick was both a true scientific genius and a Renaissance Man.

Before entering Dr. Mallick's lab, David opened the Previséo file once more to search for anything of concern. On paper, the drug looked more promising every time he read about it. After only five years, it was already well into the third and final phase of testing. Most blockbusters took up to twelve years to reach that third phase, but Previséo made lightning leaps without cutting corners.

Previséo lacked Priority Review, an FDA designation that targeted action on applications within six months. But it did have Accelerated Approval, meaning that because it could provide a solution that didn't otherwise exist for a serious condition, its approval could be based on a surrogate endpoint, or a laboratory measurement meant to predict clinical benefit.

Its testing was off the charts. The FDA had approved every stage of development so far without a blemish, and if all went according to plan Préviséo would hit pharmacy shelves as quickly as two or three years. David recalled asking Alvin why Priority Review hadn't been requested, but he hadn't really gotten an answer.

He wondered about that now more than ever.

The fact was, the only thing more impressive than Préviséo's creator was how the drug functioned. Its three-phase administration essentially neutralized diabetes, which scientifically speaking isn't the same thing as eradicating it from the body, but was still an amazing outcome.

According to Dr. Mallick, Préviséo isolated the disease from the rest of the body during phases one and two, and then nullified it during the third. This distinction was important to Dr. Mallick and a handful of scientists at Medzic, but Alvin and the other executives, himself included, didn't care what you called it.

Once the final stage was complete, which would take roughly six-to-nine months depending on the patient, the drug would begin to induce repeated generation of antibodies through a form of specialized genetic reproduction. It actually served to block the problematic, abnormal antibodies that destroyed insulin-producing cells in the pancreas and caused the diabetes in the first place. This created the long-term effect of being free of the disease altogether.

"In essence, the medicine will cause the body to continue to generate new antibodies autonomously in order to counterbalance the diabetic effects, and that counterbalance is what gives the patient the sensation of the disease having been removed," Dr. Mallick had told him during their first meeting.

"But there are no more insulin shots every day, no more fluids to drink or sugar levels to measure, no more worrying about what food is safe to eat and what food isn't?" David had asked.

"That's correct."

"So from the patient's point of view, the diabetes is gone."

"Essentially yes, but I wouldn't characterize it that way."

That was the last they spoke of the distinction. It was immaterial. While Previséo and the way it worked amazed David every time he thought about it, the patient, the *customer*, wouldn't make the distinction or care. It was the quality of life following its administration that mattered. He didn't know the specifics of how Previséo operated on a biological or chemical level, and he didn't need to know. His concern was growing the company's value and managing business development. He let the scientists understand the science.

And apparently, they understood it very well.

Human trials had shown remarkable results after only a few years, and all the experts verified that Previséo did exactly what Dr. Mallick claimed it would do. To the scientists at Medzic and the doctors who would prescribe it, Previséo was a miracle drug. To the executives involved, it was a cash cow.

After scouring the files for both Previséo and Dr. Mallick, David knew what he had to do hadn't changed. He usually went to the R&D lab at least three or four times a week, but this next visit would be different.

He didn't know what he was going to say to the smartest, most benevolent man he'd ever met. He didn't have a plan, or an idea of how he could learn whatever it was he was hoping to learn. And the notion of confronting Dr. Mallick seemed as arbitrary as it did wrong.

The only thing he knew was that if the wrong people saw him do what he was about to do, he would be in serious trouble.

22

Research and Development was the largest department at Medzic. Its reach extended to forty-four states and an industry-leading thirty-three countries around the world. It employed over 40,000 people in total, from scientists to clinicians to custodians, and it required just over eight billion dollars a year in operating expenses alone.

Its primary objective was to safely create, test and produce the drugs the Strategic Marketing department said. The Marketing and Product Management teams were responsible for identifying the right products for Sales to sell, and it was R&D's job to make that possible.

That's all these people do, David reminded himself, stepping into the guarded elevator. Whenever intimidated by their brilliance, he'd reminded himself that at the end of the day, they were just really smart people who happened to make medicine for a living.

And they failed far more often than they succeeded. At any given time, hundreds of drugs were being tested across the globe, with only fifteen or twenty making the first, and by far the easiest, of several cuts. Rejection rates were consistently in the ninety-fifth percentile or above, and it proved to David that perhaps more than intelligence or any other personality trait, the scientists who worked in R&D possessed amazing levels of perseverance. Even a sales director would lose motivation after that much rejection.

Medzic's corporate headquarters in Richmond housed the Strategic R&D team, which was just a fancy way of saying that was where the big blockbusters were developed. The brightest of the brightest worked here, taking the pioneering steps that led to new ways of life for millions of people across the globe. It all happened right here in this very building. And after six months on the job, that fact still felt mind-blowing.

When he reached the basement level and stepped out of the elevator, the sight he'd seen so many times before still didn't fail to mesmerize him. It never did.

A thick plate of double pane, soundproof glass and a yellow steel railing separated corporate visitors and big-ticket customers from the 500,000-square-foot laboratory's working space. Beyond the barriers, on both the ground level and the one above it, the men and women who really put the food on David's and the rest of the executives' plates circumnavigated the facility with an air of efficiency and purpose.

The lab could most accurately be described as organized chaos. There were individual workstations in certain areas, and clusters of up to ten in others. There were no floor-to-ceiling partitions, but there instead very clearly divided segments based on how and where the workstations were positioned relative to each other. The equipment changed based on the tests being run and no two stations were identical, but there was an organization to the space, particularly to the people who used it.

And whether standalone or part of a larger cluster, each workstation did have a few standard items: a smooth, hard surface with notepads, writing utensils and timers; drawers on the side, bright desk lights, microscopes and a series of tools on the above shelf. Roughly one hundred feet above them all, three hundred white fluorescent lights hung from the ceiling to brightly illuminate the entire space. A few people with sensitive eyes even wore sunglasses it was so luminous.

Some scientists wore static-free shoes, gas masks and HAZMAT suits made of rubber, but most wore only a white lab coat and safety glasses. He never understood how there could be such a range of personal protective equipment in the same room, but he couldn't even begin to understand what these scientists were working on. Some sat on stools holding syringes, others were reading paperwork, and others were looking through microscopes or mixing chemicals. Still others buzzed around the floor with clipboards in hand, moving from one workstation to the next and conferring with coworkers.

Along the inner walls on the ground level were windowed offices and large whiteboards littered with convoluted brainstorming notes, flow charts, and equations. Department managers needed such private space to provide executive updates, discuss budgets and handle the business side of the job, but the ones that David had spoken to over the months all longed to be on the floor where the action was. Most R&D managers got there by being good scientists, and they missed the day-to-day job once they moved up the ladder.

"Amazing, ain't it?" a security guard he didn't recognize asked him. He wore a grey shirt with a gun holster and black SECURITY hat.

"Sure is," he said, adjusting his mandated lab coat.

"We got labs all over the world. Japan, China, India, Germany, Sydney, list goes on. None quite as impressive as this one from what I'm told."

David nodded in total agreement while scanning the room.

It didn't take long to find his guy.

When not in his spacious office, Dr. Mallick was usually in or around the "cage." The scientists had unofficially bestowed the name to the twenty-by-twenty foot square area within a silver metal fence where ultra-sensitive testing was performed. The entrance had its own security guard, and only those with the highest clearance were permitted to pass. David slowly walked towards it, something that the scientists rarely did. In R&D, walking slowly indicates that someone is either carrying hazardous chemicals or completely out of his element.

It was pretty obvious which category he fell into.

David eyed Dr. Mallick just outside the cage. The man was wearing brown dress slacks and loafers beneath a large white lab coat that reached nearly to his shins. Hands clasped behind him, polka dot tie swinging in the breeze, the doctor rocked back and forth while peering over three younger scientists looking into microscopes. It seemed clear Dr. Mallick was excited about something, probably whatever it was the younger scientists were looking at, but that was far from unusual. The Chief Development Scientist was always enthused to participate in the "real" science as he'd once described it, and he had confided in David a few months ago that he missed working in the lab. That despite his success, both professionally and financially, he yearned now more than ever to be there again, practicing science as opposed to managing those who did.

That desire was reflected in the doctor's rocking motion. Mallick's wide eyes and wrinkled nose were full of anticipation.

"Hello, Dr. Mallick," he said, tapping him on the shoulder.

"David! How are you?" Mallick removed his eyeglasses and retired them to the red string that hung around his neck.

A world-renowned scientist at forty-nine, there was no telling what else this man might accomplish. He showed no signs of slowing down or regressing, which made David feel even more awkward about the imminent conversation.

"I'm okay," David said softly. "Do you have a minute?"

"For you? Always."

Dr. Mallick gave the young scientists some technical instructions David didn't understand and stepped away from the table, gesturing for David to walk ahead of him to an open space between lab stations.

"There's some incredible intravascular study going on over there," Mallick said, shaking his head. "So ... what's on your mind, David?"

Mallick always spoke like just a regular guy; like a guy who hadn't literally changed the way drugs were developed and produced at one of the largest pharmaceutical companies in existence. Like a guy who hadn't changed the world. He called him "David," as if they were college buddies catching up on old times. Such humility never ceased to both impress and stupefy him.

"I had a couple of questions about Previséo."

"Previséo?" A distinct look of curiosity covered Mallick's face. "Should I get the group together so others can participate? Or maybe we can discuss it at our next update session?"

"No, that's not necessary. I just had some questions. Plus, I don't want to wait that long."

As soon as he said it, David realized his error. Mallick's face grew keener and more curious, the doctor's eyes narrowing as he blinked them rapidly. Mallick slowly and gently rubbed his earlobe, picking up on his mistake.

"You don't want to ... wait that long?" Mallick skeptically asked.

"I just meant this would be real quick." Knowing he couldn't take the comment back, the best move seemed to be trying to downplay it.

"What's going on, David?"

"Have you run into any issues lately?"

"Issues?"

"You know ... side effects, delays, inconsistencies ... anything like that?" Not having the slightest clue what he was looking for definitely made it more than a little challenging to find. He was worried Mallick would know that he was on a fishing expedition, but he still didn't know how else to proceed.

"Nothing like that. Just what we've talked about in our discussions."

"So it's still doing well?"

"It's one of the most successful products we've ever had at this stage in the development phase."

"Can't argue with its results."

"You read my reports every week. We talk at least once a day. If something were irregular, I would certainly tell you. What's really going on here, David?"

He reminded himself that Dr. Mallick, no matter how philanthropic he was or benign he seemed, could be involved. He could be one of "them," despite the fact that David had no idea who "they" were. It struck him as highly unlikely, but he couldn't assume otherwise.

Of course, that possibility, remote as it may be, didn't change the fact that David didn't want to be here doing what he was doing. There was just no other way. He had to do everything he could to see if Jake's message meant something. He owed it to Jake.

"I'm just doing my due diligence. Jonathan's been really on me to make sure there aren't any glitches."

"He can be a bit harsh."

"Yeah, tell me about it. So you've never seen anything awkward, something you didn't expect?"

"Well, I wouldn't say that."

"Oh?"

"I didn't expect it to be as successful as it has been."

"Is that so?" David asked, the conversation antithetical to his "plan."

"You know it is. Don't act surprised. You know how this business works. Only a handful of ideas ever get off paper and into the lab, much less go anywhere after that. And the fact that the results are so promising has been a pleasant surprise."

And then he changed course.

"David," the doctor said, "usually when we discuss Previséo, you want to make sure we're on pace for release. Now you're asking me if something's wrong, pushing for it in fact. What's this all about?"

He wasn't surprised that Mallick was onto his game. Not only did David slip up by mentioning not wanting to wait, but he was also dealing with a literal genius. Try to put one past Peter Mallick and you quickly found out why he was considered one of the smartest men in the world by a whole lot of people.

He thought about just telling Dr. Mallick everything and letting a genius's brain try out the mystery, but this wasn't the time or place for that. And although he trusted the good doctor, he'd already taken a huge gamble by coming to R&D in the first place. More risk wasn't on the menu. So instead, he looked back into the doctor's genuine, sympathetic eyes and gave him the first believable lie that came to mind.

"Like I said, it's just been a long week. The pressure's building a little. I just want to make sure we've triple-checked everything, that's all. It's moving really fast, which is great, but I want to make sure we really are where we think we are."

"Couldn't agree with you more."

The deep tone of Mallick's voice and his cocked head told David that the good doctor didn't believe a word of what he just heard.

"Okay, well thanks for the time. I've got some meetings I better run off to."

"Not a problem, David. Any other questions, feel free to ask."

Just like that, the conversation was over and the doctor headed back to work. *Why,* David wondered. *Because he can.* Mallick wasn't the one who'd gotten the yearbook; Mallick wasn't the one whose buddy was murdered; Mallick wasn't the one who felt lost and didn't have a clue about what to do next. Of course the good doctor simply went back to work.

David headed back to the elevator, his VIP nametag making him feel hypocritical and underqualified.

That was it? That was your plan? Your grand solution to finding out what the hell is going on was to ask Peter Mallick if he's seen anything unusual? That's all you've got? What did you expect would happen?

23

He decided to stay in R&D for a little while longer to follow his normal routine when he ventured to the basement. Even less convinced it mattered after talking with Dr. Mallick, he still thought it best to go through the motions and mask the purpose of the visit as best he could. The three or four stops and brief touch points with a few researchers didn't take long, and he wasn't ready to go back upstairs anyway. At least down here the chances of running into Alvin were less. Or worse yet, bumping into Jonathon for a second time.

Twenty minutes after the fruitless conversation with Dr. Mallick, he checked the last item off the list and had given up on the idea, and the day, altogether. He wasn't sure what came next, but staying here was a waste of time. He was about to enter the elevator to go back upstairs when a perky young woman approached him with a beaming smile. She looked about twenty years old and wore a two-piece business suit with a too-short navy skirt and light blue button-down that accentuated her bosom.

"Are you Mr. Centrelli?" she asked in a sweet, high-pitched voice. Her voluptuous body and full lips commanded his attention without asking permission.

"That's me. What can I do for you?"

"I'm supposed to give you this."

She handed him a plain white envelope, letter-sized, sealed with a Medzic sticker. Nothing was written on the front or back. He tentatively accepted it.

"Who's it from?"

"I don't know. It was on my desk next to a note. The note said you'd be here and that you'd have a VIP nametag. It said I was supposed to bring it to you."

"That's it?"

"Yes, sir. I figured it was something classified. You know ... with you being a VIP and all," she answered, a hint of attraction in her voice as her eyes scanned him over. David silently chastised himself. *Get your mind of out of the gutter. Jake's dead, you have no idea why, and you're gawking at an intern. What's wrong with you?*

"Oh ... well, thanks," was all he could get out.

"You're welcome." The young woman gave him a slight giggle and then turned and bounced away, taking her bubbly smile and cute ass with her, leaving him alone with the white envelope.

Forcing his eyes away from her to turn his attention to the envelope, he opened it slowly, and read the brief message:

David:

Stop asking questions and leave the lab <u>now</u>. Payphone at the corner of North 10th and Bank Street. 8 p.m. tonight. No cell phone. Bring some cash. Come alone and wear gym shoes. Keep your mouth shut and burn this note. If you've ever trusted me, trust me now.

-P. Mallick

He crumpled the paper in his hand and looked around fretfully. The doctor was nowhere in sight.

24

After he'd read Dr. Mallick's note for a third time, he flushed it down the toilet and sat alone in his office for the rest of the day. Worried that leaving Medzic too early would draw attention, he set his office line to DO NOT DISTURB and prayed no one would knock on the door. The whole time he was itching to look up North 10th and Bank Street on Google Maps, but decided against it for the same reason. Who knew what kinds of monitoring or other surveillance they had on his computer?

He thought about using his cell to do the same thing. He was almost certain that was over by the Virginia State Capitol building, and a quick scan would confirm it. As he stared at the cell phone sitting on his desk, the absurdity of using an old-fashioned payphone came to mind. Who even knew those things were still around? Such antiquated technology, yet it was the medium of choice the Chief Development Scientist at one of the biggest and most high-tech pharmaceutical companies in the world had chosen.

He'd left the office at four o'clock and called Anne from a prepaid cell phone a few blocks away to tell her to check into a different hotel. He didn't want her to stay in one place for more than a few nights. She demanded to know why, but he didn't have the time or composure to go into the details, so instead he curtly told her he'd explain later. She yelled at him for barking orders and slammed the receiver down. He hadn't spoken to her since, despite calling back twice.

He understood her frustration. She was alone, and now felt even more in the dark because he hadn't had the chance to tell her about Mallick's note. And after the week she'd had, it was a very reasonable way for her to feel. But he had to prioritize tonight, and Anne Halavity would've been too much for him before meeting Dr. Mallick downtown. He needed focus, and to try to relax ... and a drink to settle his nerves.

He'd changed into jeans and a red sweatshirt to go with his sneakers. He'd been uneasy in his own home the entire time, wondering if it had been bugged or worse yet, if there were hidden cameras. Thankfully, sipping a glass of W. L. Weller Reserve after work was consistent with his normal routine.

He checked his watch.

Four minutes.

Sitting restlessly on the rigid plastic bus stop bench, he tipped the cheap metal flask back and hoped the whiskey would work its magic soon. He'd promised himself after he left Clearwater Funding that he'd cut back on the booze. It couldn't erase the past no matter how much he willed it to, and it'd resulted in too many unmemorable long nights and hazy mornings.

He had to cut back. And he would.

Just not right now.

Not that it helped much right now, anyway. The flask was more than three-quarters empty and not even burnt orange deliciousness at 90 proof could do the trick tonight.

He stared at the payphone and anticipated its ring. People walked past him left and right while he drained what was left of the whiskey in one ferocious, burning gulp.

At precisely eight o'clock, the phone began to ring.

He tossed the cheap flask into the trashcan and leapt up to grab the receiver, exhaling deeply.

"Hello?"

"Head southeast down Bank until you get to Governor Street. Take a left and head north. There's a payphone at the northeast corner of the Grace Street intersection. Be there in exactly five minutes."

The man hung up before he could say a word. It didn't sound like Mallick's voice, but he dutifully obeyed and made the quarter-mile trek regardless. Checking his watch as he jogged, David now understood why he'd been instructed to wear sneakers and felt out of breath after the short jog.

Within seconds of his arrival, the payphone was ringing.

"Yeah?" he answered, huffing.

"Leave your cell phone in the trash receptacle. Take a taxi to the corner of East Marshall and North Fifth. No Ubers or Lyft. Pay with cash. Then walk a half-mile west up Marshall Street and turn north on Monroe. When you get to the Clary Street intersection, head into GWARbar on the corner and grab a table for two under the name 'Bobby.'"

"GAWRbar ... the heavy metal place?"

Again, the caller hung up immediately. This time, however, David recognized the deep, monotonous voice. It was definitely Peter Mallick. With no other options, he raised his hand to hail the cab, questioning his sanity as he did.

25

GWARbar had an interesting story. Its owners, inspired by the heavy metal band Gwar that was formed in 1984 and was known for its overly grotesque costumes and gory décor, had obtained $50,000 through a crowdsourcing campaign to open up the restaurant a few years ago. And despite playing what many people felt was atrocious music, Gwar definitely had its following and had sold around a million records since its formation. Especially popular in the mid-nineties thanks to MTV's Beavis and Butthead — the cartoon duo had officially endorsed Gwar as its favorite band — the fan base that remained now was a much smaller but fiercely loyal cult following that had funded the bar.

It offered "gourmet junk food" that he'd heard was actually quite good, and paid tribute to its followers with loud and awful heavy metal music blaring from speakers, hideous costumes passing as uniforms, and fake blood splattered on the floor and walls. There was a sliding metal gate that he imagined represented a torture cage on some level leading to the dining tables, and large statues and colorful paintings of graphic mythological creatures also covered in fake blood.

It was dark, dingy and overcrowded for the space, but not altogether as unpleasant as he expected. Not every patron could pass for Dracula, and the nachos did look pretty tasty. Still, he couldn't imagine Peter Mallick had frequented or even ever been to such a place, or that this was where they were going to discuss Previséo or whatever it was they were going to discuss. Then it dawned on him: perhaps that was precisely the point. This was the very last place anyone would expect the Chief Development Scientist to be.

He didn't even try to make out the lyrics to the "music" blasting from every direction. Instead, he watched a group of what looked like college kids crammed together like penguins in Antarctica, huddled around a small high top and pounding drinks like water next to a framed picture of the original band members hanging on the wall.

There were a few booths to go with the high tops, but they were occupied. He put in a request for a table for two and the hostess told him it would only be five or ten minutes.

Standing near the front door, he folded his hands and asked himself if he was a businessman or Dirty Harry. What was all this about? How had he gotten into all this, and why was he complying with these crazy requests? What was he doing in this place? And was he in danger?

Moments later, a slender, young, dark-haired woman approached him, carrying a white dress-shirt-sized box with a red bow on top. She looked about twenty-five and was fairly attractive. Good body, average height, thin, and every single thing she wore was pitch black. Pants, shoes, long-sleeved untucked t-shirt, earrings, lips, eye shadow, the works. Even her eyes themselves looked black, though he wasn't sure how.

"Table for two?" she shouted, competing with the blaring heavy metal music for what was left of his hearing.

"Yeah," he replied, cupping his ear.

"For Bobby?" she asked.

"Yeah."

"Happy early Valentine's Day, sweetie," she said, handing him the box and pushing his head towards her, bringing his lips into hers with impressive force and assertiveness. Stupefied, he did what most men would've done, going with the flow and pressing his wet tongue against hers for a few delightful seconds, right up until she pulled away from the kiss just as aggressively as she initiated it.

Without so much as another word, she winked, turned away and walked back towards the bar.

Tempted to follow her, he instead stood there a bit apoplectic at first. Then he scanned the room. Nothing seemed out of place. People were enjoying their drinks, mingling and flirting. Grinding on the dance floor. There were drunken shouts from one corner of the room. Guys were bringing drinks to their latest female prospects.

105

Nothing unusual at all.

So he turned his attention to the box.

It was unwrapped and unlabeled, and there was nothing unique about the bow. Inside the box were a cheap dark-brown windbreaker, a Chicago Cubs baseball hat, and a half-sheet of notebook paper with a phone number written in pencil. Scribbled beneath that was a single sentence: Payphone in back.

He asked the hostess for change and found the payphone at the far rear end of the bar, then punched in the number. An all-too-familiar voice answered, and David covered his left ear and pressed the phone into his right to try to block out the background noise.

"Put on the hat and jacket and walk out the side entrance on the east wall. Head towards the park that's just north of Brook Road. It's called Abner Clay and it's only a few hundred feet from you now. Walk, at a casual pace. Don't run or draw attention to yourself. Pass the entrance sign and take a seat on the bench at the end of the tennis courts,"

"Is this the last time already?" he said to himself, growing tired of the cat and mouse game when he wasn't the feline.

He felt like a lab rat scurrying out of GWARbar into the next part of the evil scientist's maze with no sense of the bigger picture. Pissed, he punched his left fist with his right hand so hard it stung, and then considered quitting this little adventure right then and there.

Just leave. Just hop in a taxi and get away. Far away. Away from everything. Become a nomad on a mission.

But Jake's memory dissolved the fantasy rather quickly, and he walked towards the park instead. The five-minute walk was a desolate one. The park was closed, the streetwalkers weren't out in this part of Richmond, and it was getting chilly by Virginian standards. Strolling past the tennis courts, he kept looking in all directions to see who or what might be looking back, but he didn't see another human being. The park closed at dusk and the weather wasn't particularly inviting for a game of three-on-three or playtime on the playground.

He checked his watch when he finally spotted the bench.

8:52 p.m.

Sitting on the cold, hard metal bench and adjusting the Cubs hat, he began thinking about how much he already missed that cheap metal flask and its contents until a car in the parking lot east of him turned on its lights. He didn't see any people or other vehicles. And aside from the soft vibrating hum of muted heavy metal from GWARbar a few hundred feet away, he didn't hear anything but the wind. Then the mid-90s Honda Civic started flashing its lights, presumably at him. David hadn't seen the car before, but its age and very impressive collection of dents, scratches and rattling noises made him certain it wasn't Peter Mallick's.

But after the headlights finally turned off and the passenger door was pushed opened, the console light flashed on to reveal the doctor's face. Mallick's eyes said nothing, and his mouth even less. But the good doctor nodded, and David sauntered through the hard, dry grass over to the car one small step at a time. He didn't really believe he was in danger, but the evening's events wouldn't let him think otherwise.

"Get in," Mallick nearly whispered.

He didn't want to.

He felt alone, terrified, shocked and bemused all at the same time. And despite literally running all over Richmond just so he could have this conversation, now that he was there, he didn't want to have it. He didn't want to talk to Dr. Mallick. He felt the strongest urge to run, and he looked up towards Leigh Street on the north side of the park with wild eyes. Abner Clay was so small ... he could be to the other side of it in a minute flat. And from there, he imagined disappearing into the night.

Instead he climbed in the front seat, and the car drove off.

26

Maria Rodriguez enjoyed her job very much.

She knew the stigma the housekeeping profession possessed, but the chipper evening-shift maid never really cared about stereotypes. She saw it differently. She treated each new room to clean as a chance to make it perfect for the next guest. She loved that ... the promise each room's work offered.

"Maybe," she told herself, "this room will be for a family next. A family on vacation. I get to make their stay that much better, and I get to help the children enjoy their vacation that much more."

The job's repetitive nature was the one thing most people couldn't stand about it that she absolutely adored. Messiness simply wouldn't do, either at work or at home, and there was a proper way to address it. She was OCD. And she made the disorder work for her. In her own home, her dog's waste bags had to be fully rolled up and propped up against the side of the kitchen drawer; the toothpaste in the bathroom had to be capped and always squeezed from the bottom; the comforter had to be smoothed; and the books stacked neatly on the bedside table. All things had a place and belonged a certain way for a reason. Which was why, during her shift, her husband Ricardo and their three children were cleaning their small house just outside Richmond before Mommy got home.

There was nothing like coming home to a clean house.

On a chilly January evening, she pushed her cleaning cart down the heated third-floor hallway and observed the visitors she encountered with pleasure. A young couple moseyed out of their room, hand-in-hand, smiling at her before closing the door. A blonde-haired boy carefully held the ice bucket with both hands as he tiptoed down the hall. An older woman entered her room with a newspaper from the lobby.

She took note of the EXIT sign still flickering. "Maintenance hasn't fixed that yet?" she questioned aloud, before radioing the front desk to let them know the repair was long overdue.

When she reached the room that had recently been vacated, she opened the door and went to work. Of course following her proven routine, she first pushed the cart against the wall and smiled at the picture on top of it of her babies when they were six, four, and three.

"Precious angels," she said aloud. "Time to watch Mommy work again."

After the brief moment of thanks to God for her children and husband that she offered before every room's cleaning, she grabbed a fresh set of linens and began stripping the bed. She then removed the pillowcases and applied fresh sheets with amazing efficiency. Within minutes, she'd created a perfectly made bed with hospital corners and an inviting arrangement of decorative pillows.

After vacuuming the entire room from end-to-end, removing the wastebaskets' contents and re-organizing the advertisement display on the nightstand, her work there was now done, and she headed to the bathroom.

The bathroom was always the last, and messiest, part of the job. The floor was usually wet and strewn with used towels and dirty washcloths, travel-sized soap bars and shampoo bottles typically lay in the shower, and the countertop almost always needed a heavy scrubbing before disinfecting it all. She wagered her guess at how bad it'd be before she opened the door.

Not too messy, she thought. *The rest of the room was pretty neat.*

But she never found out.

When she flipped on the bathroom light switch, a massive explosion rumbled from the shower, and smoke and fire engulfed the entire area almost instantaneously. The eruption blasted through the window and cheap white plaster walls, completely disintegrating Room 314 within seconds.

27

Dr. Mallick turned out of Abner Clay Park and headed North on US-301 without saying a word. Driving on a near-empty road at exactly fifty-five miles per hour, he kept his hands at ten and two on the wheel and stayed in the rightmost lane of the six-lane divided highway. The windows were rolled up and the cabin temperature was set to sixty-eight, but David felt like he was sitting in front of a space heater. Sweat dripped from his forehead and his mustache area above his upper lip was moist, the result of the evening's physical activity and the tension he felt.

"What is going *on*, Dr. Mallick?" he finally couldn't take the silence and pressed Mallick, who seemed much too at ease.

Mallick didn't even turn his head much less respond.

"Why have you been running my ass all over town? This payphone, that payphone, this bar, that door, taxis not Uber, walk don't run, notes in boxes! What the hell is going on?"

Still not turning his head, Mallick replied, "That was all for your protection. You better start using your head, David. You have no idea who's watching you. I hope all that 'running around' got them off your tail, but only time will tell."

Jake's instructions dug into his mind like a splinter.

Don't trust anyone.

"You could've said something earlier."

"No, I couldn't have. I'm quite certain they were listening."

"With all due respect, Dr. Mallick, how would you know if anyone's listening?"

"I know because I need to know. Because they watch me, too."

He cocked his head back and squinted, ever so slightly opening his lips but not releasing any words. He didn't know what to expect, but it definitely wasn't that. Mallick finally glanced over briefly and must've read his curiosity. The doctor checked the rearview mirror before making a right onto Lancaster Road. He knew they were on the North Side, not too far from the Richmond Raceway, but David didn't know the area very well at all.

"David, listen to me very carefully. I'm under constant surveillance. Twenty-four hours a day. Why do you think I'm driving a rental? Don't ever approach me in public again, certainly not the way you did in the lab."

"Who is watching you?"

"I can't prove how deep this rabbit hole goes. But I know it's deep enough that even a shred of privacy has become a luxury for me, and that I have to go to these extreme lengths to get it. You need to come to that realization too."

"But who—"

"We'll get to that later." Mallick pulled into a vacant Burger King parking lot and headed towards the back. The Burger King's neon light sign was out and the parking lot lights weren't nearly bright enough. Mallick parked along at the northeast corner perpendicular to the lined spots. A small tree embankment was to David's right and the fast food restaurant's trash and recycling bins served as their front view. Mallick stopped the car, turned off the ignition, and withdrew a gun from the front pocket of his University of Virginia sweatshirt.

"But for now, why were you asking questions about Previséo?"

* * *

The second gun aimed at him in as many days was held by an unsteady hand that looked like it might inadvertently pull the trigger.

"Tell me why you were asking me about Previséo, David," Mallick repeated.

"What's wrong with you?" he forced out between massive gulps.

"I've carried a gun for longer than I care to admit. Start talking."

Mallick's hand continued to tremble as he spoke. It was as if he either regretted what he was doing or didn't know what he was doing or

111

both. But it didn't really matter. What mattered was that a man with a gun pointed at his face might panic. And when people panic, they tend to squeeze.

The parking lot lights filtering through leafless, branchy trees cast shadows against the dash. Mallick stared at him through foggy glasses, perspiration dripping from their black rims.

"Can you please put the gun down?"

"Start talking!"

This was not the Peter Mallick he knew. This person, whoever he was, was completely capable of killing him right then and there.

"Okay, okay," he took a deep breath, "it all started on Monday morning, when I found out my best friend Jake LeMoure died in a fire."

For the next fifteen minutes, he recalled as completely as he could everything that had happened over the past four days. Saying it out loud accentuated the terror, and he felt like he was in a movie, like he was some non-central character who stumbled onto something horrifying that a mere four days ago was unknown.

The kind of "something" that usually gets said non-central characters killed.

"What hotel?" Mallick asked after he mentioned his call with Anne earlier that day.

"Why?"

"What hotel?"

"The Red Roof Inn."

"Oh no ..."

He considered asking Mallick what he meant by that, but the gun urged him to let that one go and finish his recap.

"Well ... that's it," he said, his nerves jangling. "That's the whole story. And why I was asking about Previséo."

Mallick seemed to expect more just by the way his eyes remained widened, but kept his reaction otherwise stoic. He waited nervously for the doctor to say something, but Mallick only eyed him more closely, staring intently, as if trying to decide whether to believe him or shoot him.

Then Mallick lowered the gun.

"Are you sure you want to know?"

David knew he'd never forget that question.

"Right now, you can go home and pretend this was all a dream," Mallick said solemnly.

"A dream? A dream that my best friend was killed and I've been scared to sleep in my own house for a week?"

"Yes, David. A dream. A really bad dream ... even the worst kind of nightmare. The kind that may never fully go away or that could wake you up in a cold sweat for the rest of your life. But still just a dream. After enough time, your panic will settle and even your curiosity will fade. To some extent, you'll get to go back to normal life. But if we keep talking, the dream will vanish and there is no waking up."

Mallick waited with wide, moist eyes that displayed a genuineness that felt more real than anything David had seen the past week. Even Anne hadn't looked so vulnerable and desperate. Those pleading eyes convinced him to consider if Mallick was right. Maybe he could still get out. He never did want a part of it, and he certainly never wanted another gun in his face. He could still get away. It wasn't too late.

Mallick was giving him one last chance.

He wished he could take it, but David knew he couldn't back away now.

28

"My initial Concept Analysis report concluded there was a high degree of likelihood that Previséo was neither a safe nor viable long-term solution for diabetes."

"What report? I've never seen —"

"Of course you haven't. It and any others like it have been concealed quite effectively."

"What are you talking about?"

"There's a great deal you don't know, David."

He leaned away from Mallick, already regretting his decision to hear the explanation that would end the dream.

"While Previséo was a novel medical approach with great deal of promise, it also generated many unanswered questions. Too many questions. Questions that in my experience often times lead to failure during FDA testing."

"And you told the Executive Team that?"

"It was all in the report. I was as straightforward as possible. It's my responsibility to inform them of any and all impediments to success before very large investments are made. This is a high barrier to entry business, as you know."

"What'd they say?"

"That's when things got interesting. Only a few people had actually read the report."

"Who?"

"Mr. Patera, Mr. Debil and Mr. Bonnelson."

"Why only them? I'd think that kind of detailed report, on Previséo especially, would go to the entire board of directors."

"I'm getting to that."

"What'd they say?"

"They told me to continue testing, that we'd cross whatever bridges were ahead when we got there. 'This opportunity is far too great to be hindered by skepticism,' were Mr. Patera's exact words."

"You expected different? Alvin's the CEO. He's aggressive. He's paid to be an optimist, and Préviséo has a lot of potential."

"Usually in that situation, management would hold off on large investments. Wait for more testing. It's not their money to invest. It's the shareholders'. Aggressive CEO or not, not even Alvin can dictate strategy in a vacuum without approval from the people footing the bill. And if the drug doesn't get on the shelves, it doesn't make money. So when I tell them it won't, they usually listen. Especially Mr. Debil."

David paused. It was certainly odd that Jonathan Debil, the stingiest and most skeptical man he'd ever met, would react the way he did after hearing Mallick's recommendation. Why would the tight-fisted CFO push to keep funding a program doomed to fail?

"What'd you say?"

"I tried to convince them to reconsider. But they insisted, so I went ahead with the trials."

"How hard did you try?"

"When the CEO, CFO, and COO of the company tell you to do something, as long as it's legal and ethical, you do it. I presented them with the most accurate and complete data I could and provided my recommendation. But it was their decision whether to move forward or not."

"But it wasn't ethical. You told them Préviséo would fail."

"No ... I told them it had a very high probability of failing. It's their decision, David. Just because I don't agree with it doesn't give me the right to be insubordinate. And you of all people should understand that there are a lot of gray areas in life."

David's stomach did a flip-flop as he thought back over his own past choices, and he realized he was in no place to throw stones. He inhaled deeply and momentarily looked towards the mirage of freedom that lay just outside the passenger window, then slowly returned his gaze to his newfound prison.

"What happened during the trials?"

"For a while there were some pleasant surprises. Previséo showed plenty of signs of success in the very early stages. Phase 1 and Phase 2, the initial introduction to humans and early determinants of the drug's effectiveness, started out highly favorable. It assuaged and in some cases 'eliminated' the effects of diabetes." Mallick pantomimed the quotes.

"So maybe you were wrong ..."

"Nothing would've made me happier. I was very pleased at that point. Previséo was my idea, after all. Of course I wanted it to be successful. But I was also wary. The bulk of the testing was still to come and I didn't want to get my, or anyone else's, hopes up without more data."

"So then what?"

"I began non-official testing on my own to see what would happen in later stages."

"Does that happen a lot?"

"No, it's pretty rare. But it does occur for some high-visibility drugs. All of the official testing still needs to be conducted and reported by the FDA. But this was a way for me to try to learn the results ahead of time, before official trials."

"And?"

"That's when it happened."

Mallick stared ... his eyes fixed dead ahead. His lips locked together.

"What happened?"

29

Peter Mallick knew the young executive wasn't ready to hear this, but they were past the point of no return. There was nowhere else to go but forward.

He turned his head to gaze out the window, stroking his chin contemplatively, searching for the right words and not finding them.

"Near the middle of Phase 2 testing, I discovered that Previséo did remove diabetic effects from the body, but unfortunately, it also did something else. It ... it killed some of the test subjects."

"Say that again?"

"Successive tests confirmed the results. Previséo induces significant heart tissue degeneration over several years. That degeneration made the test subjects much more susceptible to extreme heart disease. In the worst-case projections, it was fatal in about twenty percent of the cases."

"Hold on a second," David exclaimed, his hand in a "stop" motion. "You know this. I mean, beyond the shadow of a doubt?"

"There's no such thing as beyond the shadow of a doubt with drug testing. But I conducted hundreds and hundreds of tests and thousands of simulations on numerous organisms with different body types, pre-existing conditions and backgrounds. The only aspect in all of those tests that remained constant was Previséo. And I got the same result every time. That's as close to certain as you're going to get."

"What other organisms?"

"Rhesus monkey, rats, different kinds of mice and certain types of squirrels."

"Did you test any humans?"

"Not at that point. But the CDER would do that in official testing."

"CDER?"

"Center for Drug Evaluation and Research. It's a special division of the FDA. In this case, it would conduct a thorough review of its own after we'd finished the initial trials specifically to verify its conclusions. As I mentioned, we hadn't even gotten to that point in formal testing yet. I was just trying to stay several steps ahead of the FDA to see what challenges might arise."

"Were you expecting to find such dire results?"

"No way. I thought Previséo would fail in the long-term, but I didn't anticipate heart deterioration. There's no way I could have foreseen that. I couldn't get the detailed results that a full CDER test would provide, but I got enough to know Previséo would never get approved."

"But official testing would take a lot longer than that."

"That's right. Pre-clinical testing usually takes three or four years at a minimum. Then Phase 1 lasts another, Phase 2 two more, Phase 3 three more after that. Then the FDA spends an additional two years on average for a final review. That's twelve years total, give or take."

"But Previséo has Accelerated Approval," David said.

Dr. Mallick nodded his head, impressed that David had seen it so quickly. "The concept itself is noble. Think about it. The accelerated approval gets drugs evaluated faster if there's no other remedy out there by using laboratory results instead of clinical tests. And Previséo is a textbook example."

"But only if the actual lab data is used."

He nodded in silence.

"How many years at that time did you think it would shave off?"

"Pretty much what all your fancy charts show today. It's hard to predict with a high degree of confidence exactly how FDA trials may go. There are more safeguards and hoops to jump through to ensure the integrity of the regulatory process. But it does drastically reduce the time it takes to get a drug approved overall, and Previséo being released in a few years isn't out of the question."

"Let me get this straight. The formal testing was favorable at that point in time, but you knew once it advanced it would get ugly?"

"Precisely."

"And no one else saw this but you?"

"I was the only one doing the advanced testing. Plus, it's deceiving because it looks really promising in the early phases ... when it's controlled. Controlled and closely monitored. But Phase 3 would be uncontrolled and administered to thousands of human subjects, and an even more detailed analysis would be conducted. When it reached that point, the data simply wouldn't support Previséo's development."

"So what did you do?"

"I immediately notified Mr. Patera and told him I needed to share my findings."

"And?"

"And that led to the meeting that changed my life forever."

"Tell me."

"He requested we meet after hours in his office. It was late, almost nine o'clock. That was atypical, but he's a busy man and I didn't think much of it. When I got there, Mr. Patera was there, along with Mr. Debil and Mr. Bonnelson. And there was another man whom I didn't recognize." He paused briefly. "I'll never forget that man for as long as I live. He was very tall and thin, about six-and-a-half-feet and maybe two hundred pounds soaking wet. And he was dressed in all black. Head to toe. But the thing that gave me the willies was his monotone expression. He wore neither a smile nor a frown and he had these dead-fish eyes. What happened that night ... it put the fear of God into me."

"Did you get his name?"

"No. When I asked, Mr. Patera told me he was a consultant, and that he'd be participating in our meeting. What was I supposed to do? I'm a scientist. I know drugs, not business. For all I know, he actually was a consultant ... but he sure didn't look like any consultant I'd ever seen."

"Then what happened?"

"I broke down my findings for Medzic's top three executives. My preliminary research indicated that the drug would counter the disease for about eleven years, all the while degenerating heart muscle tissue but at an initially very slow rate. After eleven years, patients would start to get sick. Anyone with a pre-existing condition might show signs

119

earlier, but the heart tissue deterioration remained almost asymptotic at the ten-year mark."

"Meaning?"

"Meaning that until year ten, the deterioration was relatively minimal and probably wouldn't even show up in regular blood work. But from that point on, it picked up exponentially."

"Which means people wouldn't even know for a decade what was happening."

"Yet by the end of year twenty, as much as twenty percent of them could be dead, and another forty percent could develop debilitating heart disease."

"What did the executives say?" David asked slowly.

"Mr. Debil asked me if my data was conclusive. Then he asked me if it was possible there were confounding factors that I had failed to consider. I told him that such factors would've been nullified over the course of hundreds of tests. There was enough repetition and data to confidently flush out the outliers and anomalies. The numbers I had were statistically significant and conclusive."

"And?"

"I knew what they wanted to hear. They wanted me to say that something, *anything*, other than Previséo was causing the heart tissue deterioration. I understood that. There's huge market for the drug. But the hard answer didn't change. Science had spoken. Previséo is fatal, plain and simple."

"Then what happened?"

"Mr. Patera told me my findings seemed suspicious, which surprised me because I was the only scientist in the room. Then he reminded me of the pressures of the business. About how generics would take away more than seventeen billion of revenue over the next three years, how fewer than twenty drugs were projected to meet FDA standards next year while almost three times that number did a decade ago, about what scrapping a drug like Previséo mid-development would do to the company's bottom line and the diabetic community."

"What did you say?"

"I said I understood, but the sad fact was Previséo wasn't a safe drug. And that there was no total available market number or P&L statement that was going to change that."

"You said that to those guys?"

"It couldn't have caught them too much by surprise. Not only did my initial report warn them that Previséo was a huge risk before testing began, but my job is to be brutally honest about the science. There's a reason companies are all trying to find a cure for diabetes without much success. The Juvenile Diabetes Research Foundation and several others pour millions and millions a year into it, but having the funds available doesn't make the science work. Look at all the time, money and effort that go into trying to cure cancer. It's the same reality. The people trying to find the answer are the smartest people in the world, but it's just *that* hard."

A train blared its horn in the distance and David literally jumped in his seat.

"Think about it, David. That's why of all the drugs that go through preclinical testing, only one in five thousand actually makes it. And even then the FDA monitors the drug post-release. The odds are very much against success. We all know that."

"What happened next, Dr. Mallick?" David said, his voice soft.

"They were outraged. They insisted that Previséo couldn't be to blame and that with almost nine percent of the world suffering from diagnosed diabetes, I should be more considerate of the sick. Mr. Bonnelson told me to think of the children who had Type 1 taking six shots of insulin every single day, carrying candy bars and juice packs everywhere they went, weighing their food at every meal to calculate the carbohydrate content. Mr. Debil was a lot pithier. He merely insisted I find the *real* cause of the heart tissue deterioration."

"But you stood by your data."

"What else could I do? I told them nothing would please me more than to cure children of diabetes, but that Previséo would kill those kids before they reached adulthood. Then I asked them what else I could do. I meant it to be a rhetorical question, but ..."

"But what?"

"Mr. Patera answered it. He said I was to continue testing ahead of the FDA and keep the feedback coming to them and them alone. He said that if the FDA denied Previséo's approval on the same grounds, case closed. But that I should let the FDA decide, not my unofficial research."

David's open mouth said it all.

"I told them I couldn't do that. Not only was it a huge waste of the company's money and scientific resources, it was highly unethical and in direct violation of my oath as a doctor. I told them I had to disclose my research to the FDA, and that we should stop wasting time and money on Previséo."

After a few seconds, Mallick's eyes starting to tear up, David asked the question.

"What happened, Dr. Mallick?"

"Until that point, the tall man in black hadn't said a single word. But then he spoke ... and shattered my world."

30

Peter Mallick pressed his now-sweaty palms against the steering wheel with what looked like impressive force. The doctor's jaw tightened and his face turned red. His eyes remained shut, but even in the dim light David could see that tears streamed down his cheeks.

"The tall man ... he ..."

"He what, Dr. Mallick?"

"He told me if I ever said a word to anyone about what I'd found, he'd kill my wife and kids."

Mallick gagged a few times and then quickly opened the door and hunched over to vomit into the parking lot. After emptying his stomach and a few dry heaves, he coughed violently as David remained frozen in the passenger seat. The doctor grabbed the bottle of water on the side of the door and rinsed his mouth out, then slammed the door shut.

"My babies ... he told me he'd murder my babies. He showed me pictures of my wife, the kids' bedrooms, and their schools. He gave me a copy of my son's Little League baseball schedule. And he said that no matter what I did or where they went, he'd find them. All of them. And that if I did anything Mr. Patera or Mr. Debil didn't approve of, something terrible just might happen to all of them."

"What about contacting the police?" David asked, trying to remain calm but feeling equal parts stunned and unqualified to respond. "They could keep your family safe."

Mallick curled his lip and pessimistically chuckled.

"What?" David asked.

"I think that's what Patrick Tomilson was about to do, and we know how that worked out for him."

"What makes you say that?"

"Tomilson's death is either a gigantic coincidence, or he figured out something didn't smell right at MacArthur, Barry and Tain. My guess is after he exhausted all his other options, he figured the police were his only hope."

"But what could he have known?"

"Beats me ... but he called Jake LeMoure, which meant he knew something. But instead of going to the cops, he called his friend and told him what he suspected. Maybe asked for help. Shortly after, he winds up dead."

"Why call Jake at all?"

"Maybe to see if LeMoure knew anything at all. Maybe he wanted to either verify or possibly refute a theory. We'll never know what he told LeMoure, but one thing is clear."

"What?"

"He underestimated the danger he was in."

David sighed in agreement.

"And he didn't have a clue what he was doing," Mallick continued.

"What makes you say that?"

"The fact he signed LeMoure's death warrant."

"Huh?"

"Imagine you're Tomilson. Like you said ... why contact LeMoure in the first place? Because you know something's wrong but don't have the evidence to back it up. Again, I don't know what Tomilson knew, but he knew something. So what did he do? He called up an old buddy of his from high school, someone he trusted, and asked for help."

"Maybe he knew Jake was friends with me, that he has a line to someone who worked at Medzic."

"Either way, now put yourself in LeMoure's shoes. You get a phone call from your old buddy in Houston. He works at an insurance firm that provides coverage for the same drug company your buddy just left to go work for, and he tells you what he thinks is happening."

"But then he winds up dead in a car accident," David added.

"And when that happened, LeMoure knew he was in danger."

"So what did Jake do? He found someone he trusted, his secretary, and friend for eighteen years, and told her to get in touch with the only person he could think of who might know more."

Anne's theory was all too believable now. Feeling less comfortable by the second, David scooted up the seat to sit as upright as possible.

"And if LeMoure was half as sharp as I think he was, he knew from the moment he learned about Tomilson's death that he was next. He knew he was going to die."

David's throat constricted as he thought about Jake. He mentally searched for ways to refute Mallick's theory, but came up with none.

"In any event," Mallick continued, "LeMoure must have verified Tomilson's concern to some extent, or he wouldn't have involved you. The question is, did he find anything tangible? Or was he trying to get you to make that connection? LeMoure has really impressed me, so I wouldn't be surprised if there's more to that yearbook than you think."

"How has he impressed you?"

"Are you listening to me? LeMoure took steps to save your life even though Tomilson accidentally doomed his. He didn't call, e-mail, or write you ... nothing. He sent someone unconnected to personally find you with a yearbook that, even if it fell into the wrong hands, wouldn't reveal a thing about what he was trying to tell you or even who you were. He probably told the secretary to come right back, too."

"There's got to be a way out of this. Between you and me, there's got to be a way out of this."

As soon as he said it, Mallick's face saddened. He leaned his head against the steering wheel and looked down at the floor.

"What is it?" David asked.

Mallick looked up and said softly, "On the news, they said there was an explosion on the third floor of a hotel. It was a Red Roof Inn on the south side of Richmond."

David just stared. No words came.

"They didn't say if anyone died, but there was some sort of gas leak. Several of the rooms were completely destroyed."

Anne ... had she checked out before? ...

"Do you see now why I can't just call the cops to protect my family? There's something much bigger happening here. Something we can't hide from, bargain or reason with."

Still thinking of Anne, he wasn't following the last part of whatever it was Mallick was saying. He shrugged his shoulders to indicate as much.

"It's the federal government, David."

"The government?" David turned his attention back to Mallick and tried to refocus.

Mallick shook his head slowly. "It's the only thing that makes sense."

"So you're saying that the federal government is in on this? Isn't it possible this is just about a drug company wanting more money?"

"Drug companies don't employ killers. Drug companies don't use surveillance on employees and partners. Drug companies don't control the drug regulatory approval process."

"And you think that proves the FBI or whoever is involved?"

"The FDA is a government entity, David. No matter how powerful a drug company becomes, it can't change that. Mr. Patera, Mr. Debil and Mr. Bonnelson obviously know what's going on because they were in the room when the tall man threatened my family. But even they can't get Previséo past inspection."

"What do you mean?"

"What do you think I mean? The only reason they instructed me to push Previséo ahead was because they know the FDA will approve it. You think they honestly expected it to pass on its own after all the evidence I showed them? Or that they thought maybe they'd get lucky? I told you that you've got to start using your head. They've got some federal government connection to the FDA who's going to approve Previséo. They just wanted to see if I'd do it on my own before exposed themselves."

"But why would anyone in the government do that?"

"I just had to say no, didn't I? I had to do the right thing," Mallick slammed the dash. "And now, because of me, because I had to be Mr. Noble in an ignoble world, they're watching my family every single day. Do you know what that's like, David?" His eyes were moist and his voice shaky.

"You really think it'll pass FDA testing?"

"Of course it'll pass," he said sadly, eyes downcast. "I don't know exactly how, but someone in the FDA is going to make it happen. The drug has great preliminary results and people want it desperately. It won't turn fatal until year eleven or twelve, and those victims will be the early ones. Most of the significant damage won't show up until several years later, and it'll take even longer than that to connect it back to Previséo."

"There's no way anyone in the FDA would do that."

"You're the business guru here. Imagine if every single person who had diabetes took the medication now. The only cure for diabetes on the market, and the FDA green lights it. This is a patent-protected monopoly on a magic bullet drug that actually beats a chronic disease. You know precisely how much people would pay so their children wouldn't have to suffer. They're going to clean up. The whole market is theirs for the taking."

"But the FDA doesn't see that money."

"Six or seven years later, all the drug execs and FDA personnel involved with this scam will retire and get the hell out of the war zone before the bombs start to drop. You tell me, David ... how would the government benefit from that?"

He ran a hand through his hair and tried to strip the human life factor away, to visualize the transaction like any other business deal. Forget loss of life and think dollars. It was a lot easier than he would've liked.

"Taxes. Taxes on the drug sales."

"Think even bigger. They're getting kickbacks already, more and more as the stock price goes up. I'll bet they're getting kickbacks from the insurance company on top of that. It's all about the cash, and the government's raking it in."

"So ..."

"So let me ask you ... who in the government would benefit from an influx of under-the-table liquid funds? What short-term government official would gain the most from a sudden rush of cash and a miracle drug for diabetes?"

David shook his head and Mallick realized that he'd figured it out. "That's right, David."

31

"You're out of your mind!" David said almost in a panic.

"Am I?"

"You're talking about the president. The President of the United States."

"You know I could be right. You just don't want me to be."

"I think you're crazier than a rat in a tin shithouse."

Mallick smiled. "When was Previséo's development first announced to the public?"

"What?" David was weary of trying to keep up.

"You heard me. When did Medzic first announce to the world that it was working on a cure for diabetes?" Mallick waited a few seconds and then continued on, "I'll answer for you. Previséo was announced exactly a year-and-a-half before the election. Pretty convenient timing, don't you think?"

"That doesn't mean a presidential conspiracy. The timing was based on when the drug was ready to be announced. Next you're going to tell me JFK was killed by his driver and 9/11 didn't happen."

Vigorously shaking his head, David opened the door and exited towards the rear of the car, breathing in the brisk January air while staring up towards the starry darkness. White clouds made horizontal streaks across the night sky, obscuring some of the stars, but adding to its beauty. For a brief moment, David recalled the cool evenings of his childhood under the same night sky. He remembered the way they'd sit on the porch swing, wrapped in a buffalo checked blanket and point out the constellations. It seemed like a funny thing to think about at a time like this.

Back from his brief trip to the porch of his childhood home, David returned with two thoughts. The first was about Anne. He wondered, and worried, if she'd checked out of the hotel in time. Why didn't he tell her about Mallick's note when she'd asked? Had he really not had the time to answer her questions? Did his selfishness get her killed?

His second thought was about how incredibly selfless Jake was in his final days. Twice now the theory had been stated that he knew his own death was imminent, yet he took lengthy steps to protect others, most notably David. And it no longer felt like theory. Jake had always been better than he was. He was a better employee, friend, family man, and human being. Even his last act was selfless. It was that undeniable fact that forced David to open the door and join Mallick back in the car.

"I'm not going to argue presidential conspiracy theories with you, Dr. Mallick. If you have any actual evidence, tell me now. If not, talking about it is a waste of time. You've clearly already made up your mind."

"Have you ever seen *Lethal Weapon Three*?" Dr. Mallick asked.

"What?" David asked, exaggerating the puzzled look on his face.

"It's a great movie. One of my favorites."

"Have I ever ..." his voice trailed. "What does that have to do with anything? What's wrong with you, doctor? Personally, I think you and your theory are nuts. But if by some ridiculous notion you're right, how do we stop it?"

The doctor scratched his forehead and just stared out into space. Maybe the paranoia was making the doctor really lose his mind, David thought. Ridiculous as his theory was, Peter Mallick honestly believed it, and perhaps it was driving him insane.

Then Mallick turned his head and stared at him with full clarity.

"There is no stopping this. And there is no escape. Running isn't an option. The moment you do, you're dead."

"Are you telling me or reminding yourself?"

"Remember the book Dan Brown wrote about the NSA before all the religious stories? He based it on a kid at Exeter High School in New Hampshire who wrote an e-mail that coincidentally contained the words 'shoot' and 'Clinton' in the same message."

"What's your point?"

"The very next day the Secret Service was on campus investigating. And that was in 1995. If a high school kid's e-mail evokes that response back then, can you imagine what would happen if you tried to stop this?"

"So you just want to give up?"

"The government's watching every step we take. House bugs, sure, but who knows what else? Tracking devices, spies, phone taps, wires, people looking through your computer, and your FBI file.... Got any skeletons in your closet, David? If so, I'm pretty sure they're not there anymore. You can't even imagine how little privacy you actually have at this very moment."

The skeleton comment caused David to hesitate, but he quickly forced his thoughts away from the past.

"Something this big would leak, Dr. Mallick. How many people do you think know about it?"

"I agree the number would have to be very small. Someone from the FDA, someone high up in the CIA or FBI, and someone in the Oval Office."

"Too many to keep this a secret," David said.

"I think we'd both be surprised what the most powerful people in the United States government can keep secret."

"But why would the president take that risk? It feels way too risky."

"Elections alone cost candidates millions of dollars, but think about what happens once they're in office. Funding is the crux of so many presidential decisions it's frightening. And I'm not talking about the budget funding you and I read about in the papers. Think of defense contractors, arms dealers, and military-approved contractors. Do you really think everything the president decides is in the public budget?"

"That doesn't mean he'd go along with this."

"How many decisions could be made in the White House Situation Room if funding wasn't ever an issue? There are no limits to what money like this can allow a president to do. Politics is business. And money trumps ethics."

Mallick sure didn't sound like a crazy man, but suddenly David wished he had. He shook his head on the outside, but inside was slowly starting to wonder.

"Come on, David. You're the shrewd businessman. Here I am, the scientist, trying to convince you why these people wouldn't care about the consequences. Aren't you listening?"

"Millions of people dying takes things to a whole new level."

"You're absolutely right it does. And that's why you've got to assume that if they'll do anything to keep it quiet, they'll do even more to make it successful. They've already proven they're willing to kill. Tomilson and LeMoure, maybe this Anne Halavity. They've promised to murder my family if I blow the whistle. And they've launched a plan that could kill up to twenty percent of the diabetic population. Money is clearly more important than anything else to them."

"And yet you haven't done anything to try to stop them?"

Mallick blinked his eyes with obvious fierceness. He could see a large vein bulging out of the doctor's neck.

"It's not that I don't want to stop it. It's that I can't. I can't stop this from happening, and neither can you. I wish we could."

"So if you can't beat 'em, join 'em?"

Now Mallick was biting the inside of his right cheek. He'd definitely touched a nerve. In one fell swoop, Mallick's sense of helplessness had been augmented if not overtaken by anger.

David continued. "I'm not just going on my merry way and letting this happen because you've given up."

"Listen to you, *Mr. Morality*. I wonder why you didn't feel that way nine years ago."

David slammed his clenched fist against the car door. Mallick's first reference to his past had merely taken him aback, but surprise and pause had been replaced with rage and frustration.

"That's not only totally different, but it's below the belt and you know it. How the hell do you even know about that?"

"Nothing's below the belt when it comes to your kids. And morals are always a matter of perspective. Talk to me about doing the right thing when your children have a gun to their heads. It's lovely that now you're so determined to stop it, but lest we forget, you're not even

132

willing to acknowledge what it is. Strong words said with conviction don't equate to a plan or a sliver's chance of success."

"You better believe I have my doubts ... especially since you haven't actually proven jack shit. Just because a theory is terrifying and would have strong repercussions doesn't make it true. But since you obviously don't have any real evidence, let's say for the moment you're on to something. Let's imagine that Previséo really would kill all those people, and they'd be responsible for it."

"Imagining anything else would be like assuming the freight train will stop right before it gets to you on the tracks."

"Then you know what I'm going to say. Come on, *Doctor*. Do what's right. What would Hippocrates say? You're the moral scientist here. And here I am, just the businessman, telling you that we can't sit here and let people die."

Mallick inched even closer from the driver seat and lowered his voice. "It's the government of the United States. You think you're going to outsmart them? Outrun them? Outmuscle them? What are you going to do? You tell me. What play do you see here, hot shot? You show me a plan that has a snowball's chance in hell of working and I'll listen. But until you do, I'm not risking the lives of those I love just because of a moral obligation that you really only feel because no one's threatened someone *you* love."

"I'd feel it either way, and deep down you know we can't just sit here and watch it happen." David wondered if the first part was true even as he said it.

"If you run, they kill you. If you talk, they kill you. If you snoop around where you're not supposed to snoop around, they kill you. And they still release Previséo. On schedule."

Then without warning, perhaps triggered by the thorough and terrifying information dump, Mallick burst into tears. Sobbing loudly and uncontrollably, with no visual indication of stopping, the doctor's breakdown felt almost surreal to him. Mallick buried his face in his hands and sobbed through his palms.

The same amalgamation of emotions hit David too: fear, anger, powerlessness, and shock. It was overwhelming. He again readjusted his position in the front seat and tried unsuccessfully to get comfortable. He stared at the doctor, then away, then back at him. Speechless, he decided to keep his eyes pointed towards the trash bins in front of the car, completely unaware of what to do. He'd been both right and wrong about Mallick. Right that Mallick was losing it, but wrong as to why. He was losing it because of the dilemma facing him.

Save millions of lives or your own family.

It was cliché in the movies. But in real life, it was anything but.

Mallick settled down a bit after a few minutes and looked towards the floor.

"I can't do it, David. I can't do something I know will get my family killed."

"We don't have a choice," David said looking out the window again.

When his bold statement was met with silence, he looked back over at Mallick.

The good doctor was pointing his pistol at David.

* * *

The trembling in Mallick's hand matched the tremor in his voice.

"I won't get my babies killed. And I won't let you, either. Stop your snooping around, and stop it right now. Do you understand?"

David's mouth was suddenly arid. He found it hard to breathe, let alone speak.

"I understand."

"I'm not sure you do, hot shot."

"Please, Dr. Mallick. Please put the gun down. I promise I won't say anything."

The trembling in Mallick's hand increased, as if he was no longer in control of it.

"I don't have anything else in this world. Look what these monsters have done to me. Look at what I've become. And I did it for my family.

134

I don't want to, David, but I'll kill you. To protect my family, I swear I'll pull this trigger."

32

The two most powerful men in the world sipped coffee near a small gas fireplace on a brisk January morning in Washington, D.C.

Free from the press and the Oval Office limelight for six precious minutes before leaving for Air Force One, they were in a modest sitting room at the end of The Executive Residence. Located directly between the East and West Wings, The Executive Residence had proven to be an appropriate setting for conversations such as these.

President Charles Thompson III sat in a wing chair with his right ankle resting on his left knee. His most trusted friend and astute advisor, presidential Chief of Staff Richard Krenzer, remained standing behind the couch. Each wore a dark power suit and neither smiled.

Thompson knew that being chief of staff was a tough job to begin with, and that being his was even harder. It meant dealing with a number of issues well outside the normal scope of the position, if such a thing existed. From character issues stemming all the way back to his college years to the lies he'd been caught telling recently, there was always a fight to be had or an image to protect. He envied past presidents that didn't have to explain social media posts made decades before they knew they'd be president, or intimate details of their past out in cyberspace that not even the most elite countersurveillance and PR teams could completely remove.

In truth, he was even surprised he still was where he was. But the American public was gullible and had a very short memory, and Richard Krenzer was his secret weapon that would exploit both. His ascension in politics had been due to Richard's genius, and little had changed since his first Inauguration Day five years ago. Krenzer had proven time and time again there wasn't anything political he couldn't handle.

This situation felt different though. He was coming to the end of his second term's first year in office, after a so-so first term, and the last thing he needed was for his trusted right-hand man to let him down for the first time. The economy was finally growing, but people were still critical of his character. And exposure to this would push them over the edge.

"Is the situation under control?" he circled back to the point before taking another gulp of his tepid coffee. He pondered about the point at which the beverage in his hand, once piping hot coffee, would drop in temperature into iced coffee realm. Funny thing was though, without the ice in the cup at the start, his beverage would always be considered hot coffee, perhaps just in need of reheating. He hoped that logic had something to offer his presidency and its lukewarm second term.

"As I told you before, conversations I've had indicate that it is," Krenzer replied.

"That's not the answer I was hoping for."

"It's the answer I have for you, Mr. President."

He rose from his chair and paced the room, a sight no commander in chief would want the American people to see. It reeked of anxiety and would likely shatter any confidence the people had in him. But he'd grown quite accustomed to hypocrisy over the past five years.

"Are you sure it was the right thing to do?"

Richard fixed his hazel eyes on him, combing his graying hair to the side with the groomed nails of his right hand.

"Of course it was. You put me in charge and moved on to other issues. Don't reopen the file and question my tactics now."

Richard had always spoken sternly to him, ever since the race for one of 180 seats in the Georgia House of Representatives thirty years ago. Yet another thing the American people would never witness.

"It seems the file has been reopened for me," he answered, rubbing his balding head in an attempt to gain clarity.

"Mr. President, how old are you?"

"Richard, let's stay on queue."

"It's stay on *point,* Charles. Shit! How many times do I have to tell you? Get your phrases right. You're the President of the United States ... you can't go around screwing up basic expressions. It makes you sound like a fool. Now again, how old are you?"

"Fifty-eight." He sighed, knowing where this was going.

"And in all those years, have I ever steered you wrong?"

Glasses off, he cleared his throat and looked back at Richard. "No."

"Then leave this to me and relax. Arms deals weren't an option, and we both know it. Elections were approaching, public opinion polls were plummeting, and we had to do something. There was no other way to get the funding."

Richard finally took a seat on the sofa, lowering himself down with a victorious smile.

"You told me to leave it to you, and I did. So why am I hearing about it now?"

"Mr. President, go be president. Yes, you told me years ago to fix a problem. And I fixed it. But that doesn't mean there wouldn't be any bumps in the road, a few eggshells in the omelet. It's under control. You don't want to know the details. Do your job and let me do mine."

Such was their relationship. A problem surfaced, he went straight to Richard, and the problem disappeared. Depending on the priority and sensitivity levels, how Richard dealt with it and who was compromised as a result were usually unknown factoids of little concern.

However, proven methodologies and impeccable past results didn't stop him from wanting to remind Richard who was in charge.

"This plan of yours had better work."

"Mr. President, stay out of my way and do what I tell you."

Yeah, he thought, *I'm in charge all right.*

33

"Have they forgotten who they're dealing with?" Richard Krenzer asked, a quiet calmness in his voice. With the stick he carried as the president's chief of staff, he could afford to speak softly.

"I don't think so, sir," Marcus answered into the phone. "I think they're arrogant and ignorant, a dangerous combination."

At first he was surprised that Krenzer opted for a phone call, even when he saw in the paper that the president and chief of staff were out of the country. Though there were certainly ways for Krenzer to make a secure call from overseas, it confirmed for Marcus the importance of this conversation. He tried not to let his excitement get ahead of the discussion, but there was only one reason that Krenzer would take the risk to have this call now.

Krenzer remained even keeled. "The woman is not confirmed dead yet and we've lost the doctor. That news, combined with your latest information and theory, will not please the president."

"Nor should it, sir," he replied evenly.

"I spoke with him before we departed, and I assured him that the situation was under control. Marcus, maybe it's time to stop considering these people's feelings so much."

"I couldn't agree more. On your command, I'll contact Centrelli."

"Yes ..." Krenzer hesitated, "I suppose it's time for Plan B."

"I concur, sir. These occurrences have certainly elevated the stakes."

"Now would be the time to say, 'I told you so.'"

"No time for that, sir," Marcus said, working to conceal the pride and excitement that welled up within him. "The objective is all that matters."

"I'm sure you have already, but review the tapes again. Make sure your theory is correct. I happen to agree with your assessment, but let's be certain. We don't want to create an unnecessary coincidence."

"It will be done."

"That said, execute tomorrow as necessary. First thing."

"Understood."

"Everything else is still on schedule?" the president's chief of staff asked.

"Yes, sir. I've been working with Jonathon Debil, Medzic's CFO. He's proven more reliable than Patera or Bonnelson. According to him, development is still on track."

"Make sure it stays that way. Flush out these clogs."

"I will."

"There's little upside to me knowing the details, so I'm giving you full authority to fix these problems in whatever way you deem best. But I do want them fixed, Marcus. I don't want to deliver any more bad news to the president. Consider it your responsibility and top priority from this point forward."

"I will, sir."

"Don't make me eat my words and have to call the old bastard back. He's the past. You're the future. Get the job done and use discretion."

"I appreciate the confidence. I assure you, there will be no more issues."

Marcus hung up the phone and pushed down the natural instinct to gloat. Richard Krenzer, the Chief of Staff to the President of the United States, had just passed him the operations torch. The "old bastard" as Krenzer had referred to him, was Byron Huetel, a man who had served Krenzer faithfully for many years. The day he wasn't sure would ever come had arrived. Huetel was out and he was in.

It was finally his time.

34

The wall clock in the ProFitness Gym locker room sounded its ear-piercing buzz as it did every hour, reminding exercisers of the time and snapping David out of his regrettable funk. While not as loud as the lunk alarm, used at Planet Fitness and other national fitness chains to discourage unwanted activity, such as grunting, the fact the annoying high-pitched cacophony went off every sixty minutes made it feel worse. Why they couldn't at least lower the clock's volume was beyond him. Unsuspecting guests often literally jumped back in surprise at the top of an hour.

Following the instructions of Dr. Mallick, he took the day off to call it a long weekend and was at ProFitness to sport the illusion to whoever might be watching that all was normal. He worried the whole time his house would blow up ... or something worse. Mallick's logic was that if they wanted to kill him, they would've done so already, but that sure didn't send him into a peaceful sleep at night.

The doctor had not only offered a ridiculous conspiracy theory without any proof, but he'd also refused to save millions of people and promised to kill David if he tried to play the hero. The doctor might not be clinically insane, but he hardly seemed like someone David should listen to either. However, after picturing the barrel of the doctor's gun, he decided there was little harm in at least starting out that way. He didn't really think Mallick would murder him, and even the doctor's face and trembling had in the car supported that theory, but who knew what a man would really do when pushed to the limit?

The truth was, after he verified Anne had checked out of the Red Roof Inn and was "safe" in another hotel, he didn't know what to do. And trying to figure out if Mallick would kill him didn't even feel like the most important question, so he decided to hit the gym, *hard*. To work out to maximum exhaustion in hopes that an extremely fatigued body would give him a sharper mind.

The independently owned gym shared the name of the popular fitness chain, but that was where the similarities ended. As if he could somehow sweat out the events of the past four days, he decided to delay meeting Anne at the hotel to take advantage of some of the gym's amenities and hopefully clear his mind. After a piping hot whirlpool soak and a forty-five-minute visit to the steam room, he leaned back on the hard wooden sauna wall and ran both hands through his wet hair, comingling water and sweat, and trying to reset his brain.

He replayed Mallick's words, spoken with the kind of passion that he suspected only a father could possess. The doctor's crazy theories aside, it did feel to him that Mallick would do precisely what he'd said he would. But for all he knew, Mallick was just as dirty as anyone else. So far, the doctor was the only person who'd actually threatened him, and the only Medzic employee who was clearly unstable. There were plenty of reasons to question his farfetched story and not believe a word of it. In fact, the only hard data he had implored him to do so.

The problem was, he believed Mallick.

And that was even scarier than the gun.

So what did that mean? Well, he reasoned, he had two viable options, one of which Mallick favored. But was David really going to be able to head back to the office next week and pretend everything was normal?

He pictured each and every Medzic employee he knew, imagining who might be trustworthy and who might not, and was quickly engulfed in ambivalence. Enraged with the executives, disappointed in Mallick, grateful to be alive, fearful that would change, and clueless as to what to do next, he tried to figure out a game plan. He suspected everyone and everything, but had nothing concrete go on.

After another shower and long shave, he walked out of the locker room still unsure of where to go. But as he headed towards the door, the long-haired teenager working the front desk told him he had a package. Of standard size and fairly lightweight, the UPS box had its trademark brown and red background and yellow shield logo. The fresh white label noted his name and number. But the ship-to address was missing, and his name had been written in pencil as opposed to printed. There was also no return address or label, or any other sender information included. This might be a standard UPS box, but his gut said that it wasn't a standard package.

Inside, a *Lethal Weapon 3* DVD case with a yellow USED sticker in the right corner lay surrounded by sealed air packing cushions. When David picked it up and turned it over taped to the back cover was a brief handwritten message on a green sticky note:

Thought you'd enjoy this

When he opened the case, on the DVD itself he again saw Mel Gibson and Danny Glover, standing back-to-back with guns pointed up, and Joe Pesci peering in between. There was no note, or anything unusual about the disc, as best he could tell. It looked like an ordinary copy of the old action flick. What kind of a jack-off would give him a movie after last night's conversation? Disgusted, he tossed it into his bag.

It did feel to him that the doctor was right about one thing: there was no turning back. While with enough time things might get closer to "normal," he knew they'd never go back to the way they were before that conversation. He felt trapped.

And that if he tried to escape now, he probably wouldn't live to see next week.

* * *

Before another night of surefire fruitless pondering, this time with Anne picking apart his decision-making, he opted to head to a bar for an early dinner. He hadn't eaten all day and perhaps, he encouraged himself, food would stimulate his brain.

He followed a similar A-C-D-E-B route to the one he'd taken the night before, hopping from taxi to taxi and paranoid that people were following him. It didn't matter that he didn't see anyone ... he didn't know what to look for anyway.

He only did it on the off chance that it would conceal Anne's new location. For his own secrecy, it didn't even make sense. What was the point? If he just went back to the office next week as Mallick had instructed, why do all of that running around now? How long could he do it for anyway? How many times could he turn ten-minute drives into hour-long treks without being seen? If he ran, how far would he get if it really was the federal government chasing him? And for how long could he live with himself if he didn't do anything? When he sat down at the table, he only thought of more unanswerable questions.

The approach that felt best was to try to confirm Mallick's story and cross the Previséo bridge if he ever got to it. He couldn't just go to the cops. The government was the cops. No, above the cops. If he divulged what he knew, witness protection or no, it wouldn't make a difference. Since disappearing felt impossible, his best option seemed to be taking one step at a time, starting with Mallick's theory. Yet even so, maybe that's what Jake and Patrick Tomilson had tried ... and he was pretty sure they were both smarter than he was. So how likely was it that his plan would work?

The medium rare eighteen-ounce Porterhouse and loaded baked potato minus the sour cream couldn't arrive soon enough. When the food finally did arrive, his third Maker's Mark also showed up as a delightful companion to both David and his steak. He began to cut into the beef, revealing a warm red center, and wanting nothing more than to indulge in his meal for a few minutes.

But he wasn't able to.

Just as he finished cutting his first bite and went to lay his knife down aside his plate, Ally Darley, a local news reporter with long blonde hair, flashed on the TV screen above the bar. A massive three-story white house in the background, the closed-caption text box transcribing her words made him drop his fork.

Good Evening. I'm Standing Outside The Home Of Dr. Peter Mallick, Chief Development Scientist At Medzic Pharmaceuticals In Richmond. Details Are Unavailable At This Time, But It Appears That Dr. Mallick Committed Suicide Sometime Earlier This Afternoon. A Source Close To The Investigation Has Indicated The Cause Of Death To Be A Drug Overdose, But The Richmond Police Department Will Release An Official Statement After An Autopsy Has Been Performed. Sad News Reporting From Chester, This Is Ally Darley.

35

Anne's legs lay stretched out under the sheets, her arms down her side over the bedspread. Still in her blue jeans and white button-down shirt, she tried to focus on the TV but could think of nothing except the Red Roof Inn's Room 314. Ready to jump at a second's notice, her bag fully packed and coat ready by the door, when the phone began to ring she wondered if this was it.

"Hello?"

"Are you okay? Is everything okay?" David's voice was frantic, even scared.

"What's the time?" she followed the protocol.

"Five thirty-seven p.m.," David quickly answered.

She breathed a sigh of relief that he didn't say "twenty 'til six" or something like that. Shorthand reference to the time was the warning sign. David had insisted that if one of them ever had to call the other under duress, e.g. a gun to the head, the caller needed an unsuspecting way to let the other person know. She thought he was crazy when he suggested it, but now she waited to hear it.

"David. What is it?"

"Are you okay?"

"You mean aside from almost being blown up last night?"

"Seriously, is everything okay?"

"Seriously, everything's not okay. I'll be there in a half-hour. Does the room have a DVD player?"

"Uh," she squinted her eyes to check the shelf under the TV on the small entertainment stand. "Yeah ..."

"Stay there."

"What is it, David?"

"Turn on the news."

36

David knew he'd never see his house or set foot in the Medzic office again. His life had changed more in four days than in the previous ten years. He'd gone from being in total control to being at the mercy of the unknown. His old dream of getting rich and being his own boss was replaced with simply staying alive.

He withdrew the maximum $800 from a nearby ATM and knew money would be a problem. Anne's stash wouldn't last forever, and their debit cards might soon be a problem to use. When the taxi dropped him off at the DoubleTree on the west side of Richmond, he tipped conservatively and sprinted to Room 222 on the backside.

"David," Anne said through tears, tightly embracing him as soon as he was inside. For a brief moment, all of the negative emotions became suspended. Her anger at him for not staying with her last night to protect her, her disappointment in his disbelief of Mallick's theory, her terror about being on a hit list ... it was all bound up and squeezed out in their embrace. She was alive, and her hug confirmed she knew she had him to thank. What she didn't know though, was that David needed her just as much as she needed him. They were all each other had left now.

They sat down together at the foot of the bed and watched Alvin Patera expressing his "sincere condolences to Dr. Mallick's family" on the news. The CEO looked dapper as ever in his $5,000 suit and Gucci tie. He played the part of a sorrowful and sympathetic boss well, a half-frown spread across his face as he dabbed his moist eyes with a white handkerchief.

"You heartless bastard," David yelled, slamming down the remote on the shabby comforter. It barely made a sound, just a sort of "thud," but the force of the gesture made Anne jump.

She took a deep breath and exhaled, "You think they killed him, don't you?"

"Life won't ever be the same. They could be following us right now. My shoes ... how do we know they're clean? What about my bag? I left it in my office when I used the bathroom the other day. Maybe they bugged it. What about my clothes? They could've followed me to the restaurant." It was only then that he realized how high Anne had set the thermostat, and the room's sauna-like heat began a sweat drip from his armpits like saline from an open IV.

"David ..." Anne said softly.

"Every single thing we own ... and every single person we know ... is a potential death trap."

"Then let's get new shoes and figure out what to do together."

"Even if we did somehow get away, we wouldn't be able to live with ourselves. We'd be in the same hell Mallick was in, only ours would be worse. It'd be a hell with millions of people actually *dead* because of us."

"We can't just run away."

"We still can't prove anything, Anne. All we've got it a harebrained idea from a guy who's now dead. And who, I might add, proved his insanity when he killed himself."

"You don't really think that he committed suicide."

"Of course I don't, but anyone we try to talk to will. They'll think we're as crazy as he was."

The truth was, he wasn't so certain. He could picture the ultimatum being uttered at gunpoint: *Dr. Mallick, lead us to Centrelli and Halavity and kill yourself ... tonight ... or we massacre your family.* Who could blame Mallick if that's how it happened?

"We do have some proof."

"What? What do we have? An old high school yearbook, a doctor who committed suicide, and our word that something's fishy. That's what we've got. Doesn't exactly bode well for implicating the President of the United States."

He turned towards the window and shook his head. Mumbling under his breath, he could somehow feel Anne's stare from behind, but she didn't dare interrupt his moment of silence.

"All I want to do is to sit in my chair with a bowl of Captain Crunch and watch SportsCenter without thinking about Mallick or Previséo or my life being in danger. Maybe even a Taco Bell run and a solid night of sleep if I'm feeling indulgent. That doesn't seem like too much to ask. But it'll never happen again."

"Stop it, David! Cut it out! You're not the only one who's terrified here. Now, we're going to just take each next right step. And we're going to do it together, as calmly as we can." Her eyes were watery and she seemed out of breath after the rebuke.

David was taken aback, chastised, but knew he needed the course correction. "You're right. I'm sorry."

"So back to my question. They killed Mallick, didn't they?"

"I really don't know."

"How could it be anything else?"

"Think about it from his perspective, Anne. Save his kids or millions of others? Think of the hell that decision had to be to make just once, and he had to make it every single day. He knew the right thing to do, but family is still family."

He paused, thinking of his own family. Anne watched him, openly inquisitively, as he lost his train of thought and then found it again.

"For Mallick, maybe suicide felt like the only way to not have to choose. Plus, he was heading Previséo's development. They couldn't have wanted him to be dead. Maybe he even thought his suicide would prevent it from getting released altogether."

"Or maybe they thought up a backup plan that doesn't depend on him when he resisted a few years ago," she said.

David didn't respond. He'd actually considered that very same thing.

"What do you really think happened, David?"

He watched Anne's eyes dilate further and took a seat down on the bed, his wet shirt pressing up against and sticking to his neck and chest, its wetness clinging to his bare skin.

"I have a hard time picturing Peter Mallick killing himself ..." His voice tailed off. "My guess is he either had help ... or he was strongly encouraged to do it himself."

She nodded in agreement. "Why'd you ask me about the DVD player?" she nearly whispered.

"This was delivered to my gym today." He dropped the DVD case and UPS box from his bag onto the bed.

"*Lethal Weapon 3?*"

"Mallick mentioned it last night in the car. It pissed me off when he brought it up, and I cut him off. Then it pissed me off again when I got this package. But after his death, I wonder if there's more to it."

"No kidding." Anne picked up the case to start playing it.

"Wait." David stopped her, grabbing her hand.

"Wait? Why?"

"What if it's a message?"

"A message?" She fingered the green sticky note on the back.

"I'm not certain Mallick sent this. There was no other note or sender info. If they were listening to our conversation last night in the car, this might be their way of letting me know."

Anne paused. "What do you think?" she finally asked.

"Don't have a clue. But I don't see another choice."

"Me neither. Do you think it's bugged?"

"Why not? Sure, it looks like a normal DVD. But for all I know, it's got a tracking chip built into it that activates when you hit PLAY and pinpoints your precise location so guys with machine guns can show up at your door."

37

When *Lethal Weapon 3* started playing normally, a series of bright, yellow flames over bluish water covering the screen end-to-end during the opening credits, Anne's intuition told her that David's conjecture about the DVD having an internal tracking device might be correct.

Shrugging her shoulders, after over a minute of listening to the soft acoustic guitar and watching the fire, potentially giving someone plenty of time to pinpoint their exact location, she got up to turn off the movie when suddenly the screen went blank. A few seconds later, a new image appeared:

It was Dr. Peter Mallick, sitting on a three-legged wooden stool. Each arm rested on its matching knee, and Mallick was looking straight at them. A plain white wall in the background and nothing else that she could detect, the doctor wore dark brown business slacks with a white dress shirt, a rugged five o'clock shadow across his face.

> Hello, David. Our conversation this evening led me to a revelation, and for that I both thank and curse you. For some time now, I've told myself I was a victim … that I was trapped in a horrible conspiracy through no fault of my own, and that my sole obligation was to my family. It worked. I managed to convince myself I was an innocent bystander. But after talking to you, I was forced to admit I can't hide from the truth anymore. My time has run out.

She looked over at David, no longer wondering if he had been fully forthcoming about his conversation with Mallick. When she first saw the UPS box, she couldn't help but speculate there was more to it than she'd been told. But David's raised, curved eyebrows and the perplexed expression on his face now confirmed she wasn't the only one bewildered by this video.

You made me remember there's nothing more important tomorrow than the decisions of today. My past decisions are irrevocable, which is part of the reason why we are where we are today. My hope is I can help make tomorrow better. What I have to offer doesn't make up for what I've done, but I want you to have it.

She squinted her eyes and focused on Mallick's aged face. It might've been the video's poor lighting, but it looked as pale as a sheet. In addition to its colorless hue, it was full of wrinkles and creases that complemented bulging eyes that had recently shed tears. Mallick's sluggish posture revealed extreme fatigue. A soft, raspy voice echoed his calm, sad demeanor.

In between the DVD case and back cover is a key that opens a storage unit in a facility just outside Richmond. There, beneath a duffle bag in the corner, is a safe that contains some things I want you to have. But before you retrieve them, a final word of caution. You are dealing with people who have already killed to keep their secret safe. They're quite proficient at it, and they won't hesitate to do it again. The information in the safe is a threat to them, so be very, very careful.

The revered scientist, a genius who was supposed to always have the answers, was at a loss for words. After a long pause, Mallick wiped the corner of his eye.

Tonight was the last time we'll ever speak. But before we part, I need to ask a favor. I'll make sure my death occurs before they can hurt my family. Be that as it may, what I ask is that you give my wife a message when you think the time is right. Please tell her I love her, and that I'm so sorry for leaving her behind. She knows nothing about Previséo. I kept her in the dark to protect her. I beg you to not involve her in any way because she and my kids really are the innocent bystanders I've pretended to be. Should the day ever come when the truth about Previséo is revealed to the world, there's something in the safe I want you to give her. You'll know it when you see it. But please ... not a second before.

The doctor then took a very deep breath and chuckled to himself, shaking his head as he stared down at the ground.

David, tonight you made me face myself. It's because of you that I now have the courage to do what I've known for some time I must. Soon, you'll have everything I had. Do more with it than I did. I both thank you and curse you for making me face the truth. Godspeed.

Mallick got up from the stool and walked off screen, then reappeared holding a large white poster board. Written in black marker:

U-STORE-IT
9234 SHILOH AVENUE
HIGHLAND SPRINGS, VA 23075
UNIT NO. 63

GATE PASSWORD: 0243
SAFE COMBINATION: 16-22-6

After thirty seconds, the screen went blank.

38

"*What I'd like*, Mr. Bonnelson, is an explanation. Why did the good doctor kill himself before we had the opportunity to find out what happened yesterday?" Marcus yelled.

It was nine p.m. on Friday night, and Medzic's top three executives were sitting in Alvin Patera's office for the impromptu meeting. The stunned executives' silence allowed the sound of whistling wind outside to be heard.

"You're in charge of surveillance," Larry Bonnelson responded.

"Not in the office. That is your responsibility. Or, it was."

Marcus glared at Alvin Patera, who kept quiet as he chewed on a perfectly manicured fingernail.

"Alvin, consider yourself a non-factor as of right now."

"Marcus, we had no reason to suspect anything was amiss with Dr. Mallick," Alvin began. "He'd been coming to work, doing his job, and didn't give us any indication."

"Wrong."

Marcus retrieved the DVD from the black backpack and inserted it into the machine. The footage revealed Mallick and David Centrelli standing in the R&D lab together, talking alone in plain sight. The three of them watched in silence. Larry and Alvin shot nervous glances at each other; Jonathon stared at the screen. Five minutes later, Marcus stopped the video.

"Where did you get that?" Alvin asked.

"As I said, you are no longer involved."

"But how did—"

"A few minutes later Centrelli receives a note from an intern. After he reads it, he heads back to his office, stopping off at a restroom along the way. Doesn't even look in Mallick's direction when he leaves the lab. No good-bye, no casual wave; he just ups and leaves as soon as he gets the note. I can't confirm it was from Mallick, but I have a strong suspicion it was ... and that Centrelli destroyed it in the lavatory. Why the hell wasn't I informed of their conversation?"

"It's hardly unusual for Centrelli and Mallick to talk," Alvin said.

"Unacceptable. The doctor's whereabouts were unknown for nearly seven hours last night. All of you knew that. Centrelli didn't return to his house until past eleven-thirty, and Mallick didn't get back to Chester until three in the morning."

"It's possible they got back at different times because they weren't together," Bonnelson said.

"There's too much coincidence to assume that. What we do know is both of them met in the morning, didn't speak to each other for the rest of the day, individually went AWOL after work, and now the doctor is dead and Centrelli isn't home."

"I think we should—" Patera started.

"What do you think?" Marcus asked Jonathan.

"It's possible Mallick just couldn't take the pressure any longer. He never was fully on board."

"What about the girl?" Jonathon asked.

"She wasn't in the hotel, yet her car is still parked in the lot. She's hiding, which means she knows something. And I suspect Centrelli told her to leave the hotel."

"Centrelli's completely off the grid?"

"His car, cell phone and computer haven't moved. He hasn't been to his house since this morning, and he withdrew $800 from an ATM shortly after the doctor's suicide was announced on the evening news. No activity since."

Jonathon nodded his head slightly, his thumb under his chin and index finger stretched over his lips, contemplating.

"What's your plan?"

"I need Centrelli alive. I have to assume Mallick told him everything, of course, but we need to find out who else knows. As such, I believe it's time to inform Mr. Centrelli of our insurance policy," Marcus said

156

while looking only at Jonathon. "My men have just returned with it, in hand so to speak."

"What are you talking about?" Patera asked.

"It doesn't concern you."

"Why doesn't it concern me?"

"You really are as stupid as you look, aren't you? You screw up beyond recognition and then have the audacity to question me? My supervisor is not pleased. You remember him, don't you? He's put me in charge of the whole operation, so question me again and it'll be *your* death some Medzic spokesperson will be talking about on TV."

Alvin sunk backwards into the leather Ottoman. Marcus continued without missing a beat.

"I want security video footage every three hours. Don't even think of making a decision without consulting me." He turned to Jonathon, the only one of the three not looking traumatized.

"Have you contacted Centrelli's supervisor?"

"I talked with Martin Richardson this afternoon. He thinks Centrelli is struggling with LeMoure's death."

"Do you believe him?"

"Yes. He's too stupid to figure anything out, and Centrelli's too smart to assume he doesn't know. Besides, removing him now would draw too much attention."

Larry and Alvin both looked at Jonathon in shock. They had no idea how long their CFO had been in deeper cahoots with Marcus.

"Report back to me every few hours. Red flags will be dealt with, but I agree with you for now."

"Yes, sir."

"What about Previséo?" Marcus asked Patera.

"Mallick's death won't affect production."

"It had better not, for your sake."

Alvin Patera nodded like the lame duck that he was, and Marcus turned his attention back to Jonathon. The CFO's eyes were as cold as bitter frost.

"Hang around after these two imbeciles leave. We need to talk."

39

U-Store-It was a medium-sized rundown storage facility on the outskirts of Highland Springs, a blue-collar suburb five miles east of Richmond. The town had a population of about 15,000 people comprised mostly of lower middle-class folks living on minimum wage. The rural, small-town feel was antithetical to how Mallick had lived and worked, and remembering his GWARbar experience, David figured the doctor chose it in part because no one would expect to see him there.

The cab ride took about a half-hour in no traffic and cost almost seventy bucks, eating away at their limited supply of cash. The facility was only about twenty-five miles away, but it felt like it could've been a hundred. When he saw the WELCOME TO HIGHLAND SPRINGS sign, he felt more nostalgic than anything. His brief glimpse of the town reminded him of home back in Minnesota. A place where everyone knew everyone. Where the rumor mill drove the dialogue. Where honest people worked hard for an honest wage, and people lived life day-to-day.

It was pretty much the exact opposite of where he wound up.

"Is everything okay?" Anne asked him.

"Well sure, Anne. If I were any better, I'd be twins."

"David?"

"I'm fine."

"You know it's not your fault about Mallick, right?"

"Honestly, I wasn't thinking about Mallick just then. But while we're on the subject, the man was alive yesterday, is dead today, and talked to me in between."

He'd come to terms with the fact that his actions had led to Mallick's death. It wasn't his fault, per se, but David couldn't deny that had he not approached Mallick, the doctor would still be alive. What really consumed him now was what they would find in the safe.

U-Store-It had a few hundred storage units, and David imagined that Mallick paid about as much for a year's worth as he did for a typical business lunch. A high fence that any able-bodied person could easily scale "protected" the perimeter; there were no guards and he didn't see any cameras. Aside from an archaic metal entry gate on its last legs, there was no additional security. No photo ID or key card was required to open a unit; a large CASH ONLY sign hung in the cracked office window.

At just after nine p.m., the place was empty as far as his eye could see. He punched in the password and listened to the gate's high-pitched creak. It inched open so slowly that he thought he felt his stubble grow in the waiting.

Storage unit No. 63 was in the middle of a row of others, otherwise unmarked and very unassuming. Anne used the key from the DVD case, and they saw that inside was nearly empty. David had assumed that they'd need to wade through a maze of useless boxes meant to distract intruders from the useful information, but then realized it didn't matter. If the wrong people got this far, they would find what they were looking for, decoys or no decoys.

He held the flashlight he'd picked up at a gas station and took a final look around outside, watching the gray clouds move slowly over the moon, the tree branches twitching slightly from the eastern breeze. Certain of nothing and suspicious of everything, he slowly stepped into the storage unit and pulled the roll door down behind them, facing the interior darkness with only a small beam of light.

Three large boxes stood abreast against the wall, a small grey Sentry safe and an old blue duffle bag on top of them. David figured the boxes must be filled with something solid in order to support the weight of a fire-resistant safe. It was only about one cubic foot in size, with a small black handle next to a sixty-digit combination dial, but it still looked more secure than anything U-Store-It had to offer.

He handed the flashlight to Anne and they inched forward together, unsure of whether they really wanted to see what was inside. Before moving the duffle bag out of the way, he unzipped it to see what was stuffed in so tightly.

"Whoa," he said. There were stacks of cash held together by rubber band. He picked one of them up and flipped through a stack of fifty-dollar bills. Digging into the bag with his hands and pushing stacks aside, between the stacks of 10s, 20s, 50s and 100s, there had to be over a hundred grand in all. But while part of him was relieved money wouldn't be an immediate problem, the larger part pondered what reason Mallick would have to stash this much cash. Was it just in case he had to run, or was there something even deeper? Anne's raised brows and wide-eyed stare confirmed for him that she too was surprised and even worried by the money, and had questions of her own.

"Ready?" he whispered.

"Yeah," Anne replied.

He turned the combination dial and cranked the handle open. The only thing inside was an oversized clear-plastic bag with a manila folder. He slid the bag's pink plastic zipper to the side and retrieved the folder containing about thirty sheets of paper. The first one had been typed on an old-fashioned typewriter.

If you're reading this, there's a good chance I sent you. And that I'm dead because of what you're about to see.

Let me say first: I'm a coward. A coward put into a situation that he was unequipped to deal with. I deserve no credit posthumously for my actions; I only hope it's not too late for you to make a difference.

These boxes contain detailed testing information pertaining to Previséo, a drug currently in development at Medzic Pharmaceuticals. And the information contained therein irrefutably proves that Previséo should **not** pass FDA inspection. My findings are carefully documented, abide by the strictest scientific testing and reporting standards, and are very clear on all accounts. My research shows Préviséo will turn fatal approximately eleven years after the first dosage. If it is released, it could kill up to twenty percent of the people who take it.

Yet, despite these startling conclusions, for reasons I've highlighted in the following pages, I believe Préviséo will still pass FDA testing unless action is taken to stop it. You must be careful. I have reason to believe (also highlighted in the following pages) that people have already been killed for trying to stop this conspiracy. In addition, my family has been threatened. Thus, there is little doubt what will happen to you if the wrong people find this information in your possession.

These are the **only** physical copies of this testing that I have. I doubt soft copies will be retrievable. Keep these pages safe and immediately prepare a plan to pass them on to someone you trust in the event you are killed.

Godspeed,

Dr. Peter Mallick

40

David finished reading then looked in all directions, thankful to be in such a tight space with only one entry point. Wishing he had more than a ten-dollar flashlight to counter the eerie darkness, he focused on listening. The wind outside whistled and the watch on his wrist ticked loudly. He looked at Anne, who'd backed up against the side of the unit.

The letter was dated one month ago, and its bright white paper was noticeably different and newer than the pages behind it. It suggested the letter was a relatively recent addition to the pile.

They sat on the ground next to each other, the outsides of their knees slightly touching, each leaning in to utilize the small flashlight's minimal illumination. They combed through the other pages and noted more guesswork than fact. The first example was a reference to Patrick Tomilson's death, then Mallick's theory on a connection between the FDA and MacArthur, Barry and Tain Insurance Firm. Both lacked any actual evidence, and though Mallick's circumstantial reasoning made sense, it wasn't nearly enough to prove a thing.

There was a detailed account of Mallick's meeting with the top three Medzic executives and an unidentified man two years earlier. In it, Mallick described the threat to his family in painful detail that matched what he'd said last night. In fact it was word-for-word, complete with a physical description of the tall man in black but no name or particularly distinguishing characteristics that could be used to find him.

Following that was a radical theory of government involvement and suspected structures of the deal between it, Medzic and the insurance firm. The theory piqued the imagination, but again lacked any proof. It was almost like Mallick had used the pages as a brain dump, listing all his guesses and hoping that someone would be able to connect the dots.

However, when they moved to the stacked boxes they found content that was anything but guesswork. Inside the one on top was a black notebook entitled "Previséo." It contained a very detailed description of which specific scientific tests were performed on the drug, when they were conducted and their durations.

Beneath the notebook and in the other two boxes were descriptions of and notes about those tests ... *lots* of tests. They spanned several years, and the meticulous notes both detailed the tests and confirmed exactly what the results meant. David didn't understand a lot of it, but its meticulousness was incredible, down to the minute the tests were conducted and with paragraphs of scientific explanations.

Unlike the pages in the safe, the data was methodically written and very professional. No opinions or commentary were included, just straight up facts and figures. After an hour of reading what amounted to a professionally published study, which they didn't comprehend, in the confines of a dark storage unit, they both looked at each other with a newfound weariness.

"What are we supposed to do with all this?" Anne asked, resting her head on the metal of the storage unit's back wall.

"Good question," he answered, shaking his head.

"It looks legitimate to me," she said shrugging without lifting her head off the wall.

"No offense, but you're not exactly an expert."

"Well does it look legitimate to you?" She lifted her head to eye him.

"I'm not an expert either," he added.

"You know, I think we need to understand how MacArthur, Barry and Tain fits into all of this too," Anne was nodding her head slowly.

"Why?"

"Because it seems to be a part of how this all ties together. This is a starting point." Anne pinched her thumb and index finger together to indicate the point, "But we're going to need more to build a legitimate case, even if all of the science checks out," she said sweeping her hand widely in front of her to show just how much more they'd need.

"I'm not sure it does all tie together." David said squinting his right eye and shaking his head again.

"Well what would you suggest we do then?" Anne asked pointedly.

Even better question, he thought. He brought his fingertips from both hands together and rested his mouth against his pointers, thinking through what should happen next.

"Let's regroup back at the hotel. This place gives me the creeps."

"And just leave all this here?"

"I'm not impressed with the security either, but there's nothing from the safe that'll help us this second. We know the boxes have been safe here for some time. Mallick kept them here for years if those test dates are right, and I don't think he'll be telling anyone about this place anytime soon."

"What if they followed us?"

"Then we've got bigger problems."

But her question made him realize something. Anne was more concerned with stopping Previséo than her own safety. To her, this was no longer about them. It was about millions of future victims. He felt ashamed for focusing on how they could get out of this mess.

"Plus," he added, trying to cover it up, "if they do find us, we can't have any of this on us. And it's not like we have a better hiding place."

Anne nodded, accepting his logic in principle. But the way she narrowed her eyes made him think that she saw right through his self-rationalization.

"We've got to look at the yearbook again," he continued. "I think we're missing something. Even Mallick said so."

They re-packed the files just as they were, and then he grabbed the duffle bag stuffed with cash. Anne shot him a skeptical glance that was obvious even in the dim lighting.

"We need money, Anne. No more ATMs."

Then he poked his head outside the door. Making sure, as much as an untrained person could, that no one was watching them, he quickly locked the door behind them and stashed the key twenty feet away beneath a few cinder blocks along the perimeter fence. The blocks were so badly discolored it was clear they hadn't been moved in years.

He still had the distinct feeling of being watched. It felt like eyes were roaming all over his body, itching him everywhere, like a million pesky mosquitoes. Even so, it was still safer to stash the key than to keep it on him. He and Anne had just become the only living link between the Previséo evidence and the world.

41

They were five minutes from the hotel when it happened.

It had been a nervous, quiet ride until that point. For most of that time, she sat behind the driver and either thought about the medical data they'd read or prayed they weren't seen. David hardly moved, his hands beside him on either side, looking straight ahead at the back of the passenger seat. That was when, suddenly and seemingly without reason, he stirred and yelled at the driver to stop right away. The elderly cabbie, understandably flustered, cursed as he halted the car, and she watched David dash out the door and into the light freezing rain. She quickly handed the driver $60 and then started running.

"What is it?" she screamed from behind, losing ground fast.

David only ran harder and faster. Straight through NO WALK signs on deserted Richmond streets and towards the DoubleTree Hotel without checking for cars. She gasped for air as she approached the front entrance, well behind David despite trying her best.

When she walked in the room, she found him sitting on the bed, his hand over his mouth. She knew why when she saw it.

There, on the 32" color TV, was David's house, engulfed in flames.

42

He was homeless.

No, check that ...

He was possessionless, jobless, *and* homeless.

When he heard the news briefing on the cab's radio, in particular the street name, he couldn't be sure it was his house. But the sprawling white-siding ranch flashed through his mind nonetheless. He wasn't even surprised when he saw it on the TV.

Some sixth sense.

An unmarried thirty-two-year-old with few friends and not a single picture of his family, there were only a few priceless possessions lost. A note from his mom when he was a kid was at the top of the list along with a few pictures, but overall nothing he'd miss too much. That said, it was still his home. And he was watching it burn to the ground on live television.

Anne didn't say anything, smart girl that she was. She seemed to have learned the right moments to keep quiet. He didn't want comfort or pity. He only wanted silence.

"At this time, it hasn't been confirmed whether the home's owner was inside, but authorities seem relatively certain this is a case of arson," the reporter announced with an upbeat voice that felt borderline giddy to him. It reaffirmed his resentment of reporters ... anything for a story.

The screen flashed back to the studio, the anchorwoman promising updates as they arrived. And that was it. Just like that, they were on to the next one.

He sat on the bed wordlessly for a few minutes, attempting to let go of the house, thinking about things he'd tried so hard to forget. On the bright side, he wasn't in the house.

Ironically, it was that very thought that made him suspicious.

"Why do you think they'd do that?" he asked Anne softly.

"I'm sorry, David."

"No, I mean why would they burn down my house when they know I'm not there? We assumed they planted the bomb in the hotel room because they wanted to kill us. They want us out of the picture, so they blow the room up. Pretty simple. Scary, but it makes sense."

"So?"

"So, if they had my house under surveillance, they knew I wasn't there. If their goal was to kill us, why burn it?"

"To give you no place to go?" her voice trailed off, making it more of a question than an answer.

"Perhaps, but what if there's more to it than that?"

"What do you mean by that?"

"What if they think I know something? Or you do? Maybe they know we're together and assume we're onto them. Or that Mallick and I talked before he killed himself."

He pictured the security cameras in R&D, knowing even then he was on TV for Alvin and Jonathon and whoever else to watch. But he'd made sure nothing unusual happened, so his mind quickly shifted to onlookers at GWARbar, street cameras as he took taxis all over, Abner Clay Park and its dark shadows, even the Burger King parking lot. The fact was, there were any number of ways for him to have been exposed.

And it only took one.

"Hold on," Anne broke his concentration, slowly shaking her head. "If that's true, if they assume you know something about this, *anything*, they'd also assume you wouldn't go back to your house."

"Right. But if they want to find out what we know, and they aren't sure where we are, burning the house down would be a pretty effective way to get my attention."

As Anne stared back with a blank expression, he jumped off the bed and motioned her to follow. He walked briskly, feeling more confident of his theory. It seemed almost certain, which was concerning in and of itself to him.

The DoubleTree's computer cluster was in yet another small, sweltering room near the front of the hotel. Remarkably similar to the

Red Roof Inn's only with newer equipment and more workstations, it too was empty and he took a seat at the far computer. Anne sat beside him and folded her hands on her stomach.

"David, what are you doing?"

"The fire ... it was a message."

"A message?"

He didn't answer.

Instead, he quietly logged on to the web-based version of his Medzic Outlook e-mail account. It was possible they could trace his remote access, but at this point nothing felt secure and this was all they had to go on.

His INBOX had 157 unread memos, many with an exclamation point to the left indicating high importance. He briefly sighed at how "importance" had taken on a new meaning. Then he started opening them up one by one, regardless of the subject or sender. Anne watched with conspicuous skepticism but didn't say anything.

Unread e-mail # 154, sent Friday night at 11:26 p.m., caught his attention.

From: WeNeedToMeet@gmail.com
To: DCentrelli@Medzic.com
Cc:
Subject:(no subject)

At first, he expected it to be just another spam e-mail, some dating website or ransomware scam phishing for suckers. But the message made him think:

We need to talk, David. 888.971.1474 ext. 9704

"What's the big deal?" Anne asked.

He stared at the e-mail, then hit Reply.

Who is this?

Ten seconds, later, he got an "Undeliverable" message from the Microsoft System Administrator. After another pause, he looked at Anne.

"This is strange."

"You don't get spam?"

"Sure do I, but usually it tries to drive you to a website. How often does it give you a toll-free number to call?"

"I don't know. I guess I haven't looked."

He looked at Anne and then back at the screen, rapping his fingers on the table. After quickly combing through the remaining e-mails and finding nothing significant, he checked his watch. Two a.m.

"Follow me," he said bobbing his head up and down in agreement with his newest brainstorm.

43

They hailed a yellow cab two blocks from the DoubleTree and David instructed the driver to take them to any working payphone he knew of that was a half-hour from the hotel. After a brief glance in the rearview mirror, the cabbie gave a long, slow nod. David and Anne watched the ads scroll on the seatback screens and listened to the Grateful Dead ooze from the front car speakers. The air was heavy with the scent of patchouli.

When they got there, David hopped out and motioned for Anne to stay there in the taxi. The driver didn't complain. Paying customers at 2:40 in the morning weren't everywhere to be found in Richmond and the meter was still running. Anne didn't complain either, since staying inside meant avoiding the rain, which had picked up considerably.

Standing in the payphone booth as countless raindrops danced on the roof overhead, David was as sure and as comfortable as he'd ever be to make this call.

Though that wasn't saying much.

If he was calling who he thought he was calling, they'd begin a trace as soon as possible. He'd read once that it took twenty-seven seconds to complete a trace. That seemed grossly inaccurate, but having absolutely no other idea, he decided to run with the info he had.

After dialing the number and pressing the phone against his ear, he heard a recording asking for an extension. He punched it in and waited.

Half-expecting to get "The Singles Hotline," even he was caught a bit off guard.

"Hello, David. I've been waiting for your call."

"Who is this?"

"In due time, David."

"What do you want?"

"On the contrary, I have something you want. Ten a.m. tomorrow, Corner of 7th and Clay. Sit next to the man on the bench facing the Coliseum."

"If you think I'm going to—"

"This is your last chance to hear what I have to tell you."

Then he heard a click, followed by dial tone.

He punched the numbers again, bottling his frustration. After five rings, someone finally picked up.

"Now you listen—"

"We're sorry. The number you have dialed has been disconnected or is no longer in service. Please hang up the phone and try your call again."

44

"You're not serious, David."

"What else can we do?"

"I don't know, but this isn't a good idea."

"I can't argue with that."

Tension filled the hotel room as ubiquitously as the stale air they were breathing. They were both right, and they both knew it. There was no answer for such a predicament. And after hours of circular debate, they were both too tired and too afraid to acknowledge it.

"This meeting with the people who probably killed Jake and Mallick is four hours away, and this still feels like a suicide mission," Anne said.

Yet another statement he couldn't argue with. It felt like a kamikaze ending to a war that no one else knew was happening. Like he'd be walking into a death trap.

And yet ...

"We don't have any other options, Anne. What can we do? Run? We've been running scared, afraid of these people and have no plan to speak of. How far can we go? Hide? Think about our last hotel room and tell me how long you really think this one will keep us safe. The only thing we've got going for us is the cash Mallick left, but even that won't last forever. Let's face it ... it's only a matter of time. They're going find us, Anne. At least this way we have some control over how."

"You really think that matters?"

As he pressed his forehead into his right hand and looked down, Anne put her hand on his shoulder. Her gentle rubbing was more comforting than he expected, but more than anything it reminded him how she must've felt. She was alone before they met, unsure of what to do or where to go. And if this didn't end well, she'd be alone again.

"How come you're not married, Anne?" he inquired suddenly. "Good-looking woman like you." He was exhausted and living too close to his emotional threshold to filter out questions he probably had no business asking, much less at a time like this.

"I was ... once. In another life."

"What happened?" David asked another intrusive question with a mixture of surprise and sadness.

She paused. "He died. Heart attack."

"Oh ... I'm sorry. I didn't know ..." He wished he hadn't brought it up. He'd been wondering for days why she didn't have a life to go back to, why no one missed her, but he didn't want to make her relive that.

"It's okay. It was a long time ago."

"You never wanted to marry again?"

"At first, I didn't meet anyone who measured up. Then I got used to being on my own. It's not so bad. I'm happy enough. I have my own place, enough money ..." She nervously fake-laughed. "I mean *had* my own place and money."

He put his hand over hers, which remained on his right shoulder. "I know this meeting could be a mistake. Probably is. I just don't know what else to do. Maybe we'll learn something about Jake or Préviséo, or even what we can do next."

He saw her big brown eyes fill up with tears that toppled over her lower lashes in erratic bursts. David got up and embraced her, pulling her in tightly and kissing the top of her head. Her chestnut hair smelled clean, like summer-fresh peaches, and she returned the strength of his embrace.

"It'll be okay. You keep watch from the Convention Center, just like we talked about. If anything happens, you know what to do. Take everything we've got straight to the cops. Make them listen. Don't take no for an answer."

Despite his outer optimism, on the inside he still couldn't believe that was the grand plan. To take two cabs and have Anne watch with binoculars and a camera. It felt so feeble compared to what they were up against.

45

The joy David once felt for Saturday mornings was gone.

The taxi had dropped him off at Leigh and 7ᵗʰ ten minutes early, and he slowly walked southwest towards Clay Street. The circular Coliseum made of concrete, metal and brick buttresses towered over him to his right. It was bigger than he expected, but the sun had done its damage over fifty years and there was little decoration to augment cracked piss-yellow brick. He now understood why so many in Richmond were pushing for it be replaced with a more modern plaza space.

As he passed the five-story open parking garage across the street, he kept scanning the Coliseum area in search of the bench. Large, aged maple trees lining both sides of the cobblestone sidewalk obstructed his view, but they wouldn't hinder Anne's. He pictured her on the fourth floor with a clear view of the bench and surveillance equipment in hand.

The sun was out, but the rain had cooled the air. He felt the gusts of a forty-some-degree windy day stand up all the fine hairs on his face and a flush of goosebumps with them. With no hat or earmuffs and only a light pullover, his ears were cold already and he shivered.

The park bench was technically part of the Nina F. Abady Festival Park just southwest of the Coliseum. It seemed innocuous, like any other bench in any other park, as did the elderly gentleman sitting on it.

He wore a black top hat and charcoal gray overcoat. Next to him was a tall and thin uniformed police officer — hat, gun, and holster included — who looked anything but innocuous. Even the officer's face looked angry, with its seemingly dilated nostrils and clenched jaw. The cop's straight posture and tall stature projected the image of a man you simply didn't want to piss off. As he cautiously approached them both, the older man looked up to face him.

"Hello, David. I appreciate your taking the time to meet me this morning."

The man looked seventy or so, and his face sported several wrinkles to go with white hair beneath the hat. He was neither impressively fit nor overweight. A white dress shirt and red tie complemented his top hat and overcoat.

"I'd like to introduce you to my associate, Marcus," the old man said, motioning to the officer.

The freaky "officer" was even bigger up close. He had to be 6'7" or thereabouts, with a slender waist and bulging chest, short black hair beneath his police hat that looked like it'd been cut military style, and a firm and uncomfortable handshake. His eyes were icy, his demeanor cold. David looked at the gun and wondered if Marcus was really a cop, and why he was there.

Marcus placed his bony hands on David's shoulders and started patting him down aggressively. It was paralyzing how strong the man felt, hard fingertips pushing deep into his chest and down his waistline. It felt like an animal was mauling him.

Marcus said nothing, and neither did the old man on the bench. When done frisking, Marcus nodded and stepped back without a word spoken.

"Take a seat, David."

He reluctantly agreed. Marcus remained standing, towering over him like the Coliseum. A few tourists with cameras were snapping pictures of the Coliseum, but the park was relatively empty. He saw one young family braving the weather with a stroller and dog, but otherwise the brisk temperatures had kept people away.

"I like it out here, don't you?" the old man continued. "The campus looks pretty; I like all the trees. You like trees too, don't you, David?"

He shrugged, not much caring for the small talk but preferring it to discussing the gun in Marcus's holster.

"I can tell you're uncomfortable. It's Marcus, isn't it?" the old man smiled. "He has that effect on people. I'll tell you what ... Marcus, why don't you leave us for a bit, so we can talk. You can come back in about ten minutes."

Ten minutes, David thought, watching Marcus walk towards the Convention Center. *Am I going to be dead in ten minutes?*

"Marcus can sometimes give the wrong impression. We didn't come here to hurt you."

"Apparently you think that's what I came for."

"You mean the frisking?" the old man chuckled, "I've seen crazier things, David. Besides, there are more threats to me than just weapons."

"Like a wire?"

"Sharp kid ... not that I'm surprised. I've been told you're very intelligent, and your past seems to confirm it. Great job at Medzic, before that Clearwater Funding, far from a pushover brokerage firm; full scholarship to Cornell for undergrad, and a homeowner at thirty-two. All that from a humble upbringing in rural Minnesota. Humble to say the least."

"You seem to know a lot about me. I don't even know your name."

"I prefer to keep it that way if you don't mind," the old man replied, as if asking permission. "I could give you a fake name, but what's the point?"

"Okay ..."

"Yes, you've done very well for yourself, David. Which is a function of two things: hard work and intelligence. That's why I'm sure you'll listen to me today."

"Don't you mean I *had* a house, and I *had* a job? What do you want?"

"You're insured, aren't you?"

After David didn't respond, the old man looked away briefly, staring towards the park, and then turned back to him.

"No more chitchat, David? I guess that's understandable," the old man replied.

The man was so seemingly imperturbable that it felt disconcerting. Here David was wondering if a sniper was on a nearby rooftop or if just by talking to this guy he was putting himself in the crosshairs of some maniacal plan, and meanwhile the old man was operating like some kind of trained professional. His body was motionless and the deep creases in his forehead remained equally still.

"My point is that you can be made whole," the old man continued. "I'll make the necessary arrangements to replace everything you lost and then some. You'll get a nicer house and a better job for starters. That's assuming you even want to work. If you play your cards right, you won't ever have to work again."

"What about bringing Dr. Mallick back?"

He reminded himself that he couldn't mention Jake. It was almost certain the old man knew he'd talked to Mallick, but everything about Jake, Anne, Previséo, and especially the information at U-Store-It was off limits. The old man probably knew a lot of that too, but in case not, he sure didn't want to be the one to tell him.

"That's not fair, David. The doctor took his own life. The autopsy even confirmed it this morning. You're not really going to blame me for a suicide, are you?"

"What are you? Kevorkian's evil twin?"

"I don't want to fight. But it seems like you're trying to provoke me. Can't we just enjoy the crisp winter air and a nice view and a simple conversation?"

He didn't answer.

"I guess not. Okay, David. I understand. You're upset, and you don't want to be here. I'll respect your time and get to the point. First of all, you should know that I'm an independent contractor. I have no connection to you, your company, Anne Halavity, Jake LeMoure, Peter Mallick, or anyone else. I was hired to do one thing: get you to reason with people who want to be reasonable. I know your past because I need to know it. But make no mistake, I'm here short-term for a short-term objective."

"How comforting."

"I know you've had several conversations with Dr. Mallick and Ms. Halavity. I know Ms. Halavity was LeMoure's secretary, and that you and LeMoure were close friends. It doesn't take a genius to connect the dots. I know she's in Richmond, probably watching us this very minute, recording us if you're as sharp as I think you are. And while that would present a threat to both me and the people who hired me, I'm here to work out a deal with you nonetheless."

"What kind of deal?" David tried to say it with a face as frozen as the old man's.

"Good, we're back on speaking terms. Negotiation, David. You know as well as I, it's the most important skill a person can have. Both in business and life, fighting for what one deserves is a tricky craft. But you've learned it well. We each have something the other wants. I want to know everything the doctor told you and what Anne Halavity is doing in Virginia. I want to know why you hadn't been to your house in two days and why you abandoned your sweet BMW. And finally, I want you both to give me everything you have that might be harmful to my employer."

The old man paused, as if the conversation was over. David noticed he didn't say Préviséo or anything else incriminating and figured that wasn't an accident. Then the old man calmly continued, answering the question on his mind.

"In return for your generosity, your trust, if you will, I will give you and Ms. Halavity new lives. A better life than you had. You can go anywhere and have anything that you want. Riches beyond your wildest dreams. A new job if you want it, a mansion to live in, enough money for the rest of your life, new job, cars, boats, planes, timeshares, you name it. You'll live like a king."

The old man paused and then lowered his voice a touch. "This is a great deal, David. Better than I've ever seen and, quite frankly, better than you should get. I would strongly advise you to consider taking it."

"Mallick didn't tell me anything. He said he needed to talk, but then he *coincidentally* decided to kill himself."

"Here I was trying to have a constructive, meaningful conversation, and you repay me by lying to my face," the old man answered in the same monotonic voice, shaking his head slightly.

"He didn't tell me anything."

"I've got to tell you, Mr. Centrelli: I very much dislike being lied to. It's a major pet peeve of mine. My patience is thicker than most in my profession, certainly thicker than Marcus's over there, but lies chip away at it like an ice pick."

It was clear the old man knew more than he let on, but how much? What if this was a bluff to get him to say something stupid? He was petrified about giving away more than he should, and sweat trickled down his back despite the chilly air.

"Let me make this simple for you, David. You think you know something about Previséo. Whether or not it's true, you'll find out in due time. But I'm only going to ask you once more."

The old man covered his gnarled hands with leather gloves from the overcoat pocket. "Jake LeMoure and Patrick Tomilson got similar offers. Not as good, but similar. They decided not to take them. Unfortunately, they each hit a streak of bad luck after that decision. Their families did, too."

David just stared, trying to keep it together. He realized he wasn't breathing and had to tell himself to exhale.

"I didn't want it to come to this. In all honesty, I didn't want it to come to this with Mr. LeMoure or Mr. Tomilson either. But I just don't get taken very seriously these days, and that's unfortunate. I think it's because I'm getting old. But that's neither here nor there, is it? I'm just a short-term player trying to help."

His heart was exploding. He could feel it throbbing against the inside of his half-zip, like a fighter pilot threatening to hit eject. The old man handed him a cell phone and David held it to his ear.

"H-h-hello?" said a quiet, jittery voice.

"Who is this?"

"Dave ... David? Is that ... is that you? Dave?" the voice forced out. Fear radiated from every word. He could hear teeth chattering through uneven gasps of air. He tried to place the voice but couldn't. It was too frantic, too panicky; without a smooth sentence, he couldn't recognize it.

But with the next sentence, he got it.

"David ... David, these people say ... they say you can help me."

His mouth hung open. It was a voice David hadn't heard in so long that the sound of it was shocking. Paralyzed, he searched for words that simply weren't there, pressing the phone even harder to his ear.

Then the old man jerked it away before he could say a thing.

"That will do," he said, and pressed END.

46

"It wasn't hard to find him. Douglas Lewis Centrelli, older brother to local hero David Timothy Centrelli. The one who got out of the small town."

"How ..." he didn't have the words.

"Your name isn't exactly anonymous in Lincoln County, Minnesota. Even with no social media accounts, people haven't forgotten you. I'll bet every one of the 6,000 residents knows it. One or two coffee shop conversations and boom, we've got all that's left of your family."

He stared at the trees, Doug's voice evoking emotions that haunted him.

"But it did take some effort to figure out why you haven't called or seen him in over a decade. Most siblings don't go more than a few months without speaking to each other, but when we discovered you hadn't talked in more than eleven years, we figured it was something juicy. We figured right."

His mind uncontrollably replayed the events. They'd led to his estrangement from what little family he had left, and replaced a belief in good, human decency with cynicism and heartache.

"Your own brother was screwing your fiancée," the old man said casually.

The words hung in the air like a sticky humidity.

"Terrible stuff. One day you're a twenty-two-year-old stud, the town hero that busted out of Hicksville and saw the world. Graduated from Cornell University with honors and soon after brought your bride-to-be, a beautiful, smart young woman, back home to meet your family and friends. And then ..."

He remembered it all too well.

"The next day, you're on a train back to New York by yourself. All because your brother, a worthless, unemployed slob living with your drunken father, was riding her in the house you grew up in. That must've been awful."

The old man's widened eyes and calm voice indicated he knew not just that, but the rest of the story too. David remained quiet, waiting in painful anticipation.

"But cutting him off completely ... that's pretty extreme. I mean, he *is* family. And as they say, family is everything. You're a tough cookie, David. Didn't even go back when your father died three years later. Didn't return calls, moved out of your apartment before Tiffany got back, and haven't said a word to either one of them since. But it's one thing to ignore your brother when you know he's safe in Minnesota shooting beer cans off the back porch with a .22 and drinking himself to a slow death. It's another when you know we've got him ... and to wonder what we're going to do."

The old man reached to his side and opened a briefcase David hadn't noticed. He withdrew a plain red file folder and handed it over. David's hands shook as he shuffled through pictures of Doug chained to a chair beside a table of very sharp knives and long metal pliers. Numerous close-ups revealed eleven years of changes he'd desperately avoided seeing over time. Doug was much heavier, and his pudgy face now had a thick graying beard. But his eyes were the same, and the look in them was empty, just as it had always been.

He shook his head and sighed. A gust of cool wind didn't stop David from sweating; he kept his eyes on the pictures as he flipped through a stack of about fifteen full color photos.

"He's a truck driver now, just like your father was for twenty-nine years. Still lives in your parents' old house and spends most of his time at the bar or on the porch. Has a few friends and a girlfriend, but nothing serious."

Each picture was more terrifying than the last: Doug lying nearly naked next to a pair of scissors and electric shock treatment equipment, standing next to a whip, sitting inches from a crowbar that glowed red from the fire it was held over.

"What'd you do to him?"

"Not a thing. Not yet ..."

He looked up.

"I don't want to hurt your brother. But Marcus over there ... he does. He's a freak of nature, a different kind of cat. He lives for other people's pain, especially if he gets to inflict it. Once, I saw his goons beat a ninety-one-year-old man to death with a baseball bat in front of his two children and three grandchildren just to prove a point to one of his sons. Marcus was smiling the whole time. He's not normal human being. He's pure evil. And if you don't show me the respect I deserve, he gets to do things his way."

The old man shook his head and made a repeated tisk sound.

"Your brother screwing your fiancé really messed you up, didn't it? Depression, counseling, alcoholism, insomnia ... the whole kit and caboodle. It led to your relentless focus on Number One. Lies, deceit, treating women ways you know they shouldn't be treated, not giving a damn about anyone but yourself. And so on. Given that, I can almost hear you wondering if your brother deserves pain. 'Karma's a bitch.' I can picture you saying it. I don't think so ... but you might even be willing to let him die. My point is, I needed a backup plan. In case your brother's life doesn't make you see the light, maybe Tiffany's will."

He looked up again, his eyes now laser focused. Every time he heard her name, be it a person or a jewelry store, memories followed. The ice-skating rink they'd met at, how she looked at her cousin's wedding, the times they'd shared, the memories they'd formed, and how much he loved her. Tears always followed.

Today was no exception.

"Tiffany Erin Carter. Blonde-haired, blue-eyed snow bunny from the East Coast, complete with daddy's trust fund and a smile that could light up any room. And eventually the reason that when everything went south, you went from not caring about money to making it the only thing that matters. Prove to the prissy that you can earn the money her daddy made. You sure showed her.

"I know she cheated on you, with your own brother for heaven's sake. That isn't easy to forgive, and impossible to forget. But you *loved* her. And they say that love never dies." The old man paused, and then shook his head slightly before continuing.

"She's a DCFS non-profit lawyer now, by the way; lives just outside of Fort Worth in a small ranch. Spends her days helping kids just like the ones you work with at Big Brother/Little Brother. She never did marry ... maybe because she kept hoping you might forgive her. She could be waiting for you at this very moment. Hoping for a second chance. Hoping for love. How sad is that? It's bad enough when things work out for the cheaters and not the cheated, but to me this feels even worse. To have two such young, intelligent, good-looking people who'd once planned to spend their lives together now so lonely and apart and worse off than they were together ... it's a real tearjerker. And even with what she did, I really don't think you want her to die a horrible death."

The old man started shaking his head again.

"Her parents didn't do anything to you. Neither did her friends. To lose a beautiful woman at such a young age ... that would be brutal. But I guess you know what that's like, don't you?"

"Shut the hell up!"

"It must've been hard to lose your mom when you were so young ... to spend your childhood without her love or nurturing. All you got was a heartbroken, drunken father who was never there. I'm sorry, David. You got a raw deal. But you don't want to give Tiffany's children the same, do you?"

Fear transformed to animosity, and David felt the overwhelming urge to pounce on the old man, rip off his head, and drop kick it across the park. He fantasized about crushing his old bones and beating the life out of him one blow at a time.

Nobody threatens my Tiffany, his mind screamed. The irony was as palpable as it was pathetic. She wasn't his at all.

"Control yourself, David. Don't let rage blind you from reason. All you have to do is tell me everything you know about Previséo and give me everything you've got, and I let your brother go and never introduce Tiffany to Marcus."

He said nothing.

"I'll give you whatever you want. You can go wherever you please. You're a sharp guy, David. You know this is the best deal you're going to get."

The photos of Doug in his hand and the image of Tiffany in his mind, he gave up on trying to respond.

"Tell you what, why don't you take a day to think about it. Hold on to those photos. We'll take more if you make the wrong decision. And while you're thinking it over, gather any paperwork you know you need to give me. You're too smart not to."

The old man checked his watch. "It's ten-thirty right now. I like this time of day. Let's say ... twenty-four hours even. It should be a gorgeous Sunday morning tomorrow, and it can be even more beautiful for you.

"Be here tomorrow. This bench, this time. And bring Halavity and everything you've got, and this'll all be over by eleven. But I have to warn you David ... if you don't show up ..."

The old man rose from the bench and started to walk away, then turned around.

"Be here, David. Don't make me cut Marcus loose."

47

Throughout the hour-long trek back to a hotel that was only twenty minutes away, all he could think about were Tiffany and Doug. The two of them half-dressed on the living room sofa, the piercing silence when he'd walked in, the sound of slamming the front door behind him ... and knowing his entire future had changed in an instant.

He and Anne sat on one of the queen hotel beds six inches apart, the manila folder resting between them. Pictures of Doug were inside, but Anne did David the courtesy of not looking at them.

"You haven't talked to him since?" She asked quietly.

"No."

"Has he called?"

"Used to. He gave up after four years."

"And your fiancée?"

"Ex-fiancée."

"Sorry."

"When I got back to New York the next day I packed up my stuff, all two suitcases' worth, and moved out before she got back. The lease was in her name, and I didn't have a penny to mine."

"You haven't seen her since?"

"Or talked to her."

He wasn't sure if Anne felt sorry for him or thought he was an icy bastard. And despite pretending to be indifferent, he hoped it was the former. She didn't react, other than to put a comforting hand on his shoulder.

"You have to understand what it did to me, Anne. I was twenty-two. Young, stupid, idealistic ... and completely in love. I loved her more than anything on this earth. The day we got engaged was the happiest of my life."

"I do understand, David."

"I just *knew* I'd be with her forever. Then I lost everything." He paused, shaking his head. "It was her first trip to Minnesota ... the first time she met my family."

"You got engaged before she met your family?"

"Mom was the only one worth meeting, and she died when I was eight. Cancer. Probably secondhand smoke from living with my father. Doug was ten. He was always Dad's favorite. Dad didn't even try to hide it. And after Mom was gone, nobody made him. From the time I was nine years old, I remember him taking Doug on his truck-driving runs and leaving me home."

"Alone?"

"On Doug's fifteenth birthday, Dad gave him a bottle of whiskey and a carton of cigarettes, told me to go to bed, and the two of them played cards until four in the morning. All night I prayed they'd knock on my bedroom door and ask me to come downstairs. Harder than anything I can remember ever praying for. I would've done anything to sit at that table."

Sirens from an ambulance at Johnston-Willis Hospital across the street interrupted them, and during the silence he thought back to that chilly and rainy October evening nineteen years ago. He remembered the smell of the thick, juicy roast beef sandwiches filling the air like it was yesterday, and the near-matching flannel shirts Doug and Dad wore so proudly. He'd even changed his own to try to join the club.

"The next day there were broken bottles on the floor and cigarette butts on my comics. Dad woke me up with a jerk and told me to clean up the mess."

"Oh my."

"Mom was the only decent person in the family. After she was gone, I was on my own. Until Tiffany."

"I'm so sorry David. What your father did ... that's wrong."

"I was a kid. I didn't know any better."

Of course you knew he didn't love you. You just pretended he did.

"All through high school I had one mission: get a scholarship to a college as far away as possible. Cornell was the winner, and that's where I met Tiffany."

"And you wanted her to meet them even after all they did to you?"

"They were still ... family. The only family I had."

Anne frowned, more tears in her eyes. It was too much emotion for him, and he needed this to end.

"I never saw either of them again. Dad died when I was twenty-eight. Aneurysm, though he deserved far worse. I didn't go to the funeral. But that's the last I'd heard of either of them until today."

"I *do* understand, David," Anne whispered.

He looked into her compassionate eyes and actually wanted to tell her ... to be completely honest and tell her the rest. But couldn't.

Instead he said, "We've got bigger fish to fry. What are we going to do?"

"I've been thinking about that."

"Me too. How do we know they won't just kill us anyway? If we give them everything we've got, they don't need us anymore and will kill us both. What reason would they have to keep us alive, even if we did do what they asked?"

"We could always hold some back as ransom while we're running away and signing millions of death warrants."

"Easy," he said while semi-chuckling, raising his hand. "We both know we're not giving them anything."

"Even if we tried to leverage it, they'd kill us anyway. Hiding the evidence won't keep us safe. And if we don't meet them, they're going to find us."

And kill Doug and Tiffany.

"We'll get to that," Anne said. "First, there's something you should see."

48

"I was thinking about what Dr. Mallick said. About how impressed with Jake he was and how he thought there was probably more to what Jake gave us than what we saw," Anne began.

David appeared to be listening but was clearly not following. It was the best she could hope for considering what had to be running through the poor guy's head. Believing that at least part of his mindshare wasn't consumed with his brother and ex-fiancée, she gripped the yearbook beneath the pillow, gave it a yank out from under and then kept talking, using it to clue him in visually.

"I looked through everything that Jake wrote in the yearbook and checked all the pages again."

"And?"

"And then I thought back to something we talked about earlier. Remember when I said we didn't know what Jake meant by 'you can't judge a book by its cover?'"

"Yeah. About how it was a reference to Julie Lerner."

"Right ... because she was unattractive. You said maybe that was Jake's way of making it look like a joke between friends, to throw anyone who found the yearbook off."

"And you said there might be more. I remember. What's your point?"

"Well, I couldn't shake the feeling that Mallick might be right. I started thinking about how he stashed the storage unit key behind the DVD cover, and ..."

She moved the pillow and exposed the yearbook she'd ripped to pieces. The glossy cover was peeled off, and the entire outside had been stripped of the shiny blue material that lined it. Hard, scaly white paper was underneath.

"What did the yearbook ever do to you?" he attempted to lighten the tension.

"Look what I found between the cover and lining."

She held up a folded half-page sheet of notebook paper. A plain white sheet with blue and red lines. The note was in black ink.

Captain
Go to the place I hid Mary's engagement ring on the night I proposed. It's important.
Chief
P.S. I'll miss you, hermano.

David read it several times, just as she had, moving his finger left-to-right beneath the words. His face didn't reveal much.

"You have any idea what this means?" she asked.

"Jake used to call me Captain, and I called him Chief. Long story. We both called each other hermano."

She kept a straight face regarding the odd nicknames as David stared intently at the note.

"Where'd Jake hide the ring?"

Instead of answering, David checked his watch, got up and looked out the window. He remained stationary, head down, holding up an index finger to plead for a moment of silence. She'd come to know that David thought to talk, while she talked to think. She hated that. Her anticipation only grew.

"Pack the bag and clean the room," he said. "I'll be back in fifteen."

"What? Why?"

"We're checking out," he said hurriedly, opening the door.

"Where are we going?"

"Watkins Glen."

49

She packed everything up in less than a minute and per David's request sat on the bench outside the front entrance. The pleasant low-fifties and cloudless sky did little to preserve her patience. After twenty minutes of waiting, and still uninformed as to why, she began to worry. Did David abandon her? Did he just feel the pressure and leave? Would he really do that?

Just then her peripheral vision caught a black SUV she'd never seen before with a Georgia license plate. It cut a hard right and sped towards the hotel as if in a drag race. David then slammed on the brakes, put the Chevy Tahoe in park, and left the engine running.

"Get in!" he frantically shouted through the closed front window.

"I trust this is your second car?" she asked as he sped away.

"Had to improvise," he said pointing to the console.

She bent down to look and underneath saw the hotwiring job. David kept his eyes on the road and turned onto northbound VA-76.

"Where'd you learn that?"

"It's about the only useful thing Dad ever taught me. I'm just glad I found a car in the garage old enough to do it. You can't hot wire newer cars."

"Garage?"

"For the hospital," he pointed east.

"Well if you're going to commit grand theft auto, I wouldn't draw too much attention to yourself, speed demon."

"Desperate situations called for desperate measures. If we make it out of this thing alive, I'll buy the guy a new car. One from the twenty-first century."

"It'll get reported. And that old geezer and scary-looking *cop* from the park probably have police scanners." She shook her head in disbelief.

"Risk we have to take. They want to meet tomorrow. Watkins Glen is seven hours away. We don't even have time to think about it. We can't wait around for a bus, and we can't use credit cards to rent a car. So we either sit here and wait for the sunrise, or we borrow some wheels and find out what's in the Finger Lakes."

"How long do you think we'll last when they find out?"

"Hopefully at least a day."

"And if not?"

"Then we'll worry about it when it happens. We've got enough dangerous bridges in front of us right now to worry about crossing one down the road."

At that exact moment, it dawned on her with remarkable clarity and incontrovertibility: she was tied to David and his decisions from this point forward. Regardless of how she felt, if he took a risk she'd have to take it. She checked the side mirror for flashing lights and listened intently for sirens.

At the moment, neither was present.

"We have another problem, David," she whispered as he merged onto I-95 North.

"What's that?" he asked, accelerating the Chevy into the fast lane.

"They might assume this means you're not complying with their request."

David turned his head towards her briefly, his wrinkled nose and squinty eyes silently asking what that meant.

"Your brother ... they could kill him."

He sighed, then turned his attention back to the interstate.

"I know ... but that's out of my control."

50

"We have confirmation," Byron Huetel whispered into the encrypted cell phone.

He knew his seventy-six-year-old voice sounded frail, but that just made this conversation more enjoyable. He pictured Richard Krenzer listening, knowing the president's chief of staff would not be pleased. It made him smile as he rubbed his tie at the knot, a habit for several decades now. Krenzer deserved to sweat. After thirty years of service, he took Krenzer's lack of loyalty as a direct slap in his face.

"Don't let me down, Byron."

"If you're so worried, Richard, have your pet project handle it."

"Just give me the details."

"You've never asked for details before."

"This is different."

"Because of how much your heir apparent screwed up?"

"Just give me the details."

He smiled during his deliberately long pause.

"We tracked Centrelli after I left the park bench. Triangulated positions, four teams with boots on the ground undercover. He sat there for twenty-seven minutes staring at the photos of his brother, then got into a cab and headed east."

"What time was that?"

"Just before eleven."

"Where'd he go?"

"Into a parking garage near the Willow Lawn Shopping Center in northern Richmond."

"He went to a mall?"

"Just shadow games. He bounced around in case we were following him. Ten minutes later, the cab exited with no one in back."

"You didn't go after him?"

"My goal is the information, not the people who currently possess it. It doesn't matter where Centrelli and Halavity are. It's unlikely they have it with them."

"You should've followed him."

"My objective, as you explained it, was to bail you out and obtain the information. Following Centrelli around Richmond doesn't accomplish that. If all you wanted was someone to mop up after Marcus, you should've hired a janitor."

"Anything else?"

"This afternoon a 1999 Chevy Tahoe was reported stolen from the Johnston-Willis Hospital parking garage. The owner prepaid for the spot just before nine and when he got back, the vehicle was gone."

"This guy and his garages."

"It's quite clever. Garages are one of the more difficult places to tail someone."

"Cameras pick anything up?"

"Cameras? In a Richmond parking garage?"

"What do they have?"

"An unmanned, ticket-access gate that can be manually lifted."

"That's it? Let me guess: the owner left the ticket in the car?"

"On the dash."

"Son of a bitch. When was it swiped?"

"12:36. Ninety minutes after Centrelli got in the cab."

"I'd say he didn't respond the way you planned."

"And I'd say Marcus badly underestimated Mr. Centrelli. But don't worry ... as usual I'm a step ahead of both of you. And I'll bail you out. For a fee."

"How much extra?"

"Twenty million."

"You're not just slipping, Byron. You're going senile."

"Take it or leave it, Richard."

After a short pause, Krenzer asked, "What else?"

"So, we have a deal?"

"We have a deal."

"Of course I had Centrelli followed. That's how I knew he took the car from the hospital garage. It's walking distance from the hotel he was at. His shadow games were noble, but I'm not Marcus. This kid is not going to outsmart me."

"Where is he?"

"He and Halavity are just outside New York, travelling north on Highway 15.

"They're running away?"

"It appears that way, but remember that Centrelli has until tomorrow morning to produce the evidence."

"You mean you think he could be going to get it? That it's in New York?"

"I don't know what they're doing. That's why we're following them. Acting on the assumption they're running away is the wrong move."

"They make any stops?"

"At a diner off I-95 just before four. They were back on the road quickly."

"Any idea what Centrelli's doing for money? It's been several days with no ATM activity."

"He's got a duffle bag he carries everywhere. Even brought it into the gas station bathroom with him. My guess is that he's got some cash inside."

"Are you sure they don't know you're watching them? They might be sending you on a wild goose chase."

"They'd be on their own chase, so that doesn't make a lot of sense. But I've considered a lot of things. For instance, LeMoure lived in New York. Maybe they're going to see someone he knew. Regardless, I know where they are, and we don't need the police intervention you suggested. The quieter we keep this, the better."

"Can't argue with that."

Of course you can't.

"I have to say," Krenzer continued, "the fact that they're six hours away doesn't bode well for your plan with his brother."

"Don't lecture me. You want your pretty boy to take things from here, just say the word. I'll walk away."

When no response came, he took advantage.

"Just so you know, right there is why Marcus will never be as good as I am. Marcus is a kiss ass, a politician's best friend. He's strong, and he'll do whatever's necessary in the field, but when it comes time to call the shots, he lets you walk all over him. Operations like these require someone who doesn't pucker up for anyone."

"Are you done?"

"I'll call you when I've got news."

"It's after six, so how are you going to—"

"I've already dispatched Marcus to New York. He landed and is awaiting a call from my guy tailing Centrelli. Your brown-noser is right where he belongs: leading the ground op, taking orders from me."

Krenzer's silence was even longer than he'd hoped for.

"Don't ever question me again, Richard. And deposit my fee now, as a gesture of good faith. This will all be over soon."

51

After almost eight hours on the road, the last thing David wanted to do was ask for directions. It was obvious that the fewer people they interacted with the better, but it'd been a long time since he'd been up this way and as small as Watkins Glen was, he couldn't remember how to get there. They'd long ditched their smart phones and the Tahoe didn't have GPS, so the archaic option of asking a local was all that was remained. It reminded him of using a payphone to talk to Mallick.

Watkins Glen is a tourist town of 2,500 residents at the southern tip of Seneca Lake, near the center of New York's Finger Lakes. Aside from the water, its main attractions were NASCAR races and state park hiking trails. Because of the tourist pull, there were several eateries and cafes, and even a few wineries and pubs, but David recalled feeling how small it felt. And being amazed that his best friend in Manhattan had come from a place almost as small as his own hometown.

Jake and he shared a lot in that regard, small town country boys who could either fillet a fish or clean a goose with one hand tied behind their backs, coincidentally wound up in New York City, and worked for a prominent investment firm that traded more money in one afternoon than their hometowns' total annual budgets combined.

Thanks to Mallick's bag of money, their exposure over the trip had been minimal. They got gas twice and stopped at a nearly empty diner between normal mealtimes. They'd traveled over four hundred miles, and he didn't notice anything unusual the entire time. No cars appeared to be following them and no strange encounters. But after following Franklin Street north for a mile or so, he couldn't remember the final steps and had to stop at the Sunoco gas station.

The twenty-something-year-old gas station clerk straightened him out, but the interaction further stirred his paranoia. At first the brunette seemed relaxed and friendly, but he could swear she grew nervous as they talked. He told himself he was reading into it but didn't believe that. He thanked her, and she replied with what seemed like a fake smile.

"What is this place?" Anne asked in a disbelieving voice as they pulled up to the old, unassuming yellow brick building next to Lake Seneca.

It was ten feet tall and stretched further back than the front view revealed. Despite appearing abandoned, it was one of the most frequented buildings in town during the summer. He could understand Anne's blatant surprise that their risky, one-way eight-hour drive from Richmond ended here.

"It's a boathouse."

"A boathouse?"

"See that over there?" He pointed towards the large body of water that was impossible to miss. "That's called a lake. People take boats out on it."

"What a funny guy."

"Just trying to keep things light."

"Keep trying."

"Remember when I told you Jake's parents had a boat?"

"Yeah."

"Jake proposed to Mary on it."

* * *

The boathouse was empty. It was the middle of January, just past eight o'clock on a Saturday night and the frigid New York air swept in and out of his lungs, cooling them along with his nerves. He walked slowly around to the side of the building. Anne followed hesitantly, constantly checking their surroundings.

He found a few bricks lying on the ground next to an old tire. Then he spotted a dumpster, thankfully one with wheels, and pushed it against the side of the building before climbing up. Before Anne could ask what he was doing, he smashed the brick into the second story window.

He didn't throw it, in an attempt to keep the noise down, but he still had to hit it hard enough to break glass. Doing so shattered the night's silence in a way he felt was certain the entire town would hear. Anne jumped and he kept a finger pressed to his lips. It was quiet again immediately thereafter, and he didn't see any new lights turn on, or hear anyone talking. And there were no houses super close or on the water, but he worried someone was dialing 911 even as he spread his jacket over the bottom windowsill.

"Let's go," he looked down at Anne, extending his arm.

"That dumpster doesn't seem stable enough."

"If you've got a better way to get in, let me know."

After mounting the dumpster, Anne crawled very gingerly over the broken glass that covered the windowsill and then slipped through the decaying wooden window frame. David lowered her down carefully and could tell from her open mouth that she was amazed at how big the boathouse was.

It was very dim, illuminated by only a few small lights that stayed on overnight and the full moon beaming through the windows. But there was enough to reveal an expansive open space that housed a wide array of boats: small tugboats, large sailboats, canoes, speedboats, pontoons, kayaks, and more.

To their right were stainless steel fish filleting stations and sinks with electric carving knives hanging from hooks. Against the back wall stood a workbench stocked with tools used to repair boats. The room hadn't been winterized at all. Everything was left just the way it was when one boating season ended in anticipation of the next.

The boats were arranged in tight rows and blocked visibility of anything not directly in front of them. The grid-like configuration, frigid air and dark room converted every turn into a scary blind corner, and they stayed close to each other and walked slowly. It smelled like fish and aside from the gentle reverberation of some boats bobbing on the water, it was jarringly quiet.

After a few minutes of walking around, he saw it. It was out of the water and modest in size, about seven feet long with white and blue stripes. It looked like many others, except "Krissy" was in cursive script just below the olive green tarp that covered its top.

52

"Mary retold me the story every time I saw her."

David slowly lowered the boat's ladder and climbed up just enough to unhook the clamps and flip a portion of the green cover back, providing them a narrow place to stand inside the boat. He left the majority of the cover on the vessel so that they could utilize the crawl space as a hiding place if needed.

"What story?" Anne asked.

"Jake was afraid his folks wouldn't let him take the boat out. But not only did they say yes, his mom made his dad clean it from bow-to-stern. Mary said it was spotless that night, shinier than she'd ever seen it. I asked him once what his backup plan was in case it rained. He didn't have one; it was the lake or bust. He made dinner, bought a nice bottle of wine, and they ate by candlelight under the stars. They were only twenty-one. Jake is ever the romantic." He paused, then corrected: "Was."

"Where'd he hide the ring?" Anne asked, verbally sidestepping.

"After dinner and champagne, he asked Mary to get a flashlight from the storage compartment under the driver's seat. By the time she found the box, he was down on one knee. They spent the rest of the night on the water with champagne and strawberries, just the two of them. He always said it was the very best night of his life, even better than the wedding."

David watched as Anne's eyes were slowly drawn toward the seat and wondered if she was thinking about her late husband's proposal. The thought made him slightly regret going into the details of Jake's romanticism. But he knew from personal experience that there was no way around feelings, just through them, so he crawled forward towards the seat under the portion of the boat cover that remained clamped.

Inside the compartment were a First Aid Kit, small blanket, two flashlights, solar fares, batteries, several nautical maps, a compass and the boat's registration.

And at the very bottom, a small black shoebox.

They hunched together on the floor beneath the tarp, Anne pointing the flashlight as he removed the first item, a sheet of laminated notebook paper. He started to read but didn't get past the first line.

A deafening bang erupted from the front of the boathouse. Its echo ricocheted off the walls of the boathouse like a pinball. David froze.

He wasn't sure who was there, but he knew they weren't alone.

53

The unexpected, earsplitting noise produced a terror that had her eyes tearing up instantly. David swiveled his head frantically, scanning the cavernous room for any sign of its origin.

"Someone's here," she whispered in a panic.

"Shh," David put his finger over his mouth. "Stay here. Don't make a sound. Understand? No matter what happens, don't draw attention to yourself."

She nodded, petrified, and lay down on the floor, tears collecting on the metal anchor that sat inches from her nose.

David turned off the flashlight and placed the note back in the shoebox, stuffing it in the duffle bag and wedging that against the side of the boat. Anne watched him crawl to the ladder and then stand up one inch at a time, pulling the tarp back over the boat.

She whispered for him, but he didn't respond. She buried her hands in her face and focused on the one thing in her control: not letting her erratic breathing draw attention to herself. She had no idea what David was doing, but he was literally slipping away, and she was left alone in the covered boat.

54

David crawled past another row of boats, trying his best not to make a sound. Convinced he needed to separate himself from Anne and the evidence, he hunched over and inched his head past each row slowly, hoping every time to see another empty aisle.

Each row offered a fresh dose of panic. Flashlight off, he widened his eyes to counter the darkness and tiptoed along the back end of the boathouse. As he passed the workbench, he grabbed the first thing he saw that could serve as a weapon: a rusty hammer with a wooden handle. He clutched it tightly and kept moving.

It was quiet, terrifyingly quiet. Neither he nor his potential pursuer(s) made any noise. He worried with each step that the wood would creak. His heart was exploding, but at least the temperature wasn't quite cold enough to turn his breath into fog. He wiped the thick sweat from his forehead and considered if he should remain in one place for a while. The anticipation was overwhelming; perhaps he'd be in better control if he waited.

Then he peeked around the next corner ...

The large man in the aisle was turned sideways, scanning the room with night vision goggles on. He jerked back and then slowly stood up to get a better look. The pursuer was white, dressed in black, at least three hundred pounds and had a thick, black beard. In his right hand, he held a revolver with a flashlight turned off affixed to the top of the barrel. The man swiveled his head again slowly, searching.

Searching for me.

He tried again to control his breathing and think. In every aspect but one, he was at a disadvantage. The man could see clearly with night vision; his eyes were in the dark. The man had a loaded gun; he had an old hammer. The man had probably been trained; he was shaking so much the hammer jiggled.

But he saw the man. And the man didn't see him.

The shadowy hunter moved forward along the starboard side of the boat that David now leaned against, a mere twenty feet away. He was walking towards the front of the eight-foot boat with his gun ready. It was almost as if he'd heard something and was on ready alert.

David was at the bow, standing such that his left eye could see the man on the starboard side but the boat concealed the rest of him. He knew he'd only have one shot. The man kept walking towards him. Slowly.

Keeping his head turned to the left, he shuffled his feet down the port side opposite the pursuer. The large man was now nearly at the bow, where he'd just been. He held his breath, contemplating a final time. Running wasn't an option anymore, and he couldn't just sit there waiting either. There was only one thing he *could* do. And now was the time to do it.

He slowly crawled on the floor back towards the bow and his pursuer. Squatting down beneath the boat's outer frame, he breathed and swallowed deeply. His attacker would turn the corner at the bow any second. He heard the man's soft footsteps inches away.

Now or never, David.

He threw the flashlight at the next row of boats and it hit with a loud clank. The man with the gun did what he hoped he would. Instead of focusing his attention on the source of the throw, he instinctively turned towards the noise.

David lunged out and swung the old hammer, knowing he was the batter who had only one pitch to hit and needed to swing for the fences.

The hammer met the man's temple with impressive enough force, and David's pursuer immediately went limp. Dropping the gun, he fell sideways to the floor and then landed on his back. The blow was hard enough that David was near certain he was down for the count, but he didn't stop there. Adrenaline took over and he pounded on the man's massive chest with the hammer, to the tune of cracking bone.

Then reality set in.

Had he killed a man? Blood pooled beside the body so much faster than in the movies. He kept backing up, staring at his shaky hands in terror, trying not to step on the blood as if it were hot lava.

He picked up the man's gun and shoved it into his pocket, then hurried back towards Anne. Desperate to get the hell away from the body and out of the boathouse, he panted loudly and his feet made plenty of noise before he finally reached the boat. And before he could even call to her, he found out why that was a mistake.

"Stop right there!"

Stunned beyond comprehension, he watched the tall man emerge from the shadows. He also wore night vision goggles, but David knew who it was. His face was permanently imprinted in his mind.

Marcus approached him, a large gun in his steady hand.

55

"Drop the gun and take two steps back with your hands on your head."

He was paralyzed by the voice hurled out of the darkness. He hesitated out of shock, rather than defiance.

"Now!" Marcus yelled after removing his night vision goggles and letting them drape around his neck.

Even through the dim lighting, David saw hate in Marcus's icy stare. The gargantuan man towered over him like a statue, grinding his teeth and breathing violently through his nose. David could hear vehemence in his exhales. He did as he was told, knowing he couldn't outmaneuver his large and presumably well-trained foe.

"You've been nothing but trouble, Mr. Centrelli," Marcus said without blinking. "And you've embarrassed me for the last time. Tell me where Halavity is, and I'll kill you both quickly. Make me find her, and I promise you'll both beg for death."

David looked back wildly, running through a thousand escape plans in his mind and trying to figure out how he'd embarrassed this man.

"You have five seconds to speak up before I shoot your right foot. Then we'll start again."

Standing fifteen feet away from anything he could grab or duck behind and having foolishly left the hammer by the corpse several rows over, his first instinct was to race for the door and hope for a quick death that way. A bullet in the back that passed through the heart. The five seconds had already started ticking, and no better options came to mind.

Then he saw it.

Faintly illuminated by the moon peeking through the translucent window, the boat tarp started to inch upwards ever so slightly. Just a few feet behind Marcus, he saw Anne's large brown eyes peer out from underneath.

Hope.

"Okay ..." he replied, holding up his hand. David needed to simultaneously buy time and keep Marcus's attention. "Just give me a minute. You need me. I have things that—"

"No one needs you. And tonight you will be eliminated. It's only a matter of how. Tell me where the woman is or start to suffer ..." Marcus paused and then formed a spine-chilling smile. "Like your buddy Jake."

56

Anne watched with dread from beneath the boat's cover. She couldn't stop shaking. Her arms were trembling so much she worried it would hit the side of the boat. Swallowing hard, she folded her vibrating right hand into her left palm to try to counter its quivering.

The silence wouldn't last long. Five seconds, he'd said. She clenched her fists to summon what little courage was there, imploring her desperation to take over.

He'll find you anyway.

Do it.

For David.

She flexed her arms and clenched both her fists, pumping all her adrenaline to the surface, and then ripped the tarp off. Fully exposing herself, she lunged forward with the small but heavy anchor. She threw it with both hands extended and all the force she could muster, exerting a loud grunt as she released it.

* * *

The metal anchor hit Marcus square in the face and sent him to the ground howling in pain. A gunshot ricocheted off another boat and David ducked and covered, luckily uninjured. Marcus had blood on his hands and forehead as he groaned. He was struggling to get up and though he kept losing his balance, he was still conscious. He covered his eyes and crimson face with one hand and felt blindly around the floor for the gun with the other.

Anne grabbed the duffle bag and jumped down from the boat. And in a rush of panic, they both started running. They'd sprinted out of the boathouse by the time David realized he should've grabbed the pistol and shot Marcus. Cursing himself for not thinking of it sooner, he knew now it was too late.

They sprinted to the car in the cold night's air, puffing frost from his mouth as he hogged air. Steam starting to rise from the sweat on his neck, he lost his footing and tripped. Anne whimpered from the other side of the Tahoe.

"Come on!" he shouted aloud at himself.

He finally got the car door opened and they scrambled inside just as Marcus exited the boathouse. He was still standing but very wobbly, obviously off-kilter and quite dazed from the anchor blow. Losing his balance quickly, Marcus fired the gun with one hand while still covering his forehead with the other, blood seeping out in-between its fingers. David started the car as a bullet pelted its windshield, but most of the shots missed their mark.

Loud tings and glass cracks pouring endlessly into his ears, he peeked above the dash ever so slightly. The headlights offered a clear view of Marcus's shattered nose and very bloody face. He looked like a mangled pizza, the anchor having ripped much of his forehead and cheek skin off.

"Hold on!" he yelled at Anne.

He yanked the lever switch into reverse and peeled away, the tires screeching at a deafening pitch, the bullets still coming.

Hunched over beneath the windshield's view, he drove backwards and blind for five seconds, the pedal to the metal. The SUV entered grass terrain after smashing through a wooden railing that separated a walking path from the boathouse.

Then the Tahoe jerked up a hill in reverse before coming to an abrupt stop on the steep incline. The sudden halt made their bodies lurch forward, knocking the wind out of him. He looked up a second later and saw Marcus walking towards the motionless vehicle, putting in a fresh ammo clip and firing the weapon.

A predator coming for his prey.

The windshield was completely shattered, and he could barely even see. He curled under the dash by the steering wheel and could feel the cold air coming in through the holes. The gunshots were getting louder. The headrest ripped apart as bullets whizzed through what was left of the glass.

Anne's eyes were clamped shut as she curled in a fetal position on the passenger seat floor. Marcus was fifteen feet away when he did the only thing he could think to do.

Pushing the gearshift down two notches, he pressed the gas pedal to the floor with his right hand and held the steering wheel as straight as he could with his left. Rapidly gaining speed from the quick acceleration and downhill momentum, the car plunged ahead quickly as he strained to catch a brief glimpse of where it was going. He didn't see much, the continuous flux of bullets he was driving into forced him to keep his head down, but he knew the car was going straight and tried to keep it that way.

Then he heard a loud thump and saw Marcus roll over what was left of the windshield, flying upwards over the car as it continued to move forward. He pressed down on the brake with both hands as soon as he could ... but not soon enough.

57

The Tahoe crashed into the front of the boathouse with a tumultuous thud and the impact was painful all over. Without a restraint, David lunged further towards the pedals and smacked his head on the hard-plastic interior as the airbag deployed above him. There was no blood, but it felt like a concussion.

Anne's body rammed against the dash floor beneath the glove compartment. But in contrast to him, not being in the seat saved her life. The passenger side of the windshield was now wedged against a wooden beam that protruded through the glass and inside the car, all the way to the headrest. And though bruised and battered, she was still breathing. She held her arm in obvious anguish, and her whole body wracked with sporadic tremors.

He pulled himself up from his twisted configuration and turned around to see Marcus's body lying on the ground next to yet another rapidly growing puddle of blood. It was already larger than the last, and it was growing ... right next to Marcus's head.

He tried to put the Tahoe in reverse, but the SUV didn't budge. He reached for Anne, who held up her hands in resistance. He couldn't convince her to move by herself, so he pulled her towards the driver's seat between the middle storage compartment and beam. Every muscle in his arms ached as he lowered her out the window, dropping her as slowly as he could. Both of his biceps throbbed in pain as he stretched his arms to the max to get Anne as close to the ground as possible.

She regained enough balance to land on her feet, then stumbled away from the SUV and fell to the ground after two steps. Her elbows and knees on the ground holding her up, she buried her head in her arms and howled.

When he looked at the drop, his sternum howled in protest. He'd cracked at least one rib and his head throbbed with pounding pain, and the last thing he wanted to do was lower himself out of a car window. But the mangled doors that couldn't be opened left no other choice. When he hit the ground, the sharp, pointed aches of pain attacked from every direction. He felt like a pincushion. Hunched over beside the Tahoe, barely able to stand, he heard sirens in the distance. He forced himself to laboriously trudge to Anne, who remained hunched over as if between tabletop plank reps.

"Just wait. Just wait for them," she said, distraught; agonized.

"What?"

"I can't ... I can't run. Just wait for the cops to come get us."

He looked in her eyes and no longer saw fight. Her aggressiveness, her drive to unlock the mystery and find the answers, to seek justice for Jake ... none of it was there anymore.

The sirens grew louder.

"Anne, I have to go."

"I can't come with you. I can't do this anymore. I need to stop running." Her face was drained of color, her brow sweaty, and she looked rigid and limp all at once. But it was her wide, unblinking eyes that alarmed him most.

"I can't tell you why ... but I can't stay here and neither can you." It was a plea for her life and a poor confession rolled into one. He swore under his breath, chastising himself for not letting her in on the whole plan earlier.

58

He could just picture Richard Krenzer standing there on the other end of the line like a dumbfounded fool, probably tightening his thousand-dollar silk robe until his stomach hurt.

"How could this happen, Byron?" Krenzer said.

Byron Huetel smiled wider. The silence that followed was worse than anything Krenzer could've expected to hear. He checked his cheap black-and-white wall clock, waiting for the second hand to make it to the six.

"It's ten after eleven, Richard. I called you for a reason."

"What the hell happened?" Krenzer answered.

"After what you pulled, are you really surprised?"

"What?"

"Don't you ever use my name again by the way. How dare you go behind my back for a second time."

"What the hell are you talking about?" Krenzer asked.

"I sent Marcus to New York for a reason. And it sure as hell wasn't to be undermined by your orders. Not even the commies would stoop so low. And now your precious heir apparent is dead, and you're in yet another pickle. It's clear I'm not the one who's slipping here."

"I don't have the slightest clue what you're talking about!" the chief of staff sounded genuinely incredulous.

Byron could just picture the open jaw, the blank face, the shaking head. He envisioned Krenzer having crawled out of his California king bed in his silk pajamas and his fancy robe, standing there now like the imbecile that he was.

The chief of staff's shock was both genuine and understandable, as no such order had been given. And though Byron's original plan, for Marcus to kill Centrelli prematurely, obviously hadn't panned out, this was even better. Centrelli had taken care of Marcus for him.

"Byron ... listen, I didn't give Marcus *any* orders. I haven't even talked to him since—"

"Save it, Richard. *Someone* told Marcus to apprehend Centrelli. My operative, who's also a victim of your stupidity, told me there was no stopping him. He said that Marcus was bound and determined."

"He must've done it on his own. I never gave that order."

"I guess we'll never know, will we?" Byron answered.

"Why would I lie to you?"

"I said save it."

"What does the Watkins Glen Police Department know?" Krenzer asked, changing the subject.

"Is that supposed to be a joke?"

"Well, at the very least the police know that Marcus is dead. They also probably have your operative in custody. They're probably asking him right now what the hell he was doing there."

"When I found out what happened, out of respect for the president I made sure the operative was eliminated," Byron said. "He was a decent man and didn't deserve to die. But they won't be tracing him or Marcus back to you. Certainly not back to the president. But Centrelli and the woman pose an even greater threat than we thought. They were in upstate New York for a reason."

"Do you know where they are?"

"Something for you to think about, *Dick* ... The Tahoe had bullet holes on its hood and windshield, with an anterior point of entry. And the police report indicates its tire tracks were in a relatively straight line from the top of the hill to Marcus's dead body. Do you know what that means?"

No answer.

"It means Centrelli deliberately ran him over. Marcus was shooting at the car as it approached, and Centrelli punched it to run your heir apparent's ass over. I guess Centrelli has more fight in him than Marcus thought."

"I'll ask again. Do you know where they are?"

"No."

"What *do* you know?" Krenzer let his irritation be obvious.

"Watch your tone, Richard. This was not my operation after you interfered. You didn't get me involved until you realized you needed me, then you went behind my back with my subordinate. I'm not used to such disrespect, and I'm not going to fix this for you out of the kindness of my heart. Remember who you're talking to, Mr. Chief of Staff."

The awkward silence was even more exhilarating than sex. Sensation tingled in every part of his being as he again pictured the befuddled look that had to be on Krenzer's pompous face. The man would never, *ever*, doubt him again.

"What's the next move?" Krenzer finally said.

"A navy Dodge Charger was reported stolen about a mile from the boathouse. Idiot owner left his keys in the car overnight. There aren't any leads yet, but Watkins Glen is a small town and that's a pretty big coincidence."

"You know why they were there, don't you?"

"Jake LeMoure's parents keep their boat there in the winter."

"Do you think that LeMoure left something for them?"

"I think it's possible," Byron answered.

"What else could it be? They just decided out of the blue to drive to a boathouse eight hours away?"

When he didn't respond, he heard Krenzer curse under his breath.

"Troubles?" he asked, chuckling for effect.

"Do you really think Centrelli will show up tomorrow?" Krenzer asked nervously.

"We have his brother."

"A brother he hasn't spoken to in years."

"He'll meet."

"Then what?" Krenzer replied.

"Finally, the reason I called. I'd like to confirm that you don't have any more harebrained ideas to undermine my expertise. Because if you do, just say the word and I'm gone."

"Perish the thought."

"Not a joking matter, Richard. You've got a real problem here. Two dead government operatives and another stolen car proving someone's on the loose in a tiny hick town that most people haven't heard of. I can minimize the damage, but word will get out. There might be a way to control the message and the situation, but we both know there are aspects to my ... tact ... that don't bode well for public officials and have caused consternation before."

"Fix this. You're in charge."

"You realize I'm going to have to ... do things."

"I'll brief the president."

59

In over four hours, barely a word was spoken.

Anne remained silent and shut down, physically and psychologically, that entire time. Driving yet another stolen vehicle, this time a Dodge Charger, back towards Richmond, his thoughts toggled between her well-being and the duffle bag sitting in the back seat. He'd expected some measure of silence as they processed what they'd been through, but he grew more worried as each quiet hour passed.

He was in pain, too. The sharp throb in his stomach and thumping palpitations across his tight, compressed chest made him wonder if he was having a heart attack or pulmonary embolism. But while said symptoms would presumably subside, and his wounds had all stopped bleeding, he knew the boathouse would leave more than scars. In all likelihood, he'd killed two men tonight. And though each was an act of self-defense, David knew that the motive wouldn't free him. The memories of killing would haunt him for the rest of his life.

Just after one a.m., he slowly turned his head towards Anne.

"Are you okay?" he softly whispered.

"I think so," Anne replied in a cracked voice. She didn't sound okay, more like she had smoker's cough and was falling asleep at the same time, but at least she spoke.

"Want to see what's in the shoebox?"

She paused before nodding, then reached back and grabbed the duffle bag. The first item was a letter, which she read aloud so he could keep driving.

Dave:

Last week I got a package from an old friend of mine named Patrick Tomilson. He was an attorney at MacArthur, Barry

219

and Tain Insurance Firm in Houston that represents one of Medzic's drugs in development. He told me an <u>unbelievable</u> story, then asked for my help.

At first I thought he was crazy. You will too. But then he died in a car accident, and maybe it was a fluke, but I think he was killed because of this. It scared me, but even more it made me focus on what he sent.

When I told him about our friendship, he begged me to ask for your help and died thinking I never would. I asked my secretary, Anne Halavity, to bring you a message if anything bad happened to me. I couldn't tell her about all this for her safety, but if you're reading this, I'm gone … so you know the gravity of this situation.

I'm sorry to ask what I know is no small favor, but some things are bigger than you or me. I'm worried my days are numbered bud, and you're the only one I can trust. You've <u>got</u> to try to finish what Pat began. I'll always miss and love you, Captain.

Your Friend, Jake

P.S. Please take care of Mary for me.

Anne started crying again when she re-read the last sentence and images of Jake overwhelmed his mind. They sat in silence again for a few more minutes until, driven by his best friend's plea, he asked Anne to check the rest.

Beneath the letter was a plethora of information, way more than he'd imagined. There was so much that he pulled over to a rest area to give it his undivided attention.

On top were photographs of people, some he knew and some he didn't, and each was labeled. Alvin, Jonathon and Larry were the ones he recognized. Next was an audio recorder tape of Patrick Tomilson, describing his theory with no shortage of detail whatsoever, including who was in the photos and the significance of the paperwork.

Many copies of MacArthur, Barry and Tain balance sheets, income statements and cash flows, along with a detailed explanation of how the taxes remitted were higher than they should have been. Most of the tax talk was over his head, but it sounded legitimate. Finally, there were two pages of predictions about the structured relationship between the federal government, Medzic, and MacArthur, Barry and Tain.

Tomilson, the thorough lawyer he must've been, had copies of everything: an elaborate explanation of how such fraud was possible for key members of the IRS, SEC and FDA, explaining taxation loopholes; recorded responses to Tomilson's several questions about the financial inconsistencies from the CEO; government officials photographed meeting with firm executives. It was uncanny just how much there was.

Jake added a comparison of the insurance firm's fees to all of its clients, highlighting that despite the high risk in representing Préviséo, Medzic paid less than any other client by a massive proportion. Several discrepancies between Medzic's public financial statements and the privately owned insurance firm's books were highlighted in yellow.

The takeaway was painstakingly supported by everything they'd read: Medzic was claiming higher invoices to the insurance company on tax forms so it could hide illegal kickbacks to the government, and the insurance company in turn reported almost one-and-a-half times that amount on their private company financial statements to shield the money trail. The figures not only proved the insurance firm and drug company were shielding money, but that the money was going to the only entity that could've either noticed or prevented the scam: the US government.

"This is crazy," Anne said. "Is this right? Could they actually get away with this?"

He re-read Jake's final line aloud. "So in exchange for kickbacks laundered through taxes plus future payments from additional taxes and who knows what else once the drug gets released, the government provided the legal and regulatory means to get Previséo through FDA inspection."

He stared out the dark car window and envisioned the deal: make a ton of money by getting a killer drug released on the world.

60

An hour later, the shock hadn't subsided.

"I thought Mallick was crazy. All this time, I thought ... I don't know what the hell I thought."

"This is the missing link, David," Anne said. "Between this and Mallick's test data, we've got enough to prove—"

"Who are you going to prove it to?"

She didn't answer.

"The only people who can stop this are in on it." He pressed the accelerator harder. "And trying to kill us."

"I know, but ..."

"And they have my brother."

The meeting was eight hours from now, and the two of them were still three hours from Richmond. The harsh realities hitting him in the face like a strong wooden plank, he needed to reset. He checked the Charger's fuel level and got off the highway.

He walked into the *FLYING J* to pay for the gas and bought a map of the USA and Virginia, trying not to look directly at anyone. Certain the clerk would see his face and somehow be a problem, he nervously held his breath when the elderly man handed him change and wished him a good night.

Unfolding the paper map and holding it under the car's interior lights, David realized just how dependent on phones, GPS and other technology of today he'd become. With the click of a button he used to quickly find new restaurants with reviews to explore and know exactly how to get there, but by depriving himself of those buttons this past week it became apparent just how little he could do without them.

He chose a different route back to Virginia, avoiding the interstate. It would take an hour longer, but staying on I-95 so close to Richmond in a stolen car seemed like a bad idea.

When Anne finished sifting through all the documents, pictures and voice tapes for the second time, she looked at him with fearful eyes.

"No wonder they want to kill us."

"They didn't know about this, or it wouldn't have been there."

"But they know we went to New York. It won't take long for them to figure out why."

"That's why we got out of there," he answered, sighing deeply. "Even if we don't meet them tomorrow, there was no safety in staying there."

Anne put her hand on his shoulder and nearly whispered, "But where is our safe place tomorrow?"

61

The sun had woken up, but frost still blanketed the grass and willed the green blades to hit the snooze button once more. After the standard five hours of fitful sleep, another typical Sunday awaited Walter Buck.

He settled in contentedly at the office.

It wasn't that he had to be there, lest anyone pity the man. It was that the job was all he had left. After two divorces and three children who didn't want to see him, he didn't have family, friends, or the ability to navigate complex feelings anymore. The job was the only thing he could understand or control. It didn't hurt that he was really good at it, too.

Walter's high degree of skill was the result of often eighteen-hour days back-to-back and a willingness to do what no one else would. His insane work ethic and knack for uncovering information had sealed his ascension in the news media industry. Though few people liked him, everyone respected him. And that was fine by him: respect outranked likeability.

No one knew how, but he was always a step ahead of everyone else. He told people it came from hard work, but the bosses knew better. You didn't get his results playing by the rules.

He was alone in the office this Sunday as usual. After swallowing four extra-strength Tylenol capsules to counter his hangover, he tugged the bottom of each suit coat sleeve on his three-piece Forman & Clark pinstripe and stared at the computer screen. He knew the millennials snickered behind his back about his cufflinks, silk ties, and general penchant for overdressing, but he could care less. There was casual attire and there was work attire, just like conversation and attitude, and it'd serve them well to know the difference.

The ringing phone interrupted his train of thought and caught him off guard. He turned his head and grunted. No one else would get in until ten if at all, and the damned thing would just keep on ringing if he pretended not to hear it.

Removing the half-smoked Winston Light cigarette from its familiar post between his lips, he picked up the receiver and coughed violently into the mouthpiece.

"Yeah?" he shouted.

"Walter Buck?" a strong male voice inquired.

"We're closed on Sunday morning," he said sharply.

"Listen to me very carefully, Walter. My name is David Centrelli, and I don't have time to explain, or to mince words. Your life is about to change. Do exactly as I say and you will not be hurt."

62

Ten-thirty came awfully fast.

From inside the stolen Dodge Charger at Marshall and Ninth Street, David sized up the scene as best he could through the same binoculars Anne had used from the parking garage just twenty-four hours earlier. The same old man from the day before was sitting on the same bench, wearing the same stoic expression.

Another man he didn't recognize stood nearby, much like Marcus had the day before, though he wasn't wearing a police uniform. For a split second, David considered the possibility that Marcus was a real police officer and he'd killed a cop. Unlikely as it was, he still didn't even want to think about it.

The new "bodyguard" was of average height and not as skinny as Marcus had been. He looked to be about middle-aged and had a thin brown mustache atop his upper lip and dark brown hair that fell at his shoulders. Both individuals were in dress pants and overcoats.

Anne was in position, so the next move was his. David went over the plan yet again and though they'd done everything they could, it didn't feel like enough. His heart, working overtime for nearly a week now, felt ready to explode. He was already sweating profusely despite the winter chill, and it was time.

He shivered as he exited the car, feeling almost certain he was walking to his end. When he was within twenty feet of the bench, the man standing up tapped the old man's shoulder. There was no smile or frown that followed, merely a blank stare.

David was frisked for the second time in two days and took a seat on the bench next to the old man, whose suit was now navy blue. A different top hat adorned his aging head and his black dress shoes appeared freshly polished. David, on the other hand, was in the same

227

jeans and shirt for the third straight day beneath his lightweight L.L. Bean jacket.

"I knew you'd show, David."

"You mean even after you sent your thugs to kill me?"

"It's time we had a proper introduction. You can call me Byron. Now, let's get down to business. You violated our trust yesterday."

"I didn't violate anything. I had twenty-four hours to get you all of the information I have. I was doing what you asked."

"Did you get it?"

"Why'd you try to kill me?"

"This country wasn't built on, nor is it run by, freedom, integrity, or the citizens who inhabit it. It's held together by the true glue of society. Do you know what that is?"

"I've got a feeling you're going to tell me."

"Money."

"Great story. Why'd you try to kill me?"

"I don't think you'd understand, David."

"Try me."

"The United States Government does things that people wouldn't even approve of much less fund every single day." Byron lifted both hands up slightly and shrugged. "We've got a national debt of over thirty trillion dollars, and people have no idea what the government has to do to keep them safe. They don't know ... and they don't want to know.

"You didn't answer my question."

"You are jeopardizing an endeavor that will fund a large number of important operations for this country. And improve safety for 330 million Americans. We couldn't let you do that."

"Trying the 'doing it for our country' bit, huh?" He shook his head and forced a fake chuckle. "Well, I'm not buying it."

"I told you that you wouldn't understand. It sounds like you're not interested in my offer."

"I'm interested, but for my own reasons, not because of your bullshit story about protecting the nation. You're gonna get yours, so I'm gonna get mine. I'm taking you up on your deal for the money. And my brother."

"You surprised a lot of folks when you got away last night, myself included. And believe it or not, part of me wants to thank you for eliminating Marcus. It actually helped me out in a big way. The other part thinks you've got something up your sleeve."

"All I did last night was to react. Your thugs tried to kill me, and I defended myself. That's it. There was no *planning* involved. All things considered, I say we call it even."

The old man took a long, deep breath and glanced away from the Coliseum, towards Richmond University, stroking his rounded chin.

"Where's Halavity? And the information you owe me?"

"Where's my brother?"

The old man took a cell phone out of his pocket, pressed a button, and handed it to David. The ID said UNKNOWN.

"Hello?"

"Doug, this is David. Are you okay?"

"David, look, I—"

"*Are you okay?*"

"Yeah, I'm okay. But these guys ... they—"

Dial tone.

"There you have it," the old man whispered. "He's safe and in good hands. Where's the girl?"

"Where is he?" he demanded, pretending like he actually expected to find out.

"I'm going to ask you one more time. Where's the girl?"

"Not so fast, David replied. "I've got a few conditions of my own."

"You're not in a position to have conditions."

Byron waved his hand at the man standing, and before David knew it there was a gun, concealed beneath the younger man's coat, its metal barrel pressed against his neck. The rod dug into his skin and felt like ice.

You knew this would happen. Stick to the plan.

229

"If I have to terminate our agreement right now, I will. If you give me no choice, I'll kill you right here in front of everyone. And then your brother will get it. And then we'll find Halavity. And then Tiffany."

The old man paused ... and David tried to remain composed. But knowing a conversation was going to happen is vastly different from having it.

"Don't make me do that, David."

"It's time for you to listen to me, *Byron*. Right now, Anne is watching us. If she sees anything happen to me, she'll make sure you regret it. You'll find her eventually, no doubt about it. She knows that. But not before she screws you in a way you've never been screwed. And no, I'm not telling you how. So if you think I'm bluffing, have your new monkey here pull the damn trigger. But if you want to avoid making a huge mistake, tell him to get the hell away from me and hear me out."

Bargaining with his life, Anne's, Doug's and Tiffany's ... he tried to conceal his fear by reminding himself over and over that anything but confidence would spell his doom. He reminded himself he didn't have any other choice, so he had to go all in.

The old man stared at him, his bushy eyebrows pulled in towards one another. Then he looked towards the man holding the gun and slightly nodded his head. David felt the steel pull away from his neck.

"I've heard you're a negotiator, being in Business Development and all. And I must say, you continue to impress to me. But don't think for a second that you, Halavity or the information will save you if you try to double cross me. I told you before ... I'm a contractor. Previséo doesn't make me any money. I make mine whether you live or die. So believe me when I tell you I won't hesitate."

"My brother's release and all three of us living the good life. You and your goons staying the hell away from us all forever. That's the deal you offered yesterday. When I have proof you'll honor it, I'll give you whatever you want."

"You just learned your brother is safe."

"A gun pointed at a man's head can persuade him to say just about anything."

"What do you propose?"

"I need to see him."

"He's not in Richmond."

"Sure he is."

"What makes you think that?"

"Because you knew I'd to want to see him set free."

Bryon paused, yet again just staring right at him. The silence was so frightening and awkward it felt overwhelming, and David pressed his toes against the ground as hard as he could to channel his anxiety.

"You might be a clever negotiator, David, but you don't have the upper hand. There's no way I'm bringing your brother here. And if you see him, I see Halavity."

"Once Anne sees Doug join our little party, she'll join as well."

"And where should we have this party?"

"Where the information you want so much is located."

63

The three of them walked through the small Nina F. Abady Festival Park, Bryon to his right and the other man behind him. The park was simple, offering but a few oak trees and a bronze statue of the college professor turned development professional it honored. On a brisk Sunday morning in January, there weren't many people there and it was pretty quiet. What was surprisingly unavoidable was the smell. Not of trees, mulch or flowers. Rather, the aroma must've made its way from Richmond University, where the Heilman Dining Center was evidently serving up sausage and bacon for Sunday brunch. The whole park smelled like one giant skillet. It permeated David's nostrils and reminded him of how hungry he should've been having last eaten the afternoon before, but then Bryon spoiled his appetite yet again.

"If you try to get away," Byron whispered as they approached the Broad Street crossing, "we're going to kill you, your bother, and Ms. Halavity. Then we'll move on to Tiffany and anyone who matters to Halavity." He paused a moment to stare at David, and they made solid eye contact. "Remember, we don't need you. Just do what I say and become a very rich man."

He couldn't shake the feeling of being outmatched. From the start, Byron seemed to know exactly what he was thinking. When Doug and his captor arrived, assuming there was only one, Anne would join them, pitting a best-case scenario of three highly trained professionals against David, a fifty-one-year-old woman, and an alcoholic.

Three-on-three, yes. But not even odds.

He didn't respond or say anything else during the mile-long trek. Byron's chitchat dried up and he grew noticeably irritated with walking, which David tried to take solace in but couldn't. All he could think about besides the threat of death was the lucky people they passed on the street: dressed up for church, standing outside restaurants, grabbing a Starbucks. He'd never been so jealous of normalcy.

He pointed to the sign when they approached the modern building, stopping, clenching his fists. The gun suddenly pressed into his side as the other man stepped forward. His legs were rubbery. He was still looking at the ProFitness Gym sign above the door when Byron started talking.

"Get Halavity here."

"My brother first. That was our deal. Call my brother and I call Anne. We all go in together."

"Into the gym?"

"That's where some of what you want is."

"You're lying to me, David."

"Call my brother. That was our arrangement and I've stuck to it. Anne's not showing up unless you call."

Byron retrieved his cell phone and David could see his cheekbones compress against his jaw as he punched in a number. He pressed the receiver to his wrinkly ear while David thought of yet another way things could go horribly wrong.

"Bring him."

It confirmed two things to David:

Doug's captor was watching them.

And Doug was very close.

64

Anne clutched the binoculars as if holding on for dear life.

Through the windowsill's rusted metal bars, she watched two men approaching ProFitness Gym from the east.

The one that looked to be in charge had an average build and wore dirty-blond hair pulled back into a ponytail. He was about five feet behind the other man, and Anne could see his mouth moving. He was likely giving orders.

The other man was stout and had short, black hair. His face was scruffy, covered unevenly with black stubble that was patchy in all the wrong places and a thick bulge of skin sat beneath his chin like the makings of a chunky turtleneck. The man walked somewhat stooped over — perhaps due to his position as a captive or more likely from the excessive weight he carried and the unrelenting forces of gravity. He wore a pair of jeans that failed to fit him around the waist, but rather tugged at his hips with each new step he took, making the wearing of such a comfortable fashion staple look utterly uncomfortable. His face hardly resembled David's and he was obviously much less fit, but Anne knew immediately that the man was Doug Centrelli.

That was her cue.

65

David stared ambivalently at the only family he had left.

Part of him saw the kid he played Wiffle ball with every day growing up, the older brother who taught him how to shave and how to drive. The other part recoiled at the sight of a disgusting slob that had ruined his life eleven years earlier. In the midst of the horrendous silence, he couldn't picture anything but Doug and Tiffany on that couch.

Doug's face hadn't changed much, but he'd aged poorly with weight gain and gray hair. His brother coughed twice, a smoker's cough, and appeared to struggle to stay standing up without something solid to lean against. Gray hairs covered a quarter of his balding head.

"Get the girl here," Byron said caustically.

As his peripheral vision caught Anne crossing the street, part of him wanted to scream for an abort to save her life. He knew she wouldn't, and that they would've found her if she did, but David had learned that survival instincts were difficult to overcome. He motioned towards the intersection and Byron turned to see her approaching.

"So ... you're the infamous Anne Halavity. You look a lot older in person."

When Anne didn't respond, Byron turned to him.

"Well, David, we're all here. Where's my information? I don't see Ms. Halavity carrying anything."

"I said she had information you'd want to hear, which you will. The documents are inside," he said, nodding to the gym.

"For shit's sake," Byron replied, shaking his head. He looked down at the ground and exhaled deeply. "Okay, lead on. Remember what I told you."

He walked past Doug, still picturing that couch in Minnesota.

* * *

They walked into the gym's lobby towards the front desk. David provided his ID and said he was showing some friends around, something he'd done a few times before and wasn't uncommon. The receptionist offered the prospective guests a wide smile and told him to let her know if they needed anything. The gym, always looking for new customers, encouraged members to give private tours and offered steep referral credits if anyone bit.

Sunday morning was the emptiest time of the week at ProFitness. He wasn't sure if it was church, golf, sleeping in or something else, but every time he'd been there on the seventh day of the week it was refreshingly quiet and deserted. Just past the hallway that overlooked a small basketball court, he turned towards the staircase leading to the basement level. The old man was close behind him, followed by Doug and Anne, then by the two men with guns hidden in their jackets behind them.

Thoughts of breaking free while walking down the narrow steps were fun but short-lived. The plan was in motion; there was no turning back now. When they reached the men's locker room, Byron grabbed him.

"Check it out," he ordered one of the two men. When the man reemerged thirty seconds later with a nod, they all, including Anne, entered the room.

Despite the gym's costly membership dues, the locker room was relatively small and no-fills. Two large brick pillars separated three rows of lockers with a mirror on the wall. And with fifty lockers in each bank, it was hardly ever congested and especially open on Sunday mornings.

Two guys he didn't know talked and laughed with each other as they laced up their racquetball shoes. Their ease of conversation was in stark contrast to the situation playing out before him. Could he alert these men somehow? Could he warn them or get them to call for help?

He saw Byron slightly shake his head, proving again he knew what David was thinking. He looked away from the two guys, seconds feeling like hours as they all waited for them to leave and pretended to look around.

The two gentlemen finally got up and walked towards the door, staring at Anne in obvious objection before exiting the locker room. The gunman who'd escorted Doug double-checked the rest of the locker room, holding the weapon behind his back as he peered around corners.

The bathroom was about twenty feet long and empty. Ten feet past that was the entrance to the shower room, the alarm clock mounted on the wall next to the sauna entrance. No other people were there or in the showers.

"All clear," the gunman told the old man.

"Guard the door. We'll need a few minutes."

"Yes, sir."

"Frisk them," the old man instructed. "We didn't have the proper setting to do it earlier, but let's make sure they're clean. Weapons and wires."

While being frisked, David checked the time. Almost eleven. He replayed the ideal but unlikely scenario in his mind once more.

While Anne was being frisked, the old man sneered at her.

"Consider yourself lucky. Marcus would've had more than a little fun with you."

No answer. She tried to hide it, but she was clearly humiliated.

The pat-downs finished, the old man turned to David.

"Let's see it. Now."

66

With two guns pointed at his back, his chest tightened as he turned the combination lock dial on one of the lockers in the second bank. When it snapped open, he reached inside the locker and withdrew the manila folder from beneath a plain black T-shirt and old pair of gym shoes.

Visibly shaking, he checked his watch again, submitting that time was bound and determined not to work in his favor today. Too slow at first, then too fast. Byron snapped his fingers impatiently, and he had no choice but to pass the folder to him reluctantly. He couldn't believe he was handing it over.

Byron snatched it from David's hands and opened it ravenously. Soon, the old man wasn't paying attention to David or anyone else. His eyes were fixed on the pages in the folder while the other two men kept their guns pointed at him, Doug, and Anne.

He looked at Anne and swallowed. She did the same.

"What is this crap? Where's the information from Mallick?" Byron yelled, not looking up.

I'm not going to make it, David thought to himself as he turned to shut the locker. *Time screwed me again.*

Then it happened.

67

The locker room alarm clock belted out its annoying, piercing cry at eleven o'clock sharp. It was the same boisterous noise that he'd cursed many times before, yet now he needed it. His fear that for some reason it wouldn't come as it always did was instantaneously replaced with his fear of the reaction.

The two men near Anne and Doug instantly turned around to face the source of the loud noise, their attention shifting from David. One of them even covered his ears because of the abrupt racket.

Byron was startled too, looking up from the folder and pivoting away from him. Anne shut her eyes and didn't move as the sound wailed on. Doug jumped backwards and instinctively put his fingers in his ears.

David reached back into the locker and grabbed the .45 that he'd taken from the man at the boathouse. Hidden beneath the black T-shirt, it was within easy reach. He snatched it quickly, scraping the top of his hand on the metal locker, and whipped around without even looking at the others to extend his right arm outward in a quick, fluid motion.

By the time Byron turned back around from looking at the alarm clock when the noise finally ceased, the gun was pointed right between his eyes at point-blank range. The hand that held it was hardly steadfast, but the barrel was aimed where it mattered.

David heaved, releasing a massive buildup of air from his lungs, and immediately felt exhausted and dizzy. His forehead was wet and his heart thumped so hard it hurt his chest. Despite his twitching forearm muscles, he managed to keep the weapon fairly level.

Seconds later, everyone had reacted to David's move in his or her own way. The two gunmen whipped their weapons at him with much steadier aim; Anne remained motionless; Doug's knees buckled and he fell backwards into the locker bank, sliding down into a sitting squat position. Bryon dropped the folder on the bench and smiled at him.

Smiled.

Who smiles with a gun pointed at his head?

It got so quiet he could hear a water drip from the showers. The drops seemed thunderous, and every few seconds another explosion hit the floor.

"David, I'm so disappointed," Byron whispered.

His silence prompted further discussion.

"Didn't I offer you paradise? Didn't I give you the deal of a lifetime? You had it, kid. All three of you were going to spend the rest of your life living like kings and queens. This is how you repay me?" He made a tisking sound, shaking his head. The words were so calm, his voice relaxed. Total control. Zero fear.

David, meanwhile, was still trembling, despite the fact that he had the gun.

"Tell your men to drop their weapons," he said in the sternest, most determined voice he could. It probably came off as puerile to the old man.

"Why would I do that?"

"Because if you don't, I'm going to kill you."

The old man didn't flinch.

"Are you really willing to let Ms. Halavity and your brother die?"

"You mean the brother I hate and haven't spoken to in years? The brother who's better off dead than alive? The brother you know I don't give a damn about? Yeah, I'm willing to do that. As for Anne ... whose idea do you think this was?"

It was at that point that something happened. Something that gave him the first glimmer of hope that he'd had since approaching the park bench. It was subtle, barely noticeable, but it happened.

The old man frowned.

Byron's face quickly reverted back to phlegmatic, but he saw the frown. The old man lost a tiny bit of his advantage, and that was all David needed.

Like a light switch, his hand grew stable, his words clear, his focus sharp.

"I'd rather we all just die right here, my way, than take my chances listening to you. You tell your men to drop their guns, or I drop you. They'll get me, but not before I make a modern art masterpiece out of what used to be your head."

"You won't do it."

"I'm dead regardless. At least this way I take you with me."

He tried not to wonder if he actually had the balls to do it. Doing so would only enslave his mind to doubt. Instead, he reminded himself that for the past six days he'd begged for escape. And it'd finally arrived.

One squeeze and it was all over.

"Screw you, Centrelli!" Byron said, staring at him like a rabid dog.

"Decide, or I'll decide for you."

After two of the longest seconds he'd ever experienced, He stepped towards the old man and started to do what he didn't think he could. His trigger finger was moving.

"Stop."

Byron stared him down like a ferocious snake looks at a mouse.

"Lower your weapons."

* * *

"You've permanently screwed yourselves. You realize that, right? You realize you've ruined your only chance for survival. Even if you make it out of here, you can't hide. And you won't run for long."

"Maybe you're right," David answered, pressing the .45 into Byron's forehead. "Maybe, I should just end it all right now. Three men, three bullets. Get rid of you and say the hell with the consequences." Anne picked up both of the weapons that had been lowered to the ground and pointed them shakily at their rightful owners.

"You won't do that. You might be a cutthroat businessman, but inside you're a puppy dog. And your dumbass sidekick here is way out of her league."

241

David stepped back and swung the gun into the old man's cheek, knocking him to the ground. It felt every bit as good as he'd imagined it would.

"That was the biggest mistake you'll ever make, son."

"Shut your mouth, old man."

Anne's eyes widened. Holding the other guns at the two other men, she and they remained silent as the old man spit up blood onto the floor.

"David, it's time," she finally said.

Doug was still on the ground, lying against the lockers, dazed. His tears hadn't stopped and he looked comatose. Anne jolted him up and tried to slap him back into coherence while David kept the gun pointed at the old man.

With Doug finally on his feet, she brought the other men's guns to David and walked towards the third cluster of lockers.

"What are you going to do?" Byron said. "You know running from us makes as much sense as screen doors on a submarine. You won't last, and the consequences when we find you will be that much more severe. Even you must know that now. And right before you die, I want you to think about what you passed up."

The sad part was he couldn't stop thinking about it.

The old man may have been an arrogant lunatic and ruthless human being. But he was right. They had indulged themselves and said it might work, but in reality their plan didn't stand much of a chance. He acted confident, but he didn't have a clue what he was doing and inside knew that would come back to get them. The fact they'd made it this far was a shock. And the dark horizon had him second-guessing the decision that already couldn't be undone.

68

Anne opened the corner locker and grabbed the duffle bag.

Inside it were all the supplies she'd picked up a few hours earlier, including three sets of new clothes, jackets, bike locks, and blindfolds. David had also asked for a roll of duct tape, bag of zip ties, baseball hats, and rope. Between all that, the paperwork copies she'd made, the tickets and money, the bag was bursting at the seams and fairly heavy.

"Move to the shower room, slowly," David ordered the three men after she brought the bag to him. "Don't make any sudden moves. And don't think for a second that I won't blow his brains out. I've got a full clip of ammo, and your boathouse goon was nice enough to leave me a silencer."

David had surprised her yet again. His hand was steadier, and his icy eyes, piercing focus and firm voice convinced her he wouldn't hesitate to pull that trigger. He could've been bluffing, and if so it was damn impressive. But she didn't think so. He looked like a man pushed over the edge ...

Everyone but Doug Centrelli, who was still in shock and somewhat of a stupor, silently sitting on floor against a locker, walked towards the shower room. When David reached his brother, he spoke to him in person for the first time in years.

"Doug, snap out of it. We need your help."

The older Centrelli wiped away tears with the sleeve of his shirt and looked at her. She nodded silently and he rose up and followed. The shower room wasn't terribly tight for six people, but it wasn't spacious either. David got the industrial-strength zip ties from the bag and threw them at the feet of the three men.

"Tie each other. Hands behind your backs. Save him for last," he ordered, pointing at Byron. "I'll do him."

With David inspecting, the two men did as he instructed. It was clear that Byron was highly respected and even more important than they'd originally thought. Between the two of them, the younger men could've overtaken the situation if they were willing to sacrifice his life, but they didn't hesitate to follow orders. It only added to Byron's mystique. She wondered who he really was, and who he really worked for.

"Move under those three showers and hit the floor. On your stomachs."

"Where do you think you can go?" Byron asked.

"Now!" David yelled, firing a warning shot into the tile wall. The old man stared back in disbelief. David's slight smile indicated it felt good to pull the trigger, almost as if he was relieved.

Keeper of the clock, she looked around nervously. Her job was to move things along and keep them on schedule. They both knew that eventually someone would report the blocked locker room door, and she was surprised it hadn't happened already.

"David, it's time."

All three men were now face down on the shower floor, their hands and feet bound, their clothes soaking wet from the residual water on the floor. After finishing an especially tight fasten of Byron's legs, David looked up and nodded.

69

She began by blindfolding them one at a time, pulling the cloth over their eyes and tying it tightly behind their heads. She covered their mouths with several layers of duct tape but left room to breathe through the nose. After attaching one end of each of the three bike locks to the rope that bound their feet and the other to the handicap railing beneath the communal showers, she took their wallets.

Each carried only a money clip, so their names remained unknown. Combined there was $340, but given Mallick's money that was of little relevance. The lack of ID was disappointing. She dumped the wallets and looked at David, a hint of pride in her eyes. Their assailants were bound, blind, and silenced. It was beautiful, but short-lived.

The two younger men shouted, as loud and hard as they could, judging by how red their faces grew. But the duct tape did its job and it was muffled annoyance at best. They also tried to break free from their restraints by jerking their legs to and fro, but to no avail. Byron remained quiet and still.

Doug had been standing off to the side the whole time, motionless and quiet. She grabbed his hand, and they walked back to the lockers while David stood watch in the shower room. The two of them quickly changed clothes as she hurriedly briefed him on the rest of the plan. Doug wore a look of confusion and doubt when she was finished.

She squatted down to stare at him eye level as he sat on the bench. "How we got here doesn't matter, got it? What matters is where we're going."

Doug nodded in compliance, not agreement, and they switched places with David, dumping the guns in the trashcan after running them under water to remove the fingerprints. In less than a minute, David was back in new clothes and the plan said it was time to get rid of the .45.

"Are you sure we shouldn't keep the gun?" Doug whispered to her.

"Shut up," David replied.

"We can't have weapons on us," she whispered back to Doug. "Our best chance is to keep a low profile."

"Got the tickets?" David asked, taking the duffle bag.

"Yup."

"Let's go." As they headed toward the door, Byron's sudden screaming stopped David. He approached him slowly with the gun in one hand and duffle bag in the other.

"David, we don't have time to—" she called after him.

Without warning, David fired the .45.

She involuntarily squeezed her eyes shut when he fired the second shot, then forced herself to retrace her steps back to the men to take stock of what had just happened. David stood staring at the blindfolded and howling old man. Two bullets now inside Byron, one in each leg, the wailing discernible through the duct tape was one of sheer agony. Sweat dripped down his forehead, tears down his cheeks. She actually pitied him for a second.

"That was for Jake, you son a bitch," David said with no emotion whatsoever.

Speechless, she watched David turn on the shower at full blast, as hot as possible, aiming the nozzle straight into the old man's face. Then he adjusted its flow from a gentle mist to a sharp, straight-line jet spray. The room steamed up immediately.

The old man's bawling was drowned as the water blasted his face, complementing his two bleeding legs. He squirmed back as far as the bike lock would allow, but there wasn't enough slack to escape the scalding water altogether.

"Let's go," David said, leaving the shower room.

He rinsed and dumped the .45 when he reached the sink.

She watched the whole scene in horror.

"Anne!" David yelled.

His voice snapping her out of the shock that had overtaken her, she broke the protective glass and jerked the fire alarm lever down, sending a ringing through ProFitness Gym that made the locker room's alarm clock sound like a murmur. Seconds later, the fire siren had people scrambling in a boisterous commotion.

David eased open the door and they all walked into the chaos.

70

There were more people at ProFitness than he thought, which made David even more grateful that no one had tried to get into that locker room in the span of those six minutes.

As the fire alarm continued blaring, people scrambled off treadmills and elliptical machines and out of cardio classes in search of the nearest exit. They didn't assume it was a drill, but why would they? Most gyms don't do fire drills.

The chaos gave them all the diversion they needed. The security guard and gym manager were too busy trying to control the crowds to be able to recall anyone specifically after the dust settled. The cameras were regularly blocked by moving bodies and nobody paid much attention to others as each bolted for safety.

The three of them walked just as fast as others, ducking into the crowd. The nearest exit was a side door on the bottom level, and with several others scrambling in that direction, they merely got in line. People funneled out of the weight room and basketball courts, moving in chaotic fashion despite the voice on the PA advising them to exit in an orderly fashion.

Once outside, they crossed the street and turned away from the line forming on the long, narrow sidewalk. Then they turned the corner and ran. A few blocks later, the quiet, empty, open streets made it fell it like they were miles away from the scene and commotion.

Fire truck sirens approached from a distance. Still they didn't say a word. Anne hailed a cab and he told the driver where to go, throwing in an extra $20 to step on it. With that, they were off like a bat out of hell.

"Tickets," Anne said, handing one to him and Doug.

"You know which train, right?" he asked Doug.

"Yeah."

"You sure?"

"I said yes."

"Don't screw this up too, Doug."

"I still think we should stay together," Anne said.

"We've been over this," David replied. "Can't risk it. Who knows how long it'll take, but when they find those guys in the shower room, they'll look for a group of three."

"Especially when one of them has two gunshot wounds!" she snapped.

"We're splitting up as soon as we get to the station."

He was directing them as if he had any idea what he was talking about. As if he had a clue what to do or how to do it. Because he really, really didn't. But he did know they couldn't afford to get caught and that separating was their best chance to avoid that.

"It's a quarter to twelve, which means we've got to hustle. You hear me, Doug? There's no Plan B. Get on that damned train."

Anne and Doug both nodded their heads, and he hoped that meant Doug understood that making it wasn't simply important ... it meant staying alive. The cab driver pulled to a stop and they got out. He paid, shut the door and turned to Anne.

"Go."

Then he walked into Richmond's Main Street train station and hugged Anne for what could be the very last time.

71

He stared at the screen, without words or recourse.

Having just made his way through security, trying his best to blend into the Sunday afternoon crowd with the aid of a ball cap and keeping his eyes down, he was walking towards the 12:32 p.m. Amtrak train to Washington, D.C.'s Union Station when he saw how futile that effort was.

There, on all four of the monitors above a bank of seats, he saw his name and picture, and the following above it:

WANTED
BY THE FBI FOR MURDER

The perky news reporter explained to the citizens of Richmond that David Centrelli spoke with Dr. Peter Mallick the day before his death, was last seen at ProFitness Gym earlier this morning, and should be considered armed and extremely dangerous. Then, she provided a telephone number should anyone have knowledge of his whereabouts.

There was nothing linking him to Mallick's death, no discussion of any previous violent acts, patterns or tendencies, and no evidence whatsoever presented that he'd committed any crime. Yet the label was applied, and it would stick.

It had only been thirty minutes since they left ProFitness.

"David," he heard from behind. Paralyzed by the bank of small televisions above, he hadn't noticed Anne approach him.

"That picture ..." he said, "Jake took it. It's from my visit to New York last summer. How's that for ironic?"

"David, are you okay?"

"Now I'm *really* putting you in danger."

The reporter, her bubbly personality and all, then concluded the segment:

"The FBI has cautioned that if you think you see this man, *do not* attempt to apprehend him. Rather, call the toll-free number on the screen. Mr. Centrelli is extremely dangerous, and authorities should be contacted as soon as possible to prevent further harm."

72

WANTED for murder.

The simple and obvious statement left David with the most helpless eyes she could imagine. It had eviscerated his strength from the locker room.

"They're saying I killed Mallick," David whispered.

"David, you've got to get it together."

"Everyone in Richmond will be looking for me."

"Then it's good we're leaving Richmond."

"You need to get away from me."

"No ..."

"Anne, I appreciate the loyalty, but don't be an idiot. There's no way I'm blending in now. You still have a chance. All I would do is put you in danger."

"Follow the plan."

"This changes things," he replied.

"It was a long shot to begin with, and I need you."

She'd thought those words for some time, but hearing them from her own mouth gave her great pause. She'd prided herself her entire life, ever since her husband died, on not needing anyone. But in the last week, everything had changed.

"We've got a train to catch. Let's move!" she shouted.

But he didn't. Instead, he just looked at her, eyes watery and posture hunched. He looked beaten. Not just beaten down, but beaten as in *checkmate.*

She put both hands on his shoulders and leaned in, close enough for a kiss, and then used her right hand to physically lift him chin up so that their eyes met. The travelers around them were of no consequence, and Doug was nowhere to be seen.

"Outside the boathouse you didn't give me a choice. I didn't want to go. I wanted to crawl into a hole and suck my thumb and wait for the end. But you wouldn't allow it. You carried me away from my death even though I wanted more than anything to stay."

"Murder, Anne ..."

"Enough! We've got ten minutes. It's my decision and we're sticking to the plan. I know the risks."

"I'm not sure."

"You don't have to be sure because you no longer have any say in the matter."

He closed his eyes for a long moment, and then finally opened them. "Okay. But if someone spots me, consider this my goodbye."

"I know."

"And when I'm gone, you know what to do."

"I know."

She noticed he said "when" not "if," but the thought of carrying out the rest of the plan alone was reason enough to desperately need David. She had the information, and he'd made her memorize the next steps in case he didn't make it. But knowing what to do was a lot different than having to do it.

Without another word, David turned and walked away slowly, and she disappeared into the crowd for a second time.

Walking towards the tracks, she heard "Mallick" and "Centrelli" and "not a suicide" from two different television monitors despite her best efforts to ignore them.

73

The platform had no televisions, newspaper stands, radios or any other form of communication to the outside world. At first it made David hopeful that most people, who were there before he arrived, didn't know about his WANTED status.

Except for all the cell phones. It felt like every person under seventy, and most over, was staring at one small screen or another while waiting for the train, and all he could do was hope the news wasn't on any of them.

Tugging the hat further down over his eyes, he tried to scan the area peripherally through black sunglasses. No one seemed to be pointing at or whispering near him, but that didn't stop an endless barrage of questions from flooding his mind.

Has my luck run out? What happens when someone recognizes me? Will Anne be ok? What about Doug? Should I even care what happens to him?

His hands in the pockets of his bright red jacket and jeans sporting holes around the knees, he couldn't help but think of how much had changed. A week ago, he wouldn't have been caught dead wearing this getup, especially the bright green T-shirt. His title was more than a professional status, it was a full-body image. Branding. Branding that he was determined to preserve.

Now, he just didn't want to die.

With three-day stubble that felt sharp enough to cut his finger, it appeared no one recognized him from the clean-shaven face plastered on TV or that no one had seen it. Nevertheless, he opted to look away as the train arrived.

He tried to act naturally — like all the other people just taking a trip to the nation's capital on a crisp Sunday afternoon — but he worried it wasn't working. He constantly shifted his weight, wiped his brow, shoved his hands into and out of his jacket pockets, and soon couldn't see through the dark black sunglasses they'd fogged up so much.

But he didn't dare take them off.

A few minutes later, the train was finally moving. He momentarily felt better, but it didn't last. He sat impatiently in the rearmost seat of the second car and noted the train left four minutes late at 12:36. He told himself not to focus on the what-if scenarios.

Those around him seemed preoccupied: a mother reading *Owl Moon* to her two small kids, an old man nodding off to a newspaper, a couple arm-in-arm staring out the window. He slouched in his seat and pretended to sleep, noting the emergency pull string location and the two closest exits.

And at exactly 12:55, he got up and walked towards the last car.

Passing many faces along the way, he tried not to make eye contact by tucking the hat further down and keeping his eyes pointed at the ground. Near the end of the journey, he tripped and hit the floor hard, breaking the fall with both hands and his knee.

He quickly popped up, trying his best not to call any more attention to himself than he already had. People glanced at him before returning to their cell phones and books, but he worried the damage had been done.

Idiot.

In the train's final row, Anne and Doug were seated next to each other, staring straight ahead. There was no one sitting next to them, and they weren't looking at each other.

Anne moved her dark-brown jacket from the seat next to her, and he sat down slowly, rubbing his throbbing knee through the hole in his jeans.

"Hey," he said, "try to relax. You two look like zombies staring straight ahead like that. We're trying to blend in, remember?"

"Nice landing, blend boy," Anne said.

"You guys okay?"

"You were on the news," Anne whispered, as if it was the first they'd spoken of it.

255

"I saw it. We can't talk here."

"What are we supposed to do now?" Doug said.

"Just sit tight and shut up, Doug. We'll talk when we get there."

74

The Executive Residence's office sofa next to the gaudy fireplace was the one seat on the entire God forsaken grounds that Richard Krenzer found tolerable. Its supple light-brown leather was actually comfortable, conforming to his larger-than-it-should-be ass in a way no other piece of furniture did. But sitting in it was the only good part about this meeting. Checking his watch at a quarter to seven, he wondered for how long he'd have to humor Charles. The commander-in-chief had canceled his Sunday dinner meeting for "personal reasons" and was clearly worried.

"As my chief of staff, you assured me, in no uncertain terms, that the situation was under control."

"And it is, Mr. President."

"Sure doesn't seem like it."

"It will be soon."

"What the hell does that mean?"

"I'll explain in a minute. For now, go ahead and get it off your chest." He smacked his lips and nodded, an over-exaggeration of what little value he placed on the discussion.

"What?"

"I know you, Charles. I know what you're thinking, and I know what you need to do. It's better for you to say it now, get it all out. Then, I'll tell you what happens next."

The president didn't respond. He just stared at him and pondered the condescending comment.

Then, just as he'd instructed, it happened. A mouse following the cheese, the president didn't even realize he was doing it.

"Byron Huetel has been shot. This Centrelli is on the loose. After all that talk about leaving things to you, how the hell could you let this happen? Trusting you was the biggest mistake I've made in five years of running this country!"

"Feel better, Mr. President?" he whispered, folding his hands under his chin.

"Don't smartass me, Richard. Or forget whom you serve. I'm the President of the United States!"

"And you need me more than I need you."

"You think so? Want to find out just how much I need you?"

"Don't start a game you're not willing to finish, Mr. Leader-of-the-Free-World."

He said it calmly, relaxed. And another pause confirmed just who exactly was in charge.

"You're not the only one pissed off, Mr. President. I was *beyond* angry, but I'm not going to lose control because of it."

"Does Centrelli have enough to—"

"Soon, it won't matter what he has."

"Why is that?"

"Because in fifteen minutes, the game is going to change. And when that happens, none of this is going to make a difference."

"How can you say that? You never expected to be in this situation, and you've already lost him twice." Charles shook his head before sitting down in the much less comfortable armchair. "Your promises are coming up emptier than a swimming pool in the dead of winter."

"And here I thought you got it all off your chest."

"*Damn* it, Richard!"

He let the president shake his head and sigh for another few seconds, cursing uselessly and asking rhetorical questions to himself.

Then, when Charles finally sat down, the emotion behind his "boss," he quietly responded, "The pressure's gotten to him, Mr. President. He's a bubble ready to burst, and I'm going to pop him like a zit."

"I'm not in the mood for riddles. And we're past the point of leaving the details to you. I need to know."

The chief of staff was equal parts surprised and impressed with the President's backbone. After five years of ass-kissing and hypocrisy, he figured Charles would be completely spineless.

"We're going to use the power of the media, sir. Centrelli doesn't have anywhere to go and has no contacts in D.C. He's with two people who can easily be used to identify him, and he's smart enough to know he can't run forever."

"He has run awfully well so far. And if you can do something better than anyone else, you can succeed."

"Not if you put all your eggs in one basket. Sooner or later it tips over."

"Enough metaphors. What's your plan?"

The president absorbed every word. Of course, he didn't reveal *everything*. Charles couldn't be allowed to interfere with the primary objective, and for that reason it made sense to keep certain aspects of the plan to himself.

When he finished, it was clear that the strategy had impressed the president, who leaned back and rested his foot on his knee, nodding his head.

"This will happen in fifteen minutes?"

He checked his watch.

"Twelve."

75

The three-hour, 120-mile Palmetto train ride was more relaxing than David expected. Despite the damning local news report and concern someone might spot him, the further he got from Richmond, the better he felt. And things went more or less according to plan for a change.

The ride was quiet, and the hum of the train soothing. With no televisions aboard and newspapers printed before his WANTED status was announced, the ticket he'd bought was the best $70 he'd spent in a long time. Nobody looked at him suspiciously, at least that he noticed. Doug drifted off for the ride, meaning at least he didn't have to hear his brother's unhelpful comments. Anne looked as content as she could flipping through a magazine and pretending to care about its contents.

With twice the number of platforms and three times the traffic as Richmond, Union Station made it relatively easy for them to disappear into the masses of people and vanish into the nation's capital. Acting as natural as he could, he kept his head down and walked at a casual pace straight to the taxi.

He felt tremendous relief when Anne checked them in to the Four Points by Sheraton Hotel on K Street. Shutting the door behind him, he breathed his first sigh of relief since twenty-four hours earlier when they escaped death in Watkins Glen.

But just after seven p.m., everything changed.

He was lying on the queen bed by the window next to Anne, starting to drift off, when it happened. His body overwhelmed with fatigue and his mind still racing, the pillow was still propped up behind him and the yellow notepad on his lap when he thought he heard something.

"Oh ... my ..." he could swear Anne said faintly. He was far enough into the dozing stage to half-wonder if he was dreaming. Disoriented and groggy, he slowly forced open his eyelids. And saw, on prime time television, just how much this was not a dream.

76

Anne flipped through CNN, NBC, CBS, FOX.

Same story.

Same pictures.

Same shocking reality.

In Washington, D.C., where wartime decisions were made and laws were passed, the main story on every major station was an incident at ProFitness Gym in Richmond earlier in the afternoon, where three high level members of the United States government were tied up, shot, and left for dead in the shower room.

At the center of it all was David Timothy Centrelli, a thirty-two-year-old former business executive at Medzic Pharmaceuticals. In addition to murder, he was wanted for kidnapping, assault, battery, resisting arrest, attempted murder, and treason.

Treason?

Pictures of his face filled the screen, matched with a personal history and detailed physical description. He sat up on the bed, watching the media escalate his notoriety to heights he still couldn't comprehend.

"What would drive a successful young executive to do such a thing?" the horrified-looking newswoman asked aloud from the studio, her fake eyebrows raised and pulled together.

"Right now," an FBI official said over the phone, "we're investigating several possible motives, but none has been confirmed. Regardless of the reason, viewers are urged to immediately contact authorities if they have any information. Do not try to apprehend him yourself. Mr. Centrelli and his two accomplices bound and shot three federal agents. He's extremely dangerous, and he needs to be apprehended as soon as possible."

As the question was being answered, black-and-white images from a ProFitness camera showed David walking into the gym time-stamped at just before eleven and exiting the side door less than a half-hour later.

"A security camera at Richmond's Amtrak train station shows Mr. Centrelli boarding a train to Washington, D.C. at 12:30, approximately forty-five minutes after the incident at ProFitness Gym. We're still interviewing passengers, but we do know that he arrived in Washington just before four o'clock this afternoon."

A new full screen image appeared: David, hat pulled down over sunglass-covered eyes, de-boarding the train. He couldn't have looked more elusive or sketchy if he tried.

"Mr. Centrelli is also wanted for the death of Dr. Peter Mallick, the former Medzic Pharmaceuticals Chief Scientist. His death was initially ruled a suicide, but recent evidence has indicated foul play and Mr. Centrelli is the prime suspect."

"Do you have any evidence you can share with our viewers?" the reporter asked.

"Just that the suspect's fingerprints were found at the doctor's home, and they met hours before his death."

"Do you have any information about his two accomplices?"

"Nothing I can discuss at this time," the FBI agent said as pictures of both Doug and Anne popped up on the screen. "But we do have information that suggests Mr. Centrelli is likely connected to a terrorist organization."

"Did I hear that right?" The reporter gasped, her hand over her mouth. "A *terrorist* organization?"

"That's correct. We have reason to believe he attempted to assist in the development of biological and chemical weapons for a fee, using his connections at Medzic Pharmaceuticals."

"Do you know whom he was assisting?"

"We can't verify these weapons even exist, who they may've been intended for, or whether Centrelli is connected to them or guilty of treason at all. What we can say is that the longer this man remains free, the more dangerous it may be for every American. Because of that, the

262

FBI has added Mr. Centrelli to the "Ten Most Wanted Fugitives" list and is prepared to offer a $200,000 reward for information leading to his arrest."

Rotating photos of David from childhood to a few hours ago kept coming. Scrolling text below described "the fugitive" as being born in Minnesota, a graduate of Cornell University, and currently somewhere in or near Washington, D.C.

He tilted his head back against the wall in silence. *The FBI's Most Wanted List.* The worst of the worst: Al-Qaeda terrorists, serial killers, rapists, and some of the ugliest and most sinister souls on the planet...

And him.

77

Lying on the opposite hotel bed spread eagle, David had angled his head towards the window and lay so inert that she thought twice he'd fallen asleep. He appeared physically drained, like a marathon runner who had collapsed after crossing the finish line. She couldn't even fathom how depleted he must've felt mentally.

She didn't know what to say and didn't try, but that didn't stop his brother.

"*Holy shit*, Dave," Doug said. "You're all over the news."

Apparently, Doug felt up to speed. After they'd checked in, she had tried to explain to Doug everything that had happened to them the past week. It felt strange cramming the past six days into a few minutes of brief conversation, and her tone had been less than calm. Recounting it all stirred up more emotions and evoked a general sense of dread. She felt overtired, overwhelmed, and overmatched in every area. Like kids playing a grown-up's game. But she had never expected this. The news just kept flowing, feeding the hype of the nation's top story and stringing out her emotions even farther than she thought they could stretch.

"What are we going to do?" Doug asked. "We won't be able to walk a block without someone recognizing you."

Despite a high-pitched whining in Doug's voice that made her want to punch him, he was right. The local Richmond news was one thing, but the top story on all major networks? How could they counter that? David wasn't any more of an expert than she was, and Doug was dead weight.

"Doug," David whispered with newfound strength, "would you shut the hell up for just a minute."

It didn't sound overly upset or aggressive. It wasn't annoyance or frustration. It seemed more like he was too busy thinking to talk to Doug. Honestly, that was how she often avoided conversation too, so observing David was like having an out-of-body experience and watching it unfold in real time.

She remained quiet.

Doug complied, though not without a sigh, and for the next ten minutes nobody uttered a word. David stroked his stubble, his eyes moving from side to side as though reading a book. Finally, he nodded ever so slightly and began talking.

"We're not going to do a thing."

"What?" she asked. *Maybe he's lost it completely at this point. Maybe showing up on the Most Wanted List had put him over the edge.*

"This is bait, and our only option is to not take it."

Doug jerked his head towards her in obvious protest, his puppy dog eyes pleading for concurrence. She answered the plea, but only because she needed answers herself.

"This doesn't seem like bait to me. It seems more like an aggressive move."

"It is and it isn't."

"Excuse me?" she asked.

"It doesn't change what we have to do."

"Need I remind you that since we made that plan you've become the hottest news story in the country? I'm surprised they haven't picked us up already."

Without warning, it felt like she and David had flip-flopped their pessimist and optimist roles yet again. It wasn't logical for him to not be flipping out. But they'd never been on the same page at the same time the past six days, so why start now?

"They're cutting off my options," David replied softly. "We knew they'd trace things back to us, but why wasn't there any info on you two? Why didn't they mention *your* names or give *your* life story?"

"Maybe because they don't know it?" Doug said

"Are you kidding me? They dug you up from a hole in Minnesota farmland. They dragged you to Virginia and held your sorry ass hostage to try to force my hand. Do you really think they don't know every single thing about you?"

Doug shut up pretty quickly, and she resisted the strong temptation to reengage. David was going somewhere with this, and she needed to know where.

"They're trying to pull me in, and when they do, they'll use you two as leverage to get what they want. They can still offer you two lives. Your names aren't ruined, your futures aren't tarnished. So they'll offer a new start for both of you if I sacrifice myself."

"Maybe they think we left you?" she asked.

"Probably the other way around. But it doesn't matter which."

"Because offering us new lives is an empty promise" she caught on and finished his thought. "As soon as they get what they want, they'll kill us all."

"Right. Which is why we don't really have a choice." David looked pleased that his partner was tracking.

"How do you know all of this ties back to the same people?" Doug interrupted yet again. "It could've just been a local report that made big news because they were feds. And now the FBI is involved because of what happened. I mean, you did shoot the guy."

It was a stupid question from a stupid man. She could see David's frustration written on his sideways glance, not that he tried to hide it.

"Do you really think this is the work of the Richmond Police Department?"

Thankfully, it seemed Doug decided to stop talking. The brothers stared at each other in silent judgment.

She considered David's take on the "deal" they might offer her, and it seemed plausible. If they exposed Doug and her now, as they had David, there wouldn't be much to offer by way of new beginnings.

But what she still didn't see was how their current plan would do a lick of good. Something was off ... and just before Doug *had* to interject, David was starting to tell them what.

"Why didn't they name the agents?" David continued, getting off the bed to stand up. "Why didn't they mention the guns in the trashcan? If they really wanted to pin me as a murderer, why didn't they mention Watkins Glen? I actually did kill that guy."

"You killed someone?" Doug blurted out.

"They're controlling what the public hears and what it doesn't. They generically mention two accomplices and put your picture up so people look for three people instead of one. And how'd it get so national so fast? Nobody died. Thousands of people get killed every day all over the country, and they get a blurb on the local news at best. How'd a story about three random government officials left alive in a shower room make national headlines within three hours?"

"They were federal agents, David," she said. "It's not that much of a stretch for the media to play it up."

"Someone told them to play it up. And to do it a certain way. What about the link back to Mallick? False link, I might add. My fingerprints are nowhere near Mallick's house. There was nothing at the gym that links me to Mallick, and there was no reason to bring him into this at all. This isn't a local job gone awry. The big guys ran this thing from the start. Mallick told me the president was involved, and I didn't believe him. Obviously, I was wrong."

"Now *that* seems like a stretch."

"You think my being added to the Most Wanted list is the work of amateurs?"

She paused and then nodded, conceding he had a point. "So what does it mean? How does any of this help us?"

"It doesn't *help*. It just means they're painting the picture they want right now, and using it to drive me to a last resort option. They're trying to get us to panic and make a dumb decision. Pretty smart move. Look at you. If we were separated, you might be talking to the cops already. And Doug over there would've already had his statement recorded."

She immediately felt hurt and didn't have the energy or wherewithal to hide it.

"I'm sorry, Anne. I didn't mean to offend you."

"It's okay."

"Look, the only move is to stop letting them control what the public hears and what it doesn't."

"And just how are we supposed to do that?"

"First, I need a favor ..."

* * *

Anne's initial reaction to leaving the hotel was complete disbelief and a firm no. But once he reminded her the options, she reluctantly agreed. There was no way he could show his face in public unless absolutely necessary, and Doug wasn't trustworthy.

When he heard the 4-2-3 sequenced knock they'd agreed to earlier, he checked the peephole.

"Who is it?" he asked

"Mary Poppins," Anne answered, indicating she was both alone and didn't think she was spotted during her twenty-three-minute excursion.

"Did anyone see you?" he asked as he hurriedly shut the door behind her.

"Plenty of people saw me. But no, I don't think anyone recognized me. I avoided K Street and Thomas Circle to get to Massachusetts. The store was small and I saw one camera but didn't notice anything weird."

He grabbed the bag and pulled the three jars of hair dye out and handed one to Doug.

"Dye your hair, get rid of those clothes; take some of my clothes from the duffle bag. My shirt will be a bit tight on you, but deal with it. There are also some wigs."

"I don't want to dye my hair," Doug said.

"Just do it!" Anne unexpectedly snapped at Doug.

Doug looked shocked, then grabbed the bag with a pout and walked into the bathroom, slamming the door behind him.

Anne sat down on the bed and patted it softly in a gesture that asked David to do the same.

"David," she said in a soft voice, "what haven't you told me?"

"What?"

"Everything you said makes sense. Everything except how doing nothing is somehow a good idea. They're burying us, and I'm not aware of anything in our plan that can change that. It's great you had me buy hair dye and wigs, but we're going to run out of time real quick."

"We're already out of time."

"Exactly my point. And the longer this drags out, the less we have. There's more going on than what you're telling me. Please ... don't keep holding it back."

He stared at her and inhaled deeply. She waited for his exhale and explanation to follow, but the latter never came.

"Get dressed. We'll talk later."

"David ..." She pleaded softly, then rested her weary head on his shoulder.

David brushed her hair away from her forehead with his hand and whispered, "I'm sorry, Anne."

But the explanation never came.

78

Walter Buck tipped the crystalline glass filled with Johnnie Walker Blue Label Scotch back, his fourth in two hours, which resulted in a healthy buzz. Not that he needed it. David Centrelli had given him a natural high that would last for months. His eyes fixed on the 28-inch, non-HD television that was ready to crap out any minute, he chuckled to himself as he poured drink number five.

The hour was approaching.

His computer had long been turned off and his phone disconnected for the first time in years. He replayed the sequence of events that had led him here. Coworkers balked at his unusual behavior, watching him commandeer the conference room all day Sunday and refuse to open the door. His boss asked him over the intercom if he was okay and suggested he go home. Buck told him to leave him alone for the rest of the day.

Whispering softly, he repeated what he'd been told:

Do exactly as I say and you will not be hurt.

Do exactly as I say and you will not be hurt.

Do exactly as I say and you will not be hurt.

The phone call was intimidating enough. Then there was the e-mail. The explicit instructions, the stern warnings, the crucial and specific timing. His anticipation had been building ever since the call and skyrocketed when he read the memo. He wanted then to end the overwhelming anticipation, but the last sentence held him back.

Follow my orders precisely and change your life forever.

Everything Centrelli said would happen had happened, and a few additional, positive things as well. Now was not the time to doubt him or break his rules.

So, he did exactly as he had been instructed. He sat in the same chair, wearing the same rugged clothes, holding the same small glass filled from the same bottle of scotch, watching the same clock that he'd been watching since ten after nine. Mid-afternoon, he ordered a pizza from Anthony's, but lost the will to eat when the news came on. The rest of the day he'd simultaneously felt the edginess of a schoolboy waiting for class to be dismissed and the fear of a man who knows he's being watched but doesn't know how or why.

Halfway into his fourth pack of Winston Lights, part of him felt he couldn't sit on his hands any longer. The window of opportunity was closing, and a bird in the hand was worth two in the bush. But then the memo replayed on endless loop in his mind, and the repercussions he'd been assured that would follow his disobedience left no choice.

Bottom line: he was ready. He'd done his due diligence. He'd made the preparations. He'd put in the special requests, pulled all the strings, and cashed in on every favor he had to cash in on. The work was done, and all there was to do was wait.

It'll be worth it, he told himself.

Well worth it.

79

Despite the fact he hadn't eaten in nearly two days, David still wasn't hungry. They'd ordered Noodles on 11 Chinese takeout, but while Anne and Doug both devoured their Lo Mein and Sesame Chicken in ravenous silence, the eggroll in his plastic container nauseated him until he finally closed the lid and turned on the television for the first time in four hours.

Out of the corner of his eye, he saw Anne cast a skeptical eye as he began channel surfing. Her stare grew less subtle when he refused to return it, clutching the remote and remaining focused on the screen. He knew she felt betrayed, upset that he didn't tell her everything from the beginning. But there wasn't time for regret. It made things awkward, but it's the way it had to be.

Anne's new short, vibrant red hair contrasted sharply with the previously long, flowing, dark-brown strands that felt very befitting in hindsight. She looked like an older and more homely version of Julia Roberts in *Pretty Woman*, the burning bush color evidently not so easy on the eyes when it comes to hair, but he sure wasn't about to say that. She ran her fingers through it slowly and with obvious annoyance, as though part of her identity had been cut off as well.

It *had*.

Doug's hair — what was left of it — was now brown, compliments of the dye. He refused to wear a wig, and David didn't have the energy to argue with him. The lazy ass sat on the bed nearest the window, sipping cherry soda and staring south towards the Washington Monument.

"Does anyone else think it's odd that the President might be in on all this Previséo stuff, and we're only a half-mile from The White House?" Doug asked without even looking away from the window.

Anne didn't respond and neither did he. Focused on the future and trying his best not to dive into the past, he avoided conversation with Doug like the plague and cursed the memories that would never leave. Even being a federal murder suspect with a $200K bounty on his head couldn't prevent the memories from flooding his consciousness.

Tiffany Erin Carter was *the one*. His princess; his partner for life. The past eleven years and thousands of hours thinking about what happened hadn't changed that. She still felt like his angel, put here on Earth just for him. He still cared for her and longed for her in a way no one could understand. The things he saw that January 4th had led to a hellish life sentence. The pain and confusion would never go away, yet he couldn't find a way to hate her.

Or forget her.

His newly dishwater-blonde hair didn't suit him any better than the red did Anne, but he needed to change more than anyone. He rubbed his fake bushy mustache and threw the prescription-free glasses on the table.

It was just past eleven and there was still nothing on the TV. Flipping through the channels, he started to worry.

As he grew more restless, shaking his head, Anne ramped up the conspicuousness of her stares, confused by his sudden desire to watch television. He continued to ignore her, quickly flipping through the stations.

"David, what are you doing?" she finally asked.

Almost on cue, the program silenced her.

It was one of the most popular cable news channels in America, and the headline at the top of the red screen in large, white letters read:

BREAKING NEWS FROM RICHMOND

Beneath the headline, a full-screen image showed the face of a man that Anne, Doug and pretty much everyone else outside of Richmond didn't recognize, but soon wouldn't forget.

His name flashed onto the bottom of the screen.
Walter Buck.

* * *

The illustrious talk show host was a slim African American, mid-fifties, rimless glasses, had a smile that could light up any room, and wasted no time explaining who Walter Buck was and why Buck was on the air.

"Good evening, ladies and gentlemen. Tonight's guest is Mr. Walter Buck from Richmond, Virginia. Mr. Buck has been a reporter for *The Richmond Observer* the past twelve years, and earlier this evening he appeared on his weekly spot for the local Channel 8 news update.

"But in contrast to his usually local stories, ranging from community politics to labor disputes to events occurring in and around Richmond, his report tonight alleged a massive conspiracy involving the United States federal government and the global powerhouse drug company Medzic Pharmaceuticals. It's such a compelling story, with such colossal consequences for America, that we decided you needed to hear it.

"In addition, Mr. Buck has confirmed that his source is none other than Mr. David Centrelli, who only hours ago was declared WANTED by the FBI for murder as well as a possible connection to a terrorist organization. As we all know, ladies and gentlemen, conspiracy theories are a dime a dozen," the host paused for effect. "But what makes Mr. Buck's account so compelling is that he has the evidence to prove it."

80

This is actually happening, Walter Buck thought to himself, trying to conceal the enthusiasm.

The famous talk show host's kickoff was fluid, flowing and flattering. His life had already changed in just one short minute, but now he had to maintain professionalism.

You've got one shot. Don't mess it up.

Of course, impressive as it was, the host's intro left out some details. First, that he'd given no forewarning to producers, staff members, or anyone else from Channel 8 or *The Observer* that he wouldn't be following the original script. No subtle hints, no requests for approval, no suggested change during the pre-air routine. Instead, in stunning and unprecedented fashion, he sent shockwaves to everyone, including the viewers.

Before producers even had time to process their shock and pull the plug on his rousing report, he'd spoken for two-and-a-half minutes. And in a digital world run by data bytes and social media, that was enough. The few people in Richmond who saw the report had turned to YouTube, Facebook, Twitter, blogs and a host of other outlets, ballooning the story's audience within seconds.

Buck knew that major networks employed teams of people who scanned the web for interesting local stories. And Centrelli was dead on: being first was critical. Hundreds of stories a year reach the national spotlight because of small-time reports getting communicated to big-time audiences through the web.

The story's shock factor and fresh blood had spread like a California wildfire, producing the largest audience of the year in only moments. Twenty minutes after the local report, the major network's executive producer was talking to him directly. He'd made that quite simple to do by offering his cell phone number aloud twice at the beginning of the broadcast, just as Centrelli had instructed.

The mega giant news station immediately locked an exclusive for fifty grand, had a private car drive him to a company jet on a secluded Chesterfield County Airport runway, prepped him during the one hour, 350-mile flight to New York City and now had him in the studio, telling the rest of the world the same story.

This is actually happening.

"Ladies and gentlemen," the host said, "now that you know who Walter Buck is, it's time for you to hear his story. A story so incredible you'll find it hard to believe. Mr. Buck, thank you for being here with us tonight."

"Thanks for having me," he replied. *To the millions of people watching.*

"Mr. Buck, you are aware that what you're doing may be grounds for termination and legal recourse should your accusations prove untrue?"

It was the perfect lead-in question.

"Well aware. In fact, I've already been fired by *The Richmond Observer*."

"Fired?"

"Yes, right after Channel 8 pulled me from the set."

"Why did they fire you?"

"Insubordination."

"Insubordination?"

"I didn't share the report with producers before airing."

"Why not?" the host asked.

The script played out even better live than it did in rehearsal on the plane. The host asked the question so casually, like anyone at home would be thinking as he or she followed along. It was natural, genuine. These writers were good.

"A few reasons. But mainly because I knew they wouldn't approve it."

"But doesn't termination seem a little extreme?"

"I don't really care."

"You don't care?" the host dropped his jaw.

"There are bigger issues than my job at stake. It's my duty as a reporter to speak the truth, no matter how big or small my audience may be. Just because it's not what some people want to hear or could cost me my job doesn't mean it's not the right thing to do."

"That's noble of you." The host nodded his head for emphasis.

"Just doing my job."

"So how did all this happen?"

"I was in the office early this morning when I received a phone call from David Centrelli."

"The same David Centrelli wanted by the FBI for murder?"

"Yes, but he wasn't at that point. The ProFitness gym thing hadn't happened yet."

Buck admired how even that specific line been so very carefully choreographed. Say *thing*, the writers had urged him. *Incident* sounds too official; *crime* is too negative. *Thing* will hit it just right.

"What time did he call?"

"Around five-thirty."

"And what did he say?"

"He told me his name and said, 'do exactly as I say and you will not be hurt.'"

"Wow," the host covered his clean-shaven face with his left hand, his wedding ring glistening.

"Yeah, it definitely got my attention."

"Then what happened?"

"He told me in a few hours I'd receive an e-mail. He gave me the e-mail address and subject line and said it would include an attachment containing very sensitive and important information."

The host nodded, urging him to go on.

"I was surprised, but really more skeptical than anything. He told me to wait for the e-mail and remember to follow his instructions very precisely."

"And?"

"I balked. I get a lot of prank calls, and what he was saying was hard to believe. I almost hung up it seemed so ridiculous."

"But you didn't."

"I don't know. ... There was something about the way he said it. It was almost like ... it *felt real.* You know? I can't really explain it. Logic told me he was lying, but my gut told me to listen. It was one of those moments. As a reporter, sometimes you have to follow your intuition."

"Did he say why he called *you* in particular?"

"I asked, and he said it was because I was the only reporter he knew of who would do the right thing despite the consequences."

The truth was of course far less flattering. Centrelli said he was the only one with an ego big enough to seek the limelight in spite of the consequences, and it made him smile on the inside that the American people would never find that out.

"Any idea why Centrelli would think that?"

"Well ..." he paused for effect. "Let's just say I've put myself in harm's way before by revealing unpopular truths."

"More on that later ... but first, what happened next?"

"He told me that when I read the e-mail, I'd understand."

"Did he say anything else about the memo?"

"I asked, but he said he didn't have time and abruptly hung up."

"And you didn't hear from him again?"

"No. I tried Star 69, but that didn't go anywhere. Caller ID was blank. I didn't have any way to reach him, so all I could do was wait."

The host offered the audience a heavy, camera-friendly sigh. That was his specialty, and it was perfectly timed.

"So, what did you do next?"

"I assumed he was lying. I figured I'd check for the e-mail, but other than that, it was a prank call as far as I was concerned. Crazier things have happened."

"You didn't tell anyone about it?"

"No. No one was in the office at that hour, and Centrelli told me to keep it to myself. He also didn't ask me to *do* anything. It wasn't a compromising situation ... at the time ... so it didn't feel like a big deal."

The host offered a hearty laugh and sipped his coffee. "Didn't he tell you 'do exactly as I say and you will not be hurt'? That seems like a compromising situation to me."

"Maybe, but like I said, stranger things have happened. Even the threat didn't feel that serious. *At the time.*"

"Pretty incredible, Walter," the host shifted to the first-name basis precisely on cue. "Then what happened?"

"Everything, and I do mean *everything*, changed when I got the e-mail."

"Folks, we've got to take a short break. But when we come back ... you'll hear firsthand about the frightening e-mail Walter Buck received from fugitive David Centrelli."

81

David watched Walter Buck soak up the fame on TV like a sponge pushed underwater.

Buck played the part well and, David guessed, the network set him up for success. He wore a classic-fit Ralph Lauren collared shirt with sleeves rolled up just below the elbows, silk tie with an American flag embroidered in the center, black-rimmed glasses hanging from a red string around his neck. Neither too casual nor too formal. He spoke eloquently enough on the air and appealed to a large base of people. Not too fast or too slow, the words flowed from his mouth like a river into its basin. He came off as clean-cut and professional-looking enough to retain viewers' attention but not pompous about his image. Not too conservative or too liberal. Middle-class, down-to-earth. The image of America, the voice of its citizens.

"I can't show you the email or the attachment," Buck began. "The police took them both."

"The police *took* them?" the host gasped.

"That's right. They marched into the studio, pulled me backstage, grabbed the file and told me they were confiscating it without another word. They also deactivated my email account."

"That's incredible."

"The weird thing was Centrelli told me in the e-mail both of those things would happen. I didn't believe it when I read it, but he was spot on. He also said that because of that, I had to be sure to show the e-mail and attachment on screen during the live broadcast, if only to prove they exist. It was a good thing I listened. If I hadn't, the people behind this could deny the whole thing and there wouldn't be any proof otherwise. As I understand it, images of both are all over Facebook as we speak."

"Did the police say why they took your personal property?"

"They said it was classified. A matter of national security."

"Well, then ..." the host continued, letting the dubiousness, and drama, saturate the set. "What did the memo say?"

"The first thing it mentioned was that I absolutely had to wait until my seven o'clock Channel 8 broadcast to say anything. It didn't say why, but those instructions were underlined several times. I'll tell you though: it was pretty hard after I read everything."

"When did you get the e-mail?"

"9:10 exactly."

"And you thought of disobeying?"

David watched Buck shrug and offer a slight smile, the quintessential reaction: honest and human.

"Yes, I did. I'm a reporter. I have a duty to speak the truth. And part of me wanted to do so right away. But I also have a responsibility to my sources."

And you smelled a jackpot, David thought.

"But I'll tell you," Buck said before clearing his throat, "when I saw him on TV and heard what happened, I wasn't sure *what* to do."

"What was going through your mind?"

"I was scared. Really scared. All of a sudden it felt so dangerous, and I wondered what would happen to me if I didn't obey ... or if I did. It was surreal. There were so many things running through my head that it was hard to think at all."

"Why didn't you come forward then?"

"Believe it or not ..." Buck paused, running his hand through thin salt-and-pepper hair, "his WANTED status made his story more believable."

"How is that?"

"I remembered how he said I had to wait until seven, how I couldn't tell anyone, for reasons I'd understand after I read the e-mail. He knew something big would happen. I'll bet my life on it. And when I really thought about the message and considered it might be true ... well ... that's when I realized how scary this really is."

"What is 'this' exactly?"

That's when it happened. David cracked a smile as Buck laid it on millions of viewers, a beautiful drape of fondant over the most decadent cake.

The conspiracy between Medzic, MacArthur, Barry and Tain and the feds. Previséo's tests and all the medical documentation, financial discrepancies, and numerous coincidences. Unconcerned with the numerous slander and libel lawsuits that would almost certainly follow, Buck drew the connections between the lawyer Patrick Tomilson and stockbroker Jake LeMoure, referenced pictures of the two David had provided in the e-mail that had then been shown on live television, spent a few seconds explaining their coincidentally bizarre deaths, only months apart, and tied it all back to the conspiracy.

The host held his hand over his mouth when Buck spoke of Jake LeMoure and his young wife dying in a fire. The host then rapid-fired questions ranging from David's credibility to the veracity of the claim to the convenient "evidence" that just happened to prove everything but wasn't in Buck's possession. And he did it like a shrewd defense lawyer during a strenuous cross-examination.

Yet for every question asked, Buck had an answer. Elucidating one piece of compelling evidence after another, David was certain the cross-examination approach was written to solidify truth in viewers' eyes, and it was working. Logical doubt countered repeatedly with hard evidence paved the way.

The Q&A went on for nearly fifteen minutes, all centered around two deaths, millions of potential victims, and the horror of what could very well be happening right under the American people's noses. It was written such that viewers couldn't help but root for Buck as he fielded questions meant to knock down a theory that no American wanted to believe.

But when it was done, the host was speechless and Buck was lining up for the knockout punch.

"It was hard to swallow," Buck began his closing statement. "And there's a lot I didn't understand. I'm not an attorney or an accountant, but I know it's worth investigating. Think about how much money we're talking. The only cure for diabetes. Is it happening exactly the way Centrelli said it is? I can't say yes, but I can't say no. And there's too much at stake to turn a blind eye.

"Did you ... no ... *do* believe him?"

"Everything Centrelli said that I could actually verify for myself, *everything*, has been true. The lawyer and stockbroker dying, their connection to each other, the doctor's involvement with Previséo, even what he said would happen when I went on Channel 8. Everything. I can't prove he told a single lie. So, I'm not going to throw my hands up and say and say it can't be true because it's so hard to believe. And neither should you." Buck pointed directly into the camera, like the famous Uncle Sam recruiting poster.

"Did Centrelli tell you where he is?"

"No."

"Where the rest of the evidence is?"

"Nope."

"Did he say anything else in his message?"

"Nothing."

"Have you heard from him since?"

"Not once."

"What are you going to do now?"

"I really don't know. He told me I should surround myself with people, get a damned good lawyer, and that it'd be really dangerous. Hopefully he's wrong, but it sure doesn't feel like it. The feds took everything I had, so I don't know how much of a threat I am to them, but still ... I no longer have a job, I don't feel comfortable going home, and I don't know what's next for me."

Looking directly at the host, Buck then said, "And maybe *you* should be feeling pretty uncomfortable now too. It's very brave of you to do this for the American people."

The host was shaking his head and grimacing with what felt like genuine concern. Maybe for himself.

"Walter, you're telling me here, on national television in front of millions of your fellow Americans, that this is all true ... everything from the Previséo conspiracy allegation to the way you found out about?"

"One hundred percent. Centrelli called it 'The Deadly Deal.'"

Within minutes of the interview's airing, every news station in America was replaying it. Soon thereafter, despite it being almost midnight on the East Coast, there were so many cell phone calls being made that the overloaded lines turned busy across the nation.

82

Byron Huetel knew this call would come.

"Richard, I don't know what to say," he whispered into the receiver.

"So, you *did* catch the news this evening? I wasn't sure, what with your injury and all."

Richard Krenzer sounded neither sarcastic nor angry, but decidedly unaggressive and even more stoic than he thought possible.

Both of his legs in casts and propped up on the ottoman, Byron lay helplessly in the leather lounge chair, YouTube paused on the laptop. For the first time in he didn't even know how long, tears swelled in his aged eyes. He didn't bother to wipe them, but instead let them trickle down his scaly cheeks.

"How could you?" Krenzer continued. "You used the power of this office to declare Centrelli a national fugitive, and then let this happen. The old Byron would've never allowed it."

"I–"

"Have you spoken with anyone?" The chief of staff asked him.

"No," he answered, his voice breaking.

"Don't. I'll handle things from here."

"Operation Retrograde?"

"None of your concern. Stay out of it and focus on your recovery. I'll be in touch," Krenzer nearly whispered before terminating the call.

He looked up towards the ceiling, unsurprised. Thirty-plus years of handling matters such as these had, above all, made him a pragmatist, and he knew the drill from here. There was but one thing left to do. Centrelli's plan had terminated Previséo, as well as Medzic, and all that mattered to Richard now was protecting the president and himself.

Of course he'd considered the possibility Centrelli would try to go public, as well as sabotage Previséo, eliminate Medzic leadership, and a host of other possibilities. But the medical data that Dr. Mallick had provided was overwhelming, and it jettisoned Centrelli and Previséo into the limelight far more quickly than anyone could've foreseen.

He sighed, knowing it was a moot point. The bottom line was that his job had been to stop Centrelli before the whippersnapper could implement anything. And he had failed.

Centrelli was as good as dead, and he probably knew that before he contacted Walter Buck, but the plan would go deeper. Much deeper.

A single phone call would be made, and it would be in action within hours, not days. And it would be beyond thorough. One doesn't get to be the chief of staff to the most powerful man in the world by hoping for the best or leaving anything to chance.

The old man knew better. He knew the chief of staff had an airtight lifeboat that no one else knew about. And after Centrelli's incredibly smart move, all that mattered was inflating it.

And removing all collateral damage.

83

David awoke in the hotel's twin bed in a cold sweat, his head pounding even louder than his heart. And that was saying something. He rolled towards the center of the room to find that Anne wasn't in her bed and Doug was on his back, snoring like a buzz saw on the floor between them. David flipped back the white duvet in one swift motion, sat up slowly, and wiped his wet forehead with the back of his sleeve. He rerouted around Doug's clodhoppers and then made his way to the bathroom for a shower. It would feel miraculous to wash this whole ordeal down the drain too, if that were only possible.

His face in the mirror confirmed the colossal drain the last few weeks had been on his sleep, strength and emotional wellbeing. He looked worn out, enervated, and beaten down. His skin had taken on a sallowness and his mouth felt permanently drawn. Were his teeth still white or had they yellowed too? He turned the shower handle to start the flow and was in and out in three minutes. He no longer had the desire for long showers, for luxury. He toweled off and threw on a pair of khakis and a black sweater that buttoned asymmetrically at the top, his last fresh set of clothes. His fake mustache sat on the dresser behind him as David gave himself a shave and thought through what lay ahead.

Instead of turning on the TV, he made a cup of coffee using the hotel Keurig. It was a five on a scale from one to ten, if only because he hadn't had a hot beverage in days. Not daring to venture towards the lobby for the continental breakfast, he poked his head out the door momentarily to yank the *USA Today* off the floor.

The hallway was empty, and the building was quiet. Several adjacent rooms had the do not disturb sign hanging on the doorknob, and he didn't see or hear any other guests. Still, he quickly shut the door, threw the dead bolt and closed the latch guard, breathing quickly, but quietly, like his inhaling and exhaling would somehow divulge his whereabouts.

The newspaper's front page highlighted a large, full-color picture of Walter Buck and insert-sized photo of him, the one shown on TV countless times the night before. The headline read:

FUGITIVE ALERTS WORLD TO DRUG SCAM

As he started reading the article, he heard a knock at the door.

"Who is it?"

"Mary Poppins."

Anne burst inside with what seemed like unrealistic energy. She dropped a pile of papers on the desk in a tizzy and continued shaking her head. Her short red hair was all over the place. It looked like she'd been touching a Van de Graaf generator from one of those wow-the-middle-schoolers science assemblies.

"You wouldn't believe how much is on the web," she said loud enough to stir Doug from a deep sleep.

"Where were you?"

"I was in the business center downstairs."

"Anne ..."

"There was no one there and I kept my head down. But listen ... it's on the front page of *The New York Times, Wall Street Journal, Washington Post, L.A. Times, Chicago Tribune,* and pretty much every news website you can think of. *WikiLeaks, Drudge Report—*"

"You shouldn't leave the room."

"Your biography is one of the top Google hits when you search for 'Deadly Deal,' 'Previséo,' 'Medzic,' and a whole bunch of others. One site claimed there's over a thousand blogs. And you've ... made a few enemies."

"Enemies?"

"Anti-Centrelli and pro-pharmaceutical bloggers; they claim you're faking the whole thing to cover up your crimes. Some posts supporting Medzic and the government claiming both are innocent, that you're slandering them. Pictures of you with a slash mark through your face, swastikas in the background—"

"I get it. Any supporters?" he asked.

"Sure, some people think you're a hero. There's a 'Parents with Diabetic Children' Facebook group that labeled you 'The Saving Grace.' Whistleblower sites commending you for speaking the truth, offering money to meet you, hear your story firsthand. You've also got over a dozen marriage proposals."

Shaking his head in disbelief, he pressed the ON button with his thumb.

"Story of the Hour" on local Channel 5 was showing clips of Buck's interview and giving in-depth information about David's childhood and academic career. Pictures of his mother touched a nerve and he flipped to the next channel. Buck's original broadcast on the local Richmond news was mentioned but not shown as four "experts" sat around a table debating the story's believability, concluding that it most likely wasn't accurate.

David wasn't surprised. He wouldn't believe it either had he not lived it. But it did feel strange to see his picture on television. He knew the popularity, or notoriety, was inevitable. But that didn't make it feel any less weird. He flipped through a few more stations and found more of the same on other networks.

"Buck's original broadcast is off the web," Anne said in worried voice. "I couldn't even find it on YouTube. They yanked it, David. The government pulled it."

"We knew they would. The interview is what matters. People are talking about it. The government can't stop that. If anything, removing Buck's broadcast makes it look like they have something to hide."

"But the documents, David ... Now, it's just a story without proof. What are we going to do?" Anne replied, her earlier optimism spiraling into angst. Doug had moseyed into the shower, hopefully for a while. Anne's questions were good ones, but he didn't want to deal with Doug.

"Getting the story on prime time was the easy part."

"But what now? Your picture's all over the place and you're still wanted by the FBI. Are we just supposed to hide in this hotel room for the rest of our lives?"

Anne raised her eyebrows and violently scratched her short hair. She sat down on the bed before bouncing back up as if on a spring.

He knew a happy ending, albeit more plausible than before Buck's interview, was still very unlikely. But he was surprised she didn't see it.

"The only way we could stop this was if we made sure people knew about Previséo. And the only way that was going to happen was to make the story go viral. You think I like my picture being on every TV in America? Believe me, I had a much different plan for my life a week ago.

"But now there's no chance of us ..." Anne started to say. "Wait ... what are you saying?" she lowered her voice.

"This wasn't about our survival. It was bigger than us," he repeated Jake's line from the note. "Every diabetic, every parent of a diabetic, knows about Previséo now. This was about them. There's no way Medzic will try to release Previséo now."

"Are you sure?"

"Trust me. This I actually know a thing or two about."

She plunked herself down on the springy bed with a soft "thunk" and closed her eyes. The lashes swept her cheeks like ink-colored brooms, and David could see her working it out in the clench of her fists and the rapid bouncing of her right knee. When she opened her eyes again, there was a quiet comprehension in them.

"They're going to kill us, aren't they?"

After a few seconds of silence, he nodded slightly and she nodded in return. They spoke no words in that moment, but none were needed.

David realized then that her support meant more to him than he could have expected. It was the first time in what felt like a decade that he had someone's approval for doing the *honorable* thing. He'd long suspected that the honorable part of him had died and was thankful it hadn't.

"So what now, David? You're probably right about Previséo being finished, and that's most important. But these people ... they can make stories disappear, even popular ones. The public has a short memory. In a month, the story could easily morph into how Mr. David Centrelli deceived an entire nation."

84

Twenty-six years of experience, seven positions of escalating authority, five wildly different bureau stations, three top-notch mentors, and an uncountable number of dangerous encounters still hadn't adequately prepared him for this.

After working through the night, Jerry Riley still didn't have a clue as to how deep this rabbit hole went or what he could do to stop it. He wore the same navy suit pants from the previous day, his jacket thrown on the floor in frustration in front of his cherry-colored desk hours earlier, the sleeves of his heavily wrinkled white dress shirt rolled up well past the elbows.

Buried in paperwork, he paid scant attention to the muted TV broadcasting yet another spin on the David Centrelli story. He guzzled his fifth bottle of water and got up to turn down the thermostat. Despite the bitter chill outside, his office felt like a sauna.

At just before ten-thirty in the morning, the Director of the FBI had a nightmare on his hands.

The penultimate shitshow had the public panicking at an alarming rate with no signs of slowing down. Numerous Medzic Pharmaceuticals lawsuits would soon be filed in federal court against a fugitive of the law, the US federal government, and almost every major news network for wrongful accusation. A handful of protestors were already marching the streets of Washington, a figure that was sure to increase, and there was pressure from the President of the United States to get to the bottom of this mess.

Surely, a litany of lawsuits was also heading for Medzic; they were likely figuring out their litigation strategy with lawyers who charged two grand an hour. MacArthur, Barry & Tain had already hired an outside consulting firm that specialized in perception management and a legal team to respond accordingly. Walter Buck had done even more than lawyer up. He demanded FBI protection and had assembled a team of experts, ranging from public relation specialists to civil attorneys to career planning strategists, all to protect his interests, both personal and professional.

And after eleven hours of feverish work and late-night phone calls, Jerry Riley hadn't moved the needle in terms of finding Centrelli or either authenticating or discrediting his story.

"Mr. Riley," his secretary's voice crackled through the intercom. Kimbra was usually cheery and helpful, but today she sounded irritated, his name more of a statement than a question. He couldn't blame her. She was already into her seventh hour of work today, and there was still no end in sight.

"Yeah," he said.

"Another Centrelli tip on line two for you."

He'd had an anonymous tip line announced during several morning and nightly news programs in Washington, posted on the FBI website and in a plethora of online publications and websites. Obviously, the approach wasn't optimal, as it led to an incredibly tremendous number of false leads.

However, given that surveillance teams couldn't track Centrelli even with Washington D.C.'s hundreds of cameras and the APB hadn't generated any leads, flawed as the old-fashioned tip-line method was, it was their best shot right now. That part frustrated him. Sure, a few still shots of Centrelli got captured at Union Station just before four o'clock yesterday, but a combination of electrical interference issues and a camera malfunction on First Street had lost him. Since then, the facial recognition search software hadn't produced a single match over seventy square miles, so it seemed clear to Riley that the fugitive was holed up somewhere.

After the broadcast, the public knew that the FBI was playing catch up and there was little point in hiding it. His hope was that someone — a hotel clerk, cab driver, soccer mom, whoever — would see something and then *say* something. Wasn't that what the signs on airport baggage carousels had taught us?

The line had revealed an eye-opening cast of characters. There was the python lady who was sure that she'd spotted David stealing one of her 14 snakes earlier that morning. There was the barber who said that a man fitting David's exact description had come into his shop, but after a good ol' cut and shave, he left looking nothing like him. Apparently, he'd called to warn the Feds that indeed the adage was true: looks could be deceiving. Then there was the elderly man who swore that David had helped him carry groceries into his brownstone, turned on the television, saw his own picture and fled. Finally, there was the psychic who hadn't actually *seen* David, but could *feel* that he was headed her way. She had said it was only a matter of minutes, if Kimbra wanted to stay on the line and speak with the fugitive directly.

There had been forty-seven supposed leads this morning. Kimbra had the pleasure of conducting each initial screening, and then from there, she would connect any that "passed" to him directly. There had only been one before this.

"Put him through."

He reached for the original copies of the documents Walter Buck received in the Centrelli e-mail that had already been tagged "The Memo Heard 'Round the World" on Facebook. Thumbing through the pages, he grabbed the receiver and pressed LINE 2.

"Jerry Riley."

"The Jerry Riley who is the Director of the FBI?"

The male voice sounded typical and unaggressive.

"That's right. May I ask who this is?"

"I'm surprised I got you after only a few basic questions that some savvy web searches can answer. You must be desperate."

"You've got ten seconds to convince me I should keep listening."

Another individual had assured him he was Centrelli by referencing a tattoo of the KKK on his ass, something the Director had no proof or reason to believe Centrelli even had in the first place, and then faxed a counterfeit birth certificate to the office as evidence while claiming the government had confiscated the original. Equally skeptical now, Riley waited through a moment of silence to hear this guy's approach.

"Do you have the e-mail I sent Walter Buck?"

Instantly more alert, he leaned forward in his chair, stroking day-old stubble.

"I do." He replied, trying to keep the feeling mounting inside him tamped down.

"On the second-to-last page, in the lower left-hand corner, there's a large star by a circled note. The note says, 'Keep this secret so I can verify my identity. My code number is 11162014012220140206 1984.'"

His dropped the bottle of water and its loud splash soon covered the floor. But he didn't even look down. The trace had already started and Riley checked his Timex watch to see how many seconds had passed. He needed about fourteen more seconds for a pinpoint.

"You have my attention, but I need more proof."

"I'm not in the mood to debate or give you time to complete the trace. You want to hear what I have to say? Take a chance. Otherwise, you'll hear it on the news."

"I'm listening."

"Meet me in front of Dolcezza at 9th and Palmer, just north of H Street. Come alone, Mr. Riley. It's the only way I show. A few too many people in my own government want me dead, so you'll have to forgive my lack of trust."

The voice paired determination with conviction. He sensed it was sincere, but he was still skeptical. Centrelli or Walter Buck could've given that message to someone else before agents seized the e-mail.

"If I, or one of my people watching your every step, get so much as a whiff of your not coming alone, the deal's off and you'll read about this in the papers. If you come armed, the deal's off and you'll read about this in the papers. If you're not there in eight minutes, the deal's off and you'll read about this in the papers."

It was an odd time to notice, but his hair felt bushy. He hated the feeling of overgrown hair sweeping the tops of his ears as the ceiling fan above his desk made the follicles dance. He went to the barber more frequently than most to try to stay ahead of his head, but right now he felt like a shaggy dog on a short leash ... especially as he prepared to head to Centrelli's desired location on the fugitive's terms. He checked his watch and knew that he'd have to hustle. H Street and 9th was about a half-mile from FBI Headquarters on Pennsylvania Avenue.

"Why should I risk my life to meet you? If you're really David Centrelli, then you're smart enough to know that I'm going to find you eventually."

There wasn't any hesitation, as if he expected the question.

"I called you because I know you're not involved and you want the truth. Here's your chance. You just have to decide if it's worth the risk to trust me."

A slight pause, then:

"But decide quickly. You're down to seven minutes."

85

Tourists, activists and businesspeople swarmed the area around Dolcezza Gelato & Coffee. The froufrou high-end chain had done well in Washington, D.C. and now had three locations. *Bon Appetite* had labeled it one of the best in the country, and for a mere eight dollars, folks could enjoy Tahitian vanilla bean lattes with almond milk or iced espressos with a Peppermint Mocha twist. Throw in some theatrical tumbler shaking or a pour from a towering height, and finish it with the flourish, presentation with a smile and a personalized "Here you are, Mister So-and-So", and the customers drank it up. It was the immersive experience more than the taste of the roasted beans or the syrupy flavor shots or the dark oceans of caffeine that kept them coming back.

But the types walking out of Dolcezza with their indulgent mid-morning caffeine boost in-hand contrasted sharply with the protestors who carried signs as they marched towards the White House, chanting catchy cadences that appropriately captured their disillusionment with the government. DC really was the Mecca for opposition. People fed off the energy surrounding dissenting opinions, which magnified the importance of issues that in many other cities would be drowned out. There was an intrinsic sense that here, change was possible. Majority ruled, and even though it was often a slow, painful process, people were empowered to drive their own destinies.

The main topic at the moment was Previséo and the government's supposed involvement. As groups of millennials banded together to holler their chants, David felt a surge of hope that this might just be okay. In the short-term, he was terrified of what would happen if his disguise didn't hold up. Especially with the world knowing he was in DC and his picture plastered all over the protesters' signs.

Standing in front of The United States Mint Coin Store across the street, he took another sip of his regular coffee. A large winter coat with a pillow stuffed underneath it gave the impression he was thirty pounds heavier. He wore black sunglasses to cover his eyes, and his blonde hair hung shaggily outside the Nationals cap. The fake mustache continued to itch, and he remained partially bent over to conceal his actual height.

But disguise or no disguise, he was exposed. And vulnerable.

Anne had insisted on a less public spot, which in hindsight may have been a better idea. But he needed to see Jerry Riley out in the open. He needed to remain hidden in the plain sight of the crowd. He leaned against a brick apartment building next to the bistro, watching the steady flow of people march into and out of it.

The endless stream of customers walking into and out of Dolcezza reminded him of his life only one week ago, before Anne entered it. Overpriced beverages every day, the Outlook calendar ruling his life. The $2,000 Isaia suits and fancy Berluti dress shoes, only the best, that projected success. It now seemed so arbitrary; back then he couldn't fathom that success might simply mean going to work and having a home without fearing for your life.

At that instant, Jerry Riley's incoming presence pulled him back to reality.

The Director of the FBI crossed H Street in a navy blue suit and black trench coat. His extremely short black hair belied his fifty-five years of age. Every couple of seconds, Riley ran his hands along the tops of his ears, as if pushing the already-out-of-the-way hair out of the way. *Was that a nervous tick of some sort? Was he somehow wired behind the ears?* Whatever the ear mystery was, one thing was certain: Riley was out of shape. The half-mile walk and palpable lack of sleep had him huffing air ... which was exactly what David wanted to happen. He couldn't give Riley time to form a plan. He needed the director to feel urgency, and allotting a short, specific timeframe was meant to impress upon him the need for speed.

Evidently, it had worked.

Both hands on his waist, Riley swiveled his head in all directions, his open jaw and scanning eyes forfeiting any possible attempt to blend in with the crowd. He remained stationary as Riley slowly turned around. He could see Riley, but Riley couldn't see him.

He looked for bulges around Riley's pockets and chest but didn't see any. It also didn't appear anyone else was with him, so he took the chance and walked towards him slowly, using protestors to shield him for as long as possible.

Riley's back was turned when he tapped him on the shoulder.

"Keep facing that way."

The protesters' boisterous chants kept the conversation between the two of them, and Riley did as he was told. It seemed the shouts were getting louder, and thankfully nobody noticed the director, which he hadn't considered until that moment. It wouldn't be out of the question for someone to recognize the Director of the FBI.

"Are you alone?"

"Yes."

"Turn around."

Riley's facial expression revealed ample surprise that he didn't seem to try to hide. The director's eyebrows curved inward as he squinted against the sun.

"I don't want to hurt you. I'm just protecting myself."

"I understand."

"People are watching us right now. Do anything rash, they'll make you regret it. We both want the same thing, so don't do anything stupid."

"I won't."

He could tell Riley was studying his eyes, surveying his demeanor. The director made no attempt to hide that either. After a long stare-down, he spoke again.

"David, I'm on your side as long as what you told Walter Buck is true. I won't harm you, and I'm alone. Just tell me the next move."

Assessing the risk one more time, he looked at the director and said nothing. Riley seemed genuine, but this was the Director of the FBI.

The leader of America's biggest domestic surveillance team. A master of expressions, impressions and manipulations. A veteran of covert and complex missions.

He could be really good at lying.

86

They walked a few blocks north and about a mile west, side-by-side the entire time. Anne and Doug followed two blocks back on either side of I Street. Neither he nor Riley spoke. When they entered McPherson Square, David steered them towards the hotel.

The cool breeze battered against his face and David's cheeks felt chilled. When they walked into the Capital Hilton lobby, the gust of warm air brought great relief. Keeping his head down, David led them to a generic hotel meeting room past the front desk. He played the part of a guest who'd been there before very well. Walk in with confidence and say nothing, no one questions you.

The room was pretty basic. In the middle sat a small table, made from cheap wood with eight less-than-executive-style leather chairs, four pitchers of water and two small candy dishes on top of it. No windows on any wall. Dim lighting, made even darker when he turned off all but one of the overhead incandescent bulbs.

"There's no cell service in here," David began. "But why don't you empty your pockets anyway."

Riley dug into his pants and dropped his phone, wallet, keys and a Christian prayer card on the table without hesitation.

"Take a seat."

Once Riley did, David poured himself a glass of water and offered one to him. The director declined.

"Before we get started, I want to clear something up."

"I'm listening," Riley said.

"What I'm going to tell you has conditions that you have to agree to. None of them will prevent you from doing the right thing, but a few of them might force you to bend some rules. Can you live with that?"

"I've been known to bend one here or there, depending on the rule and the situation. But I won't break any."

"Fair enough. Yes, everything I told Buck is true. One hundred percent."

"Can you prove it?"

"Yes."

"You're telling me you have actual, irrefutable documentation?"

"Anything can be refuted, Mr. Riley."

"I meant would it be good enough to hold up in court."

"Peter Mallick made detailed notes of his studies."

Riley's face turned inquisitive, but he remained silent. David then answered the question on the director's mind before he asked it.

"No, I didn't kill him. And no, I don't think he committed suicide. If he did, my guess is he was coerced. Either that or he did it as a way to protect his family."

"But you can't prove that, can you?"

"I can get close."

"What's that supposed to mean?"

"Mallick was doing advanced testing on Previséo long before anyone knew what was going on. He figured out it was fatal and told the top brass. When he did, they threatened his family if he ever came forward. So he didn't ever come forward with what he knew, but he kept all the records."

"And that's justification to put millions of lives at stake?"

"Who are we to judge? They promised to torture and murder his children and wife. What would you have done?"

No answer.

"That brings us to the first condition. Absolutely no besmirching or defaming of Peter Mallick in any way. No matter what you may find, if it harms the doctor's reputation, it stays buried. He made a mistake, a big mistake, but he more than made up for it. I don't want his name dragged through the mud now."

"Who are you to say he made up for it?"

"The world knows him as a good man, Mr. Riley. There's no reason to change that. Let's not make it even harder for his family."

"How can you trust me not to do that?"

"I'd like to think we can shake hands like men, and you'll keep your word. But you're right, I can't be sure. Which is why I'd have to use this conversation against you if you don't listen," he answered, removing his coat and exposing a small microphone clipped to his shirt pocket.

"What's it connected to?"

"A tape recorder someone has right now, capturing your promise and this entire illegal conversation. You think the networks had a field day with Buck ... imagine what they'd do with you."

87

Even as he heard his own voice tell it, the story felt too outrageous to be true.

In truth, David wanted it to feel too nightmarish to be realistic. He never wanted to grow numb to that sensation. And he never wanted to feel comfortable telling the story.

Riley listened carefully, an occasional ever-so-slight nod here and there but otherwise revealing no reaction. Saying nothing and barely blinking, Riley provided no clear sense of whether or not he believed what he was hearing. When David finished, Riley folded his hands on the table and stared without a word for almost two full minutes.

"Why are you telling me this?" Riley finally said in a gentle voice.

"Because I think we can help each other."

"No, I mean after all you say you've been through, why do you trust me?"

"I can't say I do. But it seems to me you've always done what you felt was right despite what others almost certainly wanted. Definitely pissed off a few higher-ups along the way. I don't agree with some of your decisions, but at least you stuck to your guns and didn't get political."

"Is that it?"

"I haven't seen your picture or heard your name from Jake, Patrick Tomilson, Dr. Mallick ... nobody mentioned you in the notes they left behind or in any conversations I had. That doesn't guarantee you're not involved, but it beats the alternative."

Still no reaction. This was getting eerier by the second.

"I also know you're under a lot of pressure after the Buck interview. It says on the FBI website its mission is to protect the American people."

"So it does."

"People need answers from you, Mr. Riley. To be perfectly honest, my hope is you want them bad enough to play this the right way."

"I'll play it the way I think it should be played."

"Like I said, you don't get political. Maybe my reasons aren't the best, but they're what I've got."

David took a long swig of water and tried once more to read the director's extraordinarily stoic reaction. No dice.

"Where are the documents from Mallick?" Riley said.

"We'll get there."

"And the information from LeMoure and Tomilson?"

"In a safe place."

"You do realize I can't do anything without them. Your story is remarkable, to say the least, but right now that's all it is."

"I know," he nodded his head, maintaining eye contact. "But I need to know you're on the right team before I hand anything over to you."

"You just got done telling me why you trust me."

"I never said I trusted you."

"If you don't know what team I'm on, why are we talking?" Riley seemed to be wondering if he was wasting his time.

"I had to take a chance."

"That's a big chance."

"Welcome to my world. But I wasn't going to put every egg in the Riley basket."

"Where are Halavity and your brother?"

"They're safe. Awaiting my return."

"And if you don't return safely?"

"They release everything to the world and turn the Buck interview into small potatoes. It'll be yesterday's news before you can snap your fingers. Then they'll tell the whole world about how you had the chance to bring justice to these people but decided to cover it up instead. With this conversation on tape to prove it."

Riley offered a slight chuckle. It was his first visceral reaction ... and it made David miss his imperturbability.

"Is this funny?" David asked.

"What purpose would that serve, Mr. Centrelli?"

"People need to know about this, Mr. Riley. And you need to know the truth will get out there no matter what you do to me. It's only a question of how."

"Plus, leverage against the Director of the FBI isn't a bad thing to have."

"My turn to ask *you* some questions, Mr. Riley."

"That seems fair," the Director said with a nod.

"Can you tell me anything about the men who tried to kill me?"

Riley paused, clearly evaluating how much he felt he could share.

"The man you refer to as Marcus is a former CIA operative named Leo Latrell."

"What makes you say that?"

"Cover-ups have their limits, like when a dead body is left at a scene. The Watkins Glen case file was scrubbed clean in a short time, but a corpse always leaves a trail. I couldn't find out who sent him, but through some connections and off-the-record favors, I got a name."

"You're sure he was CIA?"

"Covert operations specialist. It's the unit you see in the movies and then wonder if it actually exists in real life. Long military history before a dishonorable discharge eleven years ago following a civilian-hostage situation gone as awry as you can imagine. Been an unofficial operative ever since. Like I said, I don't know who he worked for. But I can tell you one thing ..."

"What's that?"

"He's one untouchable son of a bitch."

"I thought no one was untouchable."

"You thought wrong."

"Didn't you say cover-ups have their limits?"

"Even with the highest clearance levels, I couldn't find his name anywhere. Records are blank, data is gone. Transcripts are nowhere to be found. He's a ghost, a figment of folks' imaginations. You don't find people like that. They find you."

"You're the Director of the FBI!"

"Every position has its limits, Mr. Centrelli. Even the president."

"How comforting."

"That's a matter of perspective."

"Is there anything you can tell me?"

"Right now, I'm going to say no."

"You can't, or you won't?"

"Trust is meant to be reciprocal, Mr. Centrelli. It doesn't look good stag."

"But I've—"

"You've what? Told me a story without proof that may or may not be true, and then promised to ruin my career if I didn't do as you asked? Not what I'm looking for in a partner."

"What did you expect?" David was trying to stay calm, but he really needed this to work. And he was starting to feel exasperated.

"I didn't say I didn't expect it. I said it's not what I'm looking for in a partner."

"What do you want?" David put both arms out as he asked the question, like the martyr he could very well end up being.

"Let me look at the files. I need to see the actual documentation, real words and numbers on paper. Meet me halfway and I'll do what I can."

"Let's talk about that."

"I'm listening."

"I'll give you what you need and then some. If you're like me, which I hope to hell you are, you'll regret it as soon as you have it. But you'll get it all. In return, you give me what I want."

"Which is what, Mr. Centrelli?"

"First, a new life for all three of us. Anne and I have been running from people who are supposed to protect us. Doug was kidnapped and threatened with torture. We all need new beginnings. Clear my name of all charges and make an announcement publicly exonerating me of any wrongdoing whatsoever. Give us new identities, enough money to let us start over, homes in locations we decide, and total anonymity."

"Do you plan to leave the country?"

"I can't speak for Anne and Doug. But after running from my own government the past week, I know I'll be leaving."

"Where?"

"That's for me to decide and you to wonder."

"No deal." Riley shook his head. "Emergencies only, but I've got to be able to contact you."

"I can't imagine a situation where you would need me."

"That doesn't change the condition."

"I'll give you an e-mail. But you can't share it, and you have to leave Anne and Doug alone forever. Each of us gets on a separate plane and tells the pilot where to go once we're in the air. I'm the only one you ever contact, only if you have to. And I do mean *absolutely have to*."

"E-mail isn't enough."

"Can I really stop you from finding me?"

The director raised an eyebrow, paused, and then nodded slowly in agreement.

"Just one last condition," he said. "You have to do the right thing. If enough time passes by and that doesn't happen, then I'll release all this information on my own."

"That would take the secrecy out of your secret life."

"I'm aware."

"How noble of you."

"Don't think too highly of me. I'm pretty sure any network will give me whatever I want for an exclusive."

"You've got to let me uncover all the facts first," Riley replied.

"I'll give you plenty of time to do it your way. But you need to know that if you try to sweep this thing under the rug forever, it'll come back like a rattlesnake and bite you in the ass."

"Don't you feel guilty benefiting from this?"

"Benefiting? I'd do anything to undo the past week. And I know I'll never get a good night's sleep again, but not because I *benefited* from a damn thing. My only question is: when this is all over, will you get a good night's sleep?"

Riley sighed deeply, his eyes fixed on David's tired face.

"Let's talk about money," David said, more to break the silence than anything else.

"There's something I need to tell you," Riley responded.

"What's that?"

For the first time, Riley revealed a different emotion. Not anger or frustration. But instead ... sadness. He took a noticeably deeper breath and looked towards the floor before speaking, shaking his head.

"David, I thought you should hear it from me first ..."

88

The look on David's face indicated things hadn't gone well.

Anne sat at the hotel room's desk, trying to distract herself with a book of Word Finds she'd taken the risk to buy just to keep her sanity. Doug, after asking her question after question, acutely more alert and interested once he learned money was at stake, had finally shut his yapper and laid back on the bed, dozing in and out of a snore-laden nap. The television was on low in the background and the room's seventy-four-degree heat against the icy outdoor air was fogging up the windows to the point that she couldn't see out of them. At just after one, David finally opened the door and awoke Doug from his slumber.

After thirty seconds, twenty-eight longer than she'd expected, Doug's patience ran out.

"So ... what happened?" the older brother asked, scooting towards the end of the bed close to the desk. "You talked to the guy for over an hour."

David didn't respond. His face looked heavy. Despite the past week, his puckered forehead and knitted brows revealed a weight she hadn't seen before. David appeared more overwhelmed now than ever.

"Did he buy the microphone bit?" she asked, trying to ease into the conversation more tactfully.

David held up the wire that was never connected to anything.

"I think so."

Doug started to speak again and finally she'd had enough. The loud smack across his left cheek sounded like it hurt. She hoped so. Doug recoiled holding his face as though it might break. David erupted in a burst of laughter.

"What'd you do that for?" Doug cried.

"You talk too much!" she yelled, evoking even more laughter from David. "Shut up!"

The older brother ran to the mirror to look at his red cheek, and David took his seat on the end of the bed.

"You have no idea how long I've wanted to do that." She smiled at David, as if they'd just shared an inside joke.

"So what happened?"

"We have a deal."

"Oh?"

"Yeah," he replied, taking a seat on the bed. His laughter was gone, and whatever was on his mind when he'd first entered the room had returned. "Ten million each, plus another twenty when Riley gets the files. I checked the accounts. We've each already got the first ten."

"Are you serious?" Doug asked, apparently no longer afraid of her backhand. "That's great! When do you think we'll get the second half?"

"Shut the hell up before I do more than slap you!" David snapped. "People are *dead*. Not hurt. Not injured. Not *broken-hearted* ... Jake, Mary, Mallick. ..."

David's voice trailed off and he turned his head towards the window. "They're dead because of me. So stop celebrating yourself."

David stormed onto the balcony, slamming the door shut behind him. Doug's mouth was still ajar in bewilderment, and she understood why. Obviously, David had nothing to do with Jake's death for sure. Doug looked at Anne, asking with hand motions if he should follow his brother outside.

She shook her head and walked towards the door.

89

The frigid air came in from the east, bitter to the touch. David faced it without a coat, the fire in his gut plenty to keep him burning. His bare hands clutched the icy metal railing, and the brisk breeze blew straight into his face.

After silently replaying Jerry Riley's words in his head, he forced himself to whisper reality:

"Tiffany is gone."

How plausible it seemed that an FBI background check on him would lead to Tiffany's home in Texas eleven years after he last saw her was inconsequential. Whether or not it was actually carbon monoxide poisoning that killed her was of little importance. As was the confusing heartbreak he felt because of it. What was paramount was that she'd never married and died single. *Alone.* Far away from the family she loved and the ski slopes she relished. Just like him.

What if they'd skipped the Minnesota trip eleven years ago because of that blizzard? What if Doug had been out of town? What if he'd found a way to see past the affair? Would Tiffany be his today? The what-ifs just kept coming.

The bright afternoon sun reflected off several buildings' full-length glass windows and implored him to close his eyes in protest. Instead, he shifted his gaze upwards, taking in the vast and vivid blueness of the sky. Looking up had always been a way to remember how small he really was. And in that moment, something happened. He heard a whisper from within utter another truth: he'd been carrying the weight of her treachery around for far too long. For eleven years, more than a quarter of his life, he'd let one event shape his view of everything and everyone. And as traumatic as that event was, he had to move on. Perhaps, he thought, this week of near-death experiences had actually been a blessing in a way, intended to give him perspective and make him realize how much he wanted not just to stay alive, but to *live*.

Whatever the means for the revelation, the message was clear. He needed to let go of his hate and forgive his brother. The chains of bitterness had wrapped themselves around him. They'd grown tighter each year. And now it was time to break them. Having gown up in the church, he'd heard countless times that restoration and peace followed redemption, but this was the first time he'd ever felt it to be true. As he watched a cumulous cloud drift through the otherwise cloudless firmament, he couldn't help but smile.

He didn't even hear the sliding door, and he didn't notice Anne until his old Giants sweatshirt entered his peripheral vision. She didn't say anything.

She was so good at knowing when to talk and when not to.

"I miss him," he whispered.

"Who?"

"Jake. I miss him."

"Me too. But he'd be proud of you today."

He stared at her red hair and large brown eyes, wanting to tell her what had happened, but not sure his heart was ready.

"What's wrong, David?" Anne rested her hand on his shoulder.

"Believe it or not ... nothing." His smile spread slowly across his face.

Anne embraced him, gently at first, then gradually clutching his back and pulling him in tighter until they were deadlocked. It felt so comforting, like she would be always there when he needed her.

"David?"

"Yeah?" He looked down at her sweet face, upturned to meet his gaze.

"Don't let yesterday stop you from enjoying today." She smiled warmly. "You're a good man. And I think you forgot that for a while. So if nothing else, use this week to remember who you are and don't ever forget again."

He looked at Anne with wonder. It was as if she'd read his mind. In one short week, this woman had gotten to know him better than anyone since Tiffany.

He squeezed her hand. "Thanks for everything."

"You're welcome," she whispered. "And there's something you should see."

"I don't know if I can handle anymore new information at this point. Especially if it's bad news."

She handed him an online article printout that read:

CIA BIGWIG FEARED DEAD

Washington, D.C., According to a source speaking on the condition of anonymity, Byron Huetel, a longtime member of the CIA, is feared dead.

Limited information about Mr. Huetel, including his official title and physical description, is available. However, the source confirmed that Huetel's absence from a critical meeting prompted officials to visit his home, where his mobile phone, equipped with internal tracking devices and required to be on his person at all times, was evidently found submerged in a full bathtub. Repeated attempts to contact him have been unsuccessful.

A phone call to CIA headquarters was not returned.

He read it twice and got lost staring at the words.

"David?" Anne said.

"Yesterday, I wanted to kill him myself. I wanted to point that gun just one foot higher and pull the trigger. Today, I find out he's actually gone ..." he wiped his eyes, thinking of Tiffany, then whispered, "and I'm crying."

90

They were in a remote hanger at the northern edge of Reagan National Airport, standing next to a Bombardier Global 8000 private jet sized for seventeen people. She looked a mile south and saw the airport's closet commercial runway and an American Airlines plane taxiing on it. Doug nervously shifted his weight from side to side, probably thinking about the thirty million dollars he didn't deserve but would soon have. David stood still, but his eyes scanned every direction as if his head was on a swivel.

Jerry Riley was the only other person there. Which, despite it being David's request, still surprised Anne. No other airplanes, grounds crew, technicians or travelers. No law enforcement agents or plainclothes FBI agents accompanied the boss. And at just past midnight, that ending felt fitting to her.

That the three of them would escape alone into a moonlit sky.

A man who looked the part of a pilot emerged from behind the hangar door and approached them. Half-expecting him to pull out a gun and start shooting, she ducked behind David's seemingly massive stature. But saying nothing, the man walked past them all and walked up the airstairs that extended to the ground. It felt to Anne like the first step towards the promise of a new life.

"This will take you to Phoenix," Riley announced. She supposed he was speaking to them all, but he was looking at David. "There will be two other planes on the runway, and no one else, when you land. After this refuels, you each go your own way on your own jet. The moment you land wherever it is you're going, the confidential flight plans will be destroyed. And as soon I have the files, I'll wire the additional sixty million. No games, David. Like someone once told me, let's be men about this."

"No games on either side, Jerry. What else can we expect when we land?"

"Your new identities and documentation ... licenses, passports, social security cards, birth certificates, the works. Nobody but me knows your new names. Your reputation will drastically improve once I have the files."

David didn't answer.

"Is there something else you want?"

"You have my e-mail address if you need anything. Just leave these two alone."

"I will contact you only if it's absolutely necessary. You have my personal cell phone if you ever need me."

"I won't."

Riley nodded. "When you're ready, hop on board."

The engines already running, she and Doug quickly ascended the stairs towards new lives, but David walked towards Riley. To her shock, he extended his hand. Riley looked surprised himself, but then smiled and offered his own hand in return. Words were exchanged, but the noise from the twin turbines drowned them out.

* * *

Instead of the warm, barehanded grip Jerry Riley expected, he felt cold metal. Looking down, he saw a key on the end of a rubber purple key chain. Then he looked at the fugitive.

"Is this what I think it is?" Riley asked with a straight face, so as not to reveal anything to Anne or Doug.

"I'll call you when we land to tell you what it opens. After Doug and Anne are airborne on their next flights."

"I've been pretty trustworthy so far, have I not?"

"That's why we're still talking."

"I have to tell you, it's unusual for the FBI to work on these terms."

"Make an exception. For me."

Riley nodded.

"Mr. Centrelli, my career has taught me that the only partnerships you can count on are the ones that provide mutual benefit. On that basis, I think we'll be okay. I suppose this is goodbye. I wish you well."

Centrelli smiled and nodded his head slowly, but offered no words. Then, somewhat abruptly, the man everyone in the nation and soon the world was looking for slowly boarded the airplane and climbed into the rearmost seat, looking at him through the window.

He looked back and gave a short wave; certain that David Centrelli's last view of America's capital was of him, staring at the plane, muttering to himself.

91

The news report said the man who killed Walter Buck before turning the gun on himself was a crazy elitist member of one of several pro-drug organizations that had publicly scolded "The Deadly Deal" and all its constituents.

But considering the "crazy" gunman, as the news had already labeled him, somehow managed to get past FBI protection and used his Army training to kill Buck with one shot inside the "secure" compound...

David had his doubts.

He and Anne didn't discuss it at all, and they never would. Talking about it wouldn't reverse things or bring answers. After she showed him the article and tossed the newspaper in the trash, not another word was uttered.

The five-hour flight was uneventful, and he actually slept through most of it on the luxurious Bombardier jet. When he stepped off the plane and onto the tarmac, the Phoenix weather's stark contrast to DC was a very welcome change. Two hours before sunrise, it was almost sixty degrees.

As Riley had promised, other than two similarly sized private jets already on the tarmac when they arrived, no one else was within sight. Doug departed thirty minutes earlier on one of them, and their final handshake was equal parts contrived and awkward. David didn't even watch his brother board the plane.

That left just he and Anne in a town that would still be asleep for hours. Beneath a sky blinded by airport lights and warning beacons, they stood on the remote runway next to the two planes, pondering the end of the eight-day journey that felt so much longer.

"David?" Anne whispered.

"Yeah?"

"Are you going to stop that e-mail from going through?"

Before he met Jerry Riley at Dolcezza, he'd done two things that he shared with Anne before they boarded the plane in DC.

First, he'd sent a different news reporter, Mr. Matthew Leksa from *Richmond Times-Dispatch*, a package. Small and unassuming, the padded envelope had only two items inside. The first was a small, unmarked key far too generic for Leksa to guess what it opened. The second was the short note wrapped around it and bonded with tape:

HOLD ON TO THIS
-David Centrelli

What exactly Mr. Leksa would do with the key was open to speculation, but if he was like any other reporter David knew, he'd eagerly await further instruction and keep it to himself. David saw no reason Leksa wouldn't be just as anxious and docile as Buck was.

He'd also triggered an electronic postcard to be automatically delivered to Mr. Leksa's e-mail account in five days. Requiring only an e-mail address to sign up for a free trial of the postcard creation and delivery service, he'd done the whole thing from the hotel business center and committed the login information to memory. The postcard's note identified the safe that the key would unlock, where it was, and what Mr. Leksa could expect to find.

He had between now and Friday at 1:00 p.m. Eastern Time to cancel the message, or the whole story would come out through the reporter.

"I'll stop it when we all land safely," he replied.

"But if you do that, you can't make Riley follow through."

"Previséo's finished. We stopped it, Anne. We did what Jake asked us to do. I think Riley's got enough pressure on him to force him to do the right thing. And I think he would anyway."

She lifted her chin and eyebrows, a soft smile on her lips, waiting for his punch line.

This woman knew him too well.

"Plus, I figure that if he doesn't, I can always make an anonymous call."

She flashed him the kind of smile he'd wondered about earlier.

"Think Doug will be okay?"

"Well, let's see. His plane left a half-hour ago, so chances are he's on his third Bloody Mary by now."

"That's not what I mean."

"He'll be fine."

"He feels really bad, you know. He told me all about it ... about how much he regretted what happened. Said he's really missed you all these years."

"I'm not sure Doug misses anyone but my father, but thanks."

He wished he'd met Anne in a previous life. He could see why Jake had stayed close with her. The friendship she offered was a rare and beautiful thing, and he felt sad theirs would soon be over. He knew he'd miss her. God knew he could use a friend.

"What about you, David? Will you be okay?"

"I'll be fine. You?"

"Talk about a go-away answer. I'm scared, but think I'll be okay."

"You'll probably be scared for the rest of your life."

"Why thank you, David. You sure know how to make a gal feel good. But I'm still here. I'm alive, and I'm thankful for that."

"Well said."

"I heard it from you."

"Sure you want to be in the US when all this breaks? Reporters would throw you into the limelight next to me. They're relentless, and there's a decent chance they'll find you if you stay. Maybe sooner rather than later."

"America is my home, David. I wouldn't know what to do anywhere else."

He paused for just a brief moment before throwing it out there.

"Do you want to come with me?"

She smiled, and then looked down at her new Pumas. Pushing her red hair to the side, she sighed and looked back at him. Her eyes gave him her answer before her mouth did.

"Part of me really wants to. But I can't. This is it for me and America is home."

All four pilots, two per plane, were in their cockpits and waiting. Yet despite looking forward to this all day, he suddenly didn't want to go. The full moon, through scattered clouds, beamed brightly over the darkened runway and shined its spotlight on the incontrovertible fact.

The time had come.

"I never expected to regret this ending. But we're still alive."

"I'll miss you," Anne said softly.

They embraced long and hard, and Anne whispered into his ear.

"Jake is proud of you. Your mother, too. And I'll never forget you."

Then Anne broke free, walked to her plane, climbed the stairs, and didn't so much as look back before the plane departed. Still, he waved her off, one arm extended and the other down at his side.

Watching the sky.

Epilogue

Three Months Later

Leaning back in the straw chair, he relished the umbrella's shade, his legs outstretched onto the straw patio table. In his right hand, a virgin strawberry daiquiri; his left lay comfortably on the armrest.

He wore an orange Club Med hat to prevent sunburn. In his usual khaki shorts and Hawaiian shirt, his bare toes pointed towards the sky. His native Minnesota legs were lobster-colored despite the SPF 45 he applied twice a day. Ray-Ban sunglasses shielded his eyes; his nose was painted white with sunscreen.

Cliché as it was, ending up on a beach was all he ever wanted. The sky was still his favorite, and he thought of that blue sky in DC and its promise often. The sand was perfect, not a single darkened blemish among the trillions of white grains. A child's sandcastle stood by the shore, as if watching over the pristine sand stretching in all directions but one.

That direction belonged to the ocean, thirty feet from where he sat. It was picturesque, perhaps the only thing more beautiful than the sand. He'd never even imagined water so clear, so blue and full of shimmer. Sunlight danced across the waves like a delicate ballet set to nature's oceanic rhythm.

The small portable television was out of place for such a setting. The screen was only thirteen inches in size and its non-HD, black and white picture reminded him of the 80s. But he didn't mind because he didn't plan to watch long.

The broadcast the day before had been popular enough that the network reran it. Abandoning his will power, he decided to tune in and watch it again.

Two men in suits sat opposite one another at a small table, each holding a cup of coffee. The reporter wore black glasses and had white hair, gripping a few sheets of loose notebook paper. The other man held nothing but his mug.

"Good evening. I'm here with Jerry Riley, Director of the FBI, the man who brought to light the details of a story that has consumed the nation. Mr. Riley, I'll get right to the point. We first learned about the 'The Deadly Deal' when Walter Buck, a former *Richmond Observer* reporter, made his famous telecast on January 28th. Days later, he was murdered while under police custody. The investigation has been closed, and no additional information has been made available to the public. Why?"

"It's ongoing, and we're still gathering evidence."

"Can you share the evidence that you do have?"

"Not at this time."

"Buck claimed his source was David Centrelli, the former Director of Business Development at Medzic Pharmaceuticals. At the time, Centrelli was wanted by the FBI for the murder of Medzic Chief Scientist Peter Mallick, as well as his possible connection to a terrorist organization. Can you share anything about him?"

"We're still investigating."

"After three months?"

"Yes." Riley didn't take the bait.

"Centrelli is in fact no longer wanted by the FBI. To the contrary, he's been awarded a Presidential Citizens Medal for his help with the investigation, though he didn't accept it in person. And you, Mr. Riley, have personally as well as publicly refuted any connection to a terrorist group. Dr. Mallick has been posthumously honored also, leading many to wonder if they've been exonerated too quickly. Can you comment?"

"I think the FBI's action speak for itself."

"To add to the mystery, three Medzic executives — CEO Alvin Patera, CFO Jonathan Debil, and COO Larry Bonnelson — resigned from their positions within weeks of Buck's interview. Debil committed suicide two weeks later, and Patera and Bonnelson died in prison while facing multiple counts of fraud and larceny. Production of Previséo has ceased by order of the president, and several FDA regulations have since been put under intense scrutiny and enhanced."

"Is that a question?"

"Two partners at MacArthur, Barry and Tain Insurance, CEO Scott Zabel and COO Dwayne Miller, as well as several members of the FDA and IRS are reportedly under investigation for racketeering and tax evasion. Can you offer any details on these investigations?"

"I'm not prepared to discuss ongoing investigations."

"Let's try to find something you *can* comment on. Many people out there believe David Centrelli is still at large here in the United States. Some believe he is the person most directly responsible for this conspiracy in the first place. He worked closely with Patera, publicly commented on the benefits of Previséo for the diabetic population, and was one of the key individuals behind its development. What do you say to those who feel he needs to be investigated just as rigorously as the other Medzic executives were?"

"I say 'he was.' My office conducted a thorough investigation and concluded Centrelli isn't responsible for any wrongdoing."

"Do you have him in custody?"

"I can't say."

"You can't say, or you won't say?"

"Next question, please."

The reporter forced out an awkward chuckle, as if not sure whether to be pissed or entertained.

"There were reports Centrelli was with two other people. A man about his age with a beard rumored to be his brother, and a woman with red hair. Yet even now, months later, we know very little about either. Can you offer any insight?"

"The only person we've spoken to is David Centrelli."

"Neighbors in Minnesota reported Doug Centrelli missing shortly after Buck's report. Do you know where he is?"

"That is immaterial at this time."

"In other words, 'next question.'"

"I suppose so," Riley replied, returning the chuckle.

"Many Americans believe this would need presidential support to get as far as it did. In fact, over sixty percent of the country thinks President Thompson may've been directly involved. And you can't blame them ... considering the rather coincidental deaths of the Medzic executives, Walter Buck, and Peter Mallick, as well as the sudden disappearance of David Centrelli."

"The FBI worked with the DOD and Homeland Security, as well as the Senate Oversight Committee. After a detailed review, we concluded there isn't any evidence President Thompson had prior knowledge of it."

"It's apparent we won't be learning much from you today."

"I'm sorry to disappoint, but conspiracies usually aren't as extreme as the public assumes they are. I'm reporting the facts."

"There is one question on everyone's mind I think you can answer. How do we prevent the next government conspiracy? It feels like we got lucky this time."

"The federal government employees over four million people on a three-hundred-billion-dollar budget. The vast majority of those people are honest, law-abiding citizens who just want to do a good job. On top of that, there are literally hundreds of precautionary processes, checks and balances, and visibility protocols in place."

"But?"

"But it's not obviously perfect, either. They won't catch everything. Our nation's citizens have some responsibility, and we need their help. We've made changes, many of which you've referenced tonight. But the truth is, 'The Deadly Deal' should remind us precisely why we need people like David Centrelli."

He turned the television off and stared into the ocean again, a dubious expression across his face. The ordeal was over but the real perps, whoever they were, got away. Could it have gone as high as the President, or his inner circle within the government? Or maybe a wealthy private citizen with the funds to buy protection? Or both? He'd never know, and he had to find a way to be okay with that.

The undulating water crested into yet another perfect wave before collapsing into bubbly white waters. David smiled as he watched Anne desperately trying to surf. She would gain balance on the board and then immediately demonstrate how temporary that balance was. Her arms would flail and her feet would teeter from side-to-side in a frantic attempt to get it back.

Then she'd tumble facedown into the clear, cool water, as she had countless times over the last several weeks. She'd flip, get tumbled by the undertow, then re-surface exhausted and gasping for air. David took a sip of the daiquiri and smiled. He'd watch the cycle repeat itself, time and time again, just like the formation of the waves.

And it'd never get old.

CPSIA information can be obtained
at www.ICGtesting.com
Printed in the USA
JSHW022324240523
42207JS00003B/234